praise for simmons

Not My Boy

"A missing child, a family with multiple secrets, and a cast of characters that are complicated and fully realized…*Not My Boy* lands the reader in the middle of a mystery that is propulsive and impossible to put down."

—Julie Clark, *New York Times* bestselling author of *The Last Flight*

"When tragedy strikes in *Not My Boy*, a privileged neighborhood is turned upside down—and no man, woman, or even child is above suspicion. Kelly Simmons has spun a nail-biter that will have you questioning how quickly we can turn on the people we hold dear, and how far we might go to keep our deepest fears from being realized."

—Jessica Strawser, bestselling author of *Not That I Could Tell*

"*Not My Boy* is a dark, rich tale of a mother's absolute love for her unusual son and of the hazards of sisterhood. Simmons is at the top of her game here, writing with confidence and candor, never hitting a wrong note or taking a false step. I felt as though Hannah, the heroine, was leading me by the hand through the dense woods surrounding her home—emblematic of her life and of the pitfalls of family allegiances—and confiding in me all her secrets. Atmospheric, tense, and authentic to the core, *Not My Boy* will catch you in its thrall and hold you there until the very last page."

st bestselling author
Stories We Never Told

"Kelly Simmons has created a chilling tale of suspense and intrigue. Filled with sharp insights about the fierce protectiveness and envy that define a close-knit family, *Not My Boy* kept me turning the pages late into the night."

—Angie Kim, international bestselling author of *Miracle Creek*

Where She Went

"Intense, compelling and provocative. This cinematic cat-and-mouse thriller beautifully explores the depths of a mother's loving persistence, and the terrifying vulnerability of a daughter's determination and bravery. Fans of Lisa Scottoline and Kate White—and *Mean Girls*—will race through the pages of this riveting story of dark secrets, duplicity, and hauntingly realistic danger."

—Hank Phillippi Ryan, nationally bestselling author of *The Murder List*

"Kelly Simmons's *Where She Went* is the complex, twisty story of a college student who may or may not be in over her head and a mother who will do whatever she must to save her—whether her daughter realizes she needs saving or not. Fans of smart, sophisticated suspense will love Simmons's bold, relentless, and yet utterly relatable heroines. Highly recommended!"

—Karen Dionne, author of the #1 international bestseller *The Marsh King's Daughter*

"Kelly Simmons tackles every empty-nesting mom's worst nightmare: your college freshman disappears without a trace. With engaging dual narration between the mother and her missing daughter, Simmons weaves a page-turning, topical story you'll remember long after the end."

—Kaira Rouda, *USA Today* bestselling author of *Best Day Ever* and *The Favorite Daughter*

"Beautifully dark, totally devastating and so riveting you might find yourself gripping the pages, *One More Day* is about the holes in our lives and how we struggle to fill them, the love of parent for child, and the secrets that define us. Absolutely mesmerizing."

—Caroline Leavitt, *New York Times* bestselling author of *Is This Tomorrow* and *Pictures of You*

"*One More Day* is an absolutely riveting book. It's a rare novel that combines intrigue and suspense with so much heart—but that's what makes it one of my favorite new books of this winter."

—Sarah Pekkanen, bestselling author of *Things You Won't Say* and *The Opposite of Me*

also by
kelly simmons

NOT MY BOY

KELLY SIMMONS

sourcebooks
landmark

Published by Sourcebooks Landmark, an imprint of Sourcebooks
P.O. Box 4410, Naperville, Illinois 60567-4410
(630) 961-3900
sourcebooks.com

Library of Congress Cataloging-in-Publication Data

Names: Simmons, Kelly, author.
Title: Not my boy / Kelly Simmons.
Description: Naperville, Illinois : Sourcebooks Landmark, [2021]
Identifiers: LCCN 2020019106 (trade paperback) | (epub)
Subjects: LCSH: Psychological fiction. | Domestic fiction. | GSAFD: Suspense fiction. | Mystery fiction.
Classification: LCC PS3619.I5598 N68 2021 (print) | DDC 813/.6--dc23

LC record available at https://lccn.loc.gov/2020019106

Printed and bound in Canada.
MBP 10 9 8 7 6 5 4 3 2 1

For my sister, who does not live next door. Yet.

one

HANNAH

As the moving and storage truck pulled away from the curb, Hannah Sawyer waved as if friends were leaving instead of her, a stranger, staying. The two young movers had wrapped her IKEA furniture in blankets like it was custom-made. Watching a box of ordinary white plates delicately touch down on her wood floor brought a sting of tears to her eyes. That some men could be so careful, so aware of the breakable world.

It had poured just the day before, a too-warm Thursday, flooding Tamsen Creek, muddying the trails that wound through the lower eastern part of the neighborhood, across the street and down the gulch from Hannah. A rain like that could give rise to another world: earthworms, grubs, centipedes. It could also weaken cardboard and drown electronics, and Hannah had looked to the sky repeatedly throughout the day, worried it would start again.

As they'd put down brown paper to protect her floors from mud, Hannah had asked them if they'd done any jobs yesterday, and the guys had said yeah, the water had risen so high in their client's driveway, they couldn't use the dolly or hand trucks.

Her son, Miles, had listened intently, maybe pondering rain and earthworm capture or, Hannah thought, considering moving furniture as a career. He asked questions about their equipment. They'd shown him how to work the hydraulic lip of the truck. The intoxicating smell of oil, gasoline, and rubber. Did anything else in Miles's middle-school world of algebra and video games smell like that? It reminded Hannah of the grinding start of the car wash, so different from the detergent wave, rising and foamy, at the end.

If her son wanted to own a moving company, she'd be fine with that. Totally. She wasn't going to be one of those moms who insisted on engineering, medicine, consulting. They were off to a good beginning, she thought. She wished she had video of it all to show her ex-husband, Mike. *There*, she'd say. *See your son's smile? He's fine now. He was just acting out at the other school to get your attention. Trying to be tough to compete with you. Didn't you tell me once you had to eat the cheek of the first fish you caught? Smear the blood of the first deer across your forehead? Did you make the mistake of telling him that shit, too?*

"So I guess if the rain stopped, the rumors aren't true," the driver had said as he finished and loaded up the last of the quilted blankets, folded in even squares, stacked just high enough that they wouldn't fall.

"What rumors?" she had asked, tensing a little. He was young, barely out of high school, but which one? Could he know someone else in her former neighborhood, a child at Miles's old school?

"More of an old legend, I guess," he said, wiping his hands against his jeans. "Not that you're, you know, old."

"Illuminate me," she said.

"That Tamsen haunts this whole street cuz he's pissed his heirs broke up his estate into all these properties. Figured that was maybe why the previous owners of your house had trouble selling."

She blinked. "Trouble?"

She'd bought from the couple directly, introduced by her sister. No brokers, no fees. Hannah had assumed she'd been at the front of the process, not the end. Her forehead wrinkled in annoyance, confirming her old status. Not because she believed in ghosts but because she believed her sister had known something and kept it from her. Another one of Hillary's stupid tests?

She thought of her sister at the walk-through days before, shrugging at the balloons tied to the copper mailbox across the street, saying she didn't know the people, their kid was young, third marriage, she'd heard. Inside, surveying the sanded floors, fresh paint, new wallpaper hung in the kitchen and bathroom. How little time it had taken to walk through a house so snug, how nothing at all could have happened except for the dance of *you go first, no, you* outside the bathroom. And yet for all the exclamations of *floors look awesome, love the paint color*, Hillary's eyes had narrowed—Hannah hadn't imagined it—at the black-and-white toile wallpaper in the kitchen. Trying to place the historical print? The hill, the hound, the picnic, the tiny fox ears hiding in the bushes, which Hannah hadn't seen until the paper hanger had pointed it out with his wide, callused finger, and she couldn't decide if it was funny or tragic. Hillary's look reminded her of how she used to side-eye Hannah's flaking nail polish, never saying a word, then proclaiming, "What? Nothing. Don't be paranoid," when Hannah asked what was wrong.

"I'm sure it's nothing," the driver had said. "Just rumors and a little rain."

"Right," she had said. "No need to be paranoid."

"Exactly."

The driver had closed the back of the truck and saluted to Miles, who stood on the porch.

She had tipped him a hundred dollars, and before he said thanks, he also said *whoa*. She supposed it was too much for a small house. She'd also paid the contractor that week, paid him overtime to finish so it would just be done and she wouldn't have to do that on top of everything else before the school year began. No matter about the cost. The monthly retainer from Boxt Pharmaceuticals would be there by the end of the week, and everything she'd done to get herself and Miles into this carriage house without Mike, without the boys from their old school district, would be worth it.

She paused for a moment on Brindle Lane. From this vantage point, she could almost visualize how the neighborhood, which held nearly fifty sprawling homes, no two alike, was once one enormous 120-acre estate. The sycamore trees flanking the road like soldiers. The sloping hill up Brindle Lane, past Hillary's house, splitting into four or five lanes—Rose Lane, Linden Lane, others she couldn't remember—before dipping back down to the covered bridge to the Tamsen farm, the only five acres that remained in the Tamsen family. The steep drop across from her driveway to the east that led to the creek and the gulch and all the walking trails that eventually rose and twisted back into the lanes. And behind her house, through another copse of trees, Brigham's Ford Road, running parallel to her street, connecting to the other tributaries at the southern crest.

All those homes, people, pets, and yet, cushioned by landscape and leaf, so little noise.

As she walked back up to the driveway, she heard no cars passing, no dogs barking, no basketballs bouncing. Just Tamsen Creek, bubbling and alive.

Soon, next door, around the brick circle, up the wide bluestone steps that led to the double entry doors, Hillary would be back, carrying in Morgan's stuff from camp. Hillary's husband, Ben, would return from his business trip or his office in Malvern or wherever he was, and they'd all be together. Miles had already asked when Ben and Morgan would be home, glancing out the kitchen window in a way that made Hannah both happy and sad.

They would begin a new September together in the same great school district, a life as fresh and satisfying as newly sharpened pencils. Sisters as neighbors, cousins hanging out with cousins, their mother, Eva, just a few neighborhoods away, with a promise to babysit at any time.

Wasn't that the vision? Wasn't that the dream? Wasn't that everything they'd ever wanted in the first place? They were a team, ever since their father had died, helping each other muscle through, filling in for the other's weakness. They'd split up their homework in high school: Hannah did the art and English; Hillary did the science and math. Together, they had made the dean's list and gotten scholarships to colleges ten miles apart. And whenever Hannah faltered, even as she faced her inevitable divorce, Hillary was there to remind her of their childhood chant: *rock, paper, scissors, Sawyer.* The Sawyers were the hardest, sharpest substance of all. Always. Hannah, a year and a half younger, always behind; Hillary teaching her, taunting her to keep up, with her schoolgirl rules and tests. Hannah shuddered sometimes, thinking of the stupid shit they used to do. *The cocoa test. The bathtub pledge.*

As she stepped back onto her porch, she heard the distinct sound of a box cutter ripping through duct tape. She thought at twelve and a half, Miles was too young for knives and tools, but she had made an exception for the move. It seemed absurd to make him ask for it; how would anything get put away?

Pocket knives were just one of the things she and Mike had fought about, bitterly. Mike built furniture and wanted Miles to learn to whittle. He also hunted for ducks and wild turkey and had always imagined a son by his side, field dressing, bird-dogging. No, she'd said. But a boy needs some wild in him. A boy needs adventures, he'd said. *Miles likes books about adventure*, she'd told him. *Not actual adventure.* And Mike had looked at her as if she was insane.

Miles was inside unpacking, just as he'd been told to. But still, something told her to go. To check. To linger in the doorway and watch.

He crouched low over the box, all angles, elbows and knees, thin and folded like a grasshopper, and it was only when he stood up, his back to her, that she was surprised, once again, how tall he was getting, almost her height, how old he sometimes looked. How particular he was now about his hair, the length in front always so much longer than she liked, falling into his eyes. Suddenly, he reached back with one hand and put the box cutter in the back pocket of his jeans, blade up, practiced, just the way the moving guys had. Her breath caught for a second in her throat.

The box he'd opened was color coded for her bedroom, not his. Had he carried it into his room, knowing? Or had she made another mistake, one of many, one of thousands, and told the movers to put it there?

He stepped toward the back of the room, carrying something, brushing pale packing peanuts onto the floor. Then he raised the scope of Hannah's green binoculars up to the window, his pale wrists exposed, his arms too long for their sleeves. She was certain she heard something in his throat, aching and small, like the jawing sound cats made when they watched birds.

"Miles," she said in a low voice.

He hesitated for just a second. "I know," he replied. His voice half an octave deeper, cracking.

She didn't know what he saw in the backyard; she didn't ask. He handed the binoculars to her behind his back, not turning to her, not meeting her eyes. Even when she leaned over and yanked the box cutter from his jeans pocket, he did not turn around and look at her.

But when she went to her bedroom window later and held her binoculars up to the darkening sky, she saw something flutter around the corner of the house, between her property and her sister's.

Iridescent, lifting, like the pearly butterfly wings worn by children on Halloween.

Or perhaps just the passing sweep of a hawk or owl, catching the last glimmer of sunset.

two

EVA

I love my daughters equally. I'll go one further: when they were little, I sometimes didn't think of them as two. I considered them one entity, a unit, as if my lyrical naming had fused them together.

If someone had interviewed them in high school instead of now, stuck a microphone in their faces the way I watched those shameless news people try to, they would have told the truth instead of lying. They would have said they once thought of themselves the same way. Two halves of the same whole, damaged apart, perfect together. They would admit as much now, wouldn't they?

Do they think I didn't know they split up their homework, cheated for each other? If I hadn't been racked with grief over Joe's death, the debts, the deceits, I suppose I would have confronted them about it. I would have told them that despite their father's issues, it was okay to be flawed, to be bad at something. That no one would love them less.

But that would have been a lie. Because although I love my own children equally, I can't say the same for my grandchildren.

Did I know what no one else knew?

Is that why my jaw clenched when I saw one of the children first and only relaxed when the other ran into the room?

Maybe it was fortuitous that I hadn't bought the carriage house next to Hillary after all. (Although I still, even now, have trouble bringing myself to call it Hannah's house.) Oh, I'd had my eye on it for years, had gone back and forth with an agent and the owners but had never said anything to my girls about the possibility because, well, didn't a mother want to be *invited*, so she didn't feel like she was intruding? And didn't it take approximately forever for an adult child to recognize her mother is getting older and might need assistance nearby? Wasn't that why neither of them thought of me first? Oh, I hope it was. I do hope.

Margot, my real estate agent, had been furious over the whole thing. She'd spoken to the couple a year beforehand, and they'd promised to let her know if they ever considered selling, even directly. They'd bandied ridiculous numbers about, but Margot didn't blink an eye or try to tell them they were dreaming (which was what she told me). She told them she had the ideal buyer, highly motivated, no contingency, that would more than make up for her reduced fees and that I was family. Family! I was one of those stories you put in someone's mailbox with pictures of your children that persuade you! Margot was a few years behind Hannah in school, a beautiful girl, but she could be aggressive. I'd wanted someone aggressive. Was that my mistake? Was it her mistake?

I may never know.

I had to laugh the way it all went down. Outbid by my own child? How on earth did that happen, when Hannah was not exactly flush? Margot was decidedly less amused, was furious, threatening. Her face on the signs swinging from so many homes I'd admired did not show this side of her! She said she had a few other ideas, not to panic. She told me to sit tight. I told her not to ever say anything to anyone, ever, lest my daughters be angry with me.

Or believe that I had caused all the events in some minor, odd way.

That was the last thing a mother needed. More blame.

I tried not to let this disappointment keep me from being happy for my daughters and from swinging by that first evening Hannah and Miles moved in. I was curious what color she'd painted the rooms. How she'd arrange her furniture. If she'd hang curtains or blinds. I'd always thought it was a curtain-y house, a cottage, soft. But my dreams for it wouldn't be her dreams, I knew.

Hannah was in the back bedrooms, unpacking, and didn't hear my knock at the door, so I went inside, walking between cartons, and called her name. The walls were a pale color between green and gray, which looked nice with the black casement windows, which, I happened to know from Margot, were all new, replaced last year.

"Be right out," she yelled.

I handed her a small plate of frosted brownies, one of Miles's favorites, and she brushed her dusty hands off before taking it from me.

"Shall I wipe down some cupboards, unpack china, lay a fire, make myself useful?" I asked.

"No," she said, "I'm almost ready to stop. Long day."

She asked me if I wanted tea, and I said no.

"Where's Miles?"

"He ran down to look at the creek," she said. "I couldn't keep him cooped up any longer after all this rain."

"Had to go skip some stones?"

"Probably."

Every surface, chair, and sofa had a box on it, and although it wasn't even eight o'clock, my daughter seemed tired, so I didn't linger. I told her I'd come by in a couple of days and to call if she needed me. She hugged me goodbye, thanked me for the brownies, but didn't walk me to my car. She went back into her bedroom, and I went out alone.

And that's why she didn't see what I saw as I sat in my car and buckled my seat belt.

A tiny girl carrying a fishing net much taller than she was, waving goodbye to Miles as he crossed the street. Here one day, and already he had a little friend.

three

HANNAH

Hannah woke up Saturday before six, obsessing a bit over the work she had to do. Finalize the edit of the Peace Corps memoir. Article prep for Boxt, one last newsletter for an online printing company, memoir timeline for the woman with five names she called the Philanthropist. Three given names and a hyphenated last name. She'd broadly proclaimed to Hannah that she was honoring her Catholic father, her feminist mother, and her Jewish husband, as if this sentence would make a great memoir all on its own.

She got up and walked through the boxes. Terrible habit, working early in the morning. She was so tired by 10:00 p.m., right when Miles started staying up too late and pushing limits. This schedule was not going to work in high school. She opened her computer on the dining table and started on the newsletter, but in a few minutes, a shaft of light broke through the front window at an angle that was too orange and insistently beautiful to ignore.

She unlocked the door and grabbed the broom, swept a few dewy blades of grass off the porch in the pale orange light. If it was this pretty every morning, she might have trouble settling in to work. The sun rose across Brindle Lane, illuminating the landscaped property directly across the street, the driveway sloping down to a barely visible house, shrouded in ivy, shaded by maple trees, mature oaks, a Japanese cherry closer to the house. The heavy rains had made everything almost too green, overly lush, the leaves grown wide and tall, like giant hands on a child. She could only see glimpses of the sprawling stone house behind it, a piece of the gray shutters, the triangle top of a copper-roofed cupola rising above. Only a slice of a door painted a dark color, not bright like some in the neighborhood, showing off like bold lipstick. The balloons from the walk-through long gone now, but a short piece of red ribbon had been missed at the back, waving slightly in the wind.

Soon enough, in winter, trees stripped bare, she'd be able to sit on her porch and see more of the house and its owners. Now the only thing clearing the trees was a verdigris weather vane spinning above the cupola. She squinted. A fox? No, a rabbit.

She ignored the dew and her bare feet and stepped out onto her lawn, stretched, grateful. Work could wait a minute or two.

She had plenty to explore. Lanes and paths to hike, trails to run, up into the woods that ringed the Tamsen farm off Gotham Road. Hillary said everyone ran or walked on the trails; it was sometimes annoying how many people and dogs and kids you ran into.

Hannah stood on her lawn, stretching in her pajamas, enjoying the faint scent of what looked like Hillary's new plantings near her mailbox. Beds of moss, ringing what had to be pale yellow witch hazel, her mother's favorite flower. Shit, Hannah thought. She had to remember to call her mother. She'd been a little distracted when she'd stopped by.

"Did you camp out? Kinda wet for that."

Ben stood halfway down his driveway, smiling, dressed in jeans and a dark blue T-shirt, holding a fat Sunday paper. Still had it delivered once a week, though he read everything else online. Old school in a few ways, but she knew the trendy leather headphones around his neck had probably cost thousands of dollars.

She smiled back. "Maybe these are my regular clothes," she said.

"Business casual?"

"Writer casual. The most casual of all the casuals."

"I guess your sister didn't warn you about the strict neighborhood dress code," he laughed. "I'm supposed to come get you guys for breakfast, but I was waiting until maybe dawn broke? And until my headache cleared?"

"She's not cooking already."

"Of course she is," he said and smiled.

Hannah loved how deeply Ben understood her sister, how he always seemed to marvel at her even while he shook his head at what she was doing.

"Are you hungover, Uncle Ben?"

"Maybe a tad."

"Okay, go take some Advil and give me a minute."

Hannah went inside, changed into leggings, a tank top, and a flannel shirt, which wasn't much different from her pajamas, but at least she had a bra on. She left a quick note for Miles and started across the lawn, imagining some delicious egg dish or something drizzled like scones. Hillary had more cookbooks than Hannah had books. But then, Hannah's carriage house, the former estate's servants' quarters, didn't have room for them anyway. It had been somewhat expensive considering it only had one bathroom, but it also had a fireplace and a porch and her sister next door, and when Hillary had called her and told her the owners were selling directly, Hannah didn't hesitate. She had just enough from the divorce settlement for a down payment. Miles needed a new school, and she and her sister had talked about living in the same neighborhood since they were kids. When had they played house, they'd imagined it this way, always. Of course they hadn't figured on the disparities in career, husbands, income. Hadn't imagined that what looked like home to one of them wouldn't necessarily look like home to the other.

When Hannah reached the driveway, her email alert pinged in her shirt pocket. She took her phone out, glanced at it. From Boxt Pharma but not her project's manager—a name she didn't recognize. Probably a confirmation of her direct deposit or something. She rapped her knuckles three times on the front door and then stepped back and opened the email, just to check. Just to see what this new person had to say.

She heard Hillary's deep, throaty laugh on the other side of the darkgray double doors, a sound as familiar to Hannah as an ice cream truck. Even when her sister was at her toughest, that laugh could make everything better. Hillary's hair was damp from the shower, darkening the gold highlights. She looked more like her sister, more like herself, Hannah thought, when her hair was wet.

"Welcome to the 'hood," she proclaimed, wrapping Hannah in her left arm, the arm that didn't have an oven mitt dangling from a hand.

"Thanks," Hannah said.

"What's wrong? You're making that face you make."

"The face I make when I lost my newest, biggest client?"

"Fuck," Hillary replied.

"Yeah. Just got an email. Project manager gone, project terminated."

"See, this is why women drink. Seriously."

"Oh, well," Hannah said. "Onward, right? I'll figure it out, get a kill fee or something."

She was aware that her mouth was moving, that she was talking and walking toward the kitchen, completely standing upright, but she wasn't sure she could eat. She felt sick and stupid and had to go back over her emails and the project terms they'd agreed to and try to figure out how the hell she could salvage something out of this. She sat at the kitchen island and drank her sister's organic coffee in the hand-thrown mug, but part of her wanted to bang her head against the cold marble and scream. This was the last thing she wanted to deal with.

"So," Hannah said, drawing in a breath, "how was the drive back from Vermont?"

"Interminable," Hillary said. "Can you smell the mold from the laundry room? Next year, I'm going to throw out her grimy clothes. So the move went smoothly? Miles seem okay? So far so good?"

"So far. But then, he hasn't been to school yet."

"Ugh, bullies. He's probably scared to go. Did you ever find out the reason? I mean, not that any reason is valid."

"Nope," she answered quickly, too quickly.

"Well, teenage boys can be such assholes. Obviously, you of all people know that. I mean, girls can be, too, but we were smarter about it. Knew when to keep our mouths shut."

Hillary frequently referred to them as "we." Did she do that always, Hannah wondered, or just when she was around? Just one grade apart, they'd shared a room and had never been separated until Hillary went to college. That had been a rough year for Hannah, who'd felt unmoored. She'd had friends from the yearbook staff and from volunteering for the annual play; she had even had a boyfriend on and off, but increasingly, she had been removed from them all. Floating above their inane conversations. Judging their stupid parties and electronic dance music. Maybe they'd felt her disdain. Maybe they'd hated her, too. Maybe she'd asked to be hated back. Maybe she'd just needed some darkness in her life for her college essay—wasn't that what someone had accused her of after Hannah had confided in her?

"So does he like his new bedroom? Kids can be so weird about their rooms. Remember that sort of chubby girl who lived on our old street and accused her mother of buying her fat furniture?"

"You can't say 'chubby' anymore."

"Cross it off your list then. I suppose 'husky' is also out of the question."

When she was younger and first thought of being a writer, Hannah had kept lists of words she liked and wanted to use. *Irascible. Frisson. Carabiner.* She could still chant that ancient list like an incantation.

Hillary kept talking at her usual rapid pace, about introducing Hannah to her book club and organizing a party for the kids and carpooling, they absolutely had to carpool, but Hannah was only half listening when she heard Morgan shriek, "Aunt Hannah!" as she ran into the room ahead of Ben, who still had headphones around his neck.

"Not so loud, Morgan, please," Ben said.

"Hey, Bug," Hannah said, breathing in the strawberry fragrance of her niece's hair.

"Where's Miles?" she said, looking around as if they were hiding him.

"He's still sleeping."

"Can I go wake him up?"

Hannah hesitated.

"Sure," Ben replied. "Is the door open?"

"Yes, I think, but—"

"But what?"

"I'll walk with her," Hannah said.

"This little nugget slept in a tent and hiked up mountains all summer. I think she can make it downhill alone," Ben replied, tickling her. "Can't you? Huh?"

"Hannah needs to maybe go deal with some work stuff," Hillary said.

"Yes," Hannah said. "Understatement of the year."

"Wait a minute! Oh. My. God. Ben," Hillary said dramatically, eyes widening. "Darling husband Ben! I just realized you should introduce Han to that nonprofit group you're working with! Aren't they doing some articles and a documentary?"

Ben's mouth fell open a bit, hanging in the air.

"No, it's okay," Hannah said quickly. Something was off; she felt a flush in her neck that told her so. This wasn't like Ben to hesitate. It was totally like Hillary, however, to push too far.

"No, no, no, I mean yes, they are, that's…a great idea."

"I don't want to impose, Ben. It's—"

"No, don't be silly. Let's schedule a time, and I'll give you the lowdown, and you can see if it's a good fit. You're on LinkedIn, right? All your stuff?"

Hannah nodded, and Hillary smiled broadly. She loved nothing more than connecting things, making it all add up. Her biology degree and years of lab research were an anomaly, Hannah thought. Her sister could have been a Hollywood agent, a Wall Street dealmaker.

Hannah tried to hop down from the stool, but she slid the last few inches in her leggings, as if the wood had been oiled.

"Morgan, let's surprise Miles together," Hannah said.

"Okay, but bring him back for breakfast. We have bacon," Hillary called after them.

Morgan grabbed Hannah's hand as they walked, swinging it.

"Remember how you and Uncle Mike used to swing me up?" Morgan said.

"Yes," she said and smiled. She'd been so light as a toddler, Hannah had been afraid she'd let go and tumble off into space, all momentum.

How long had it been since Miles had reached out toward his mom? Was this the difference of gender, of being a bit younger, or of nature? Miles had never been a very cuddly child. Even when he was sick, he seemed to barely tolerate her brushing his hair off his forehead. But Morgan was still a little smush, small, bird-boned for eleven and a half. Hannah wondered if Morgan would ever hit a growth spurt; she worried that her sister's healthy meals weren't giving her enough fat. Still, she had her father's friendly blue eyes and her mother's gold-flecked hair. She was the kind of tween, Hannah thought, who would suddenly blossom one summer, come back in September wearing a push-up bra, and shock the whole class.

As they approached the porch, Hannah saw something that looked almost like a nest clinging at the opposite edge. She let go of Morgan's hand. Hadn't she just swept the porch?

"Hang on, Bug," she said. Hannah walked across the planks to nudge it with her toe. Reddish brownish. Hair? Or fur?

"Miles!" Hannah yelled sharply as she lunged for the door. "Wake up!"

As if she didn't know he was already up.

Miles had always loved his cousin. The pictures of Miles holding her as a newborn on his toddler lap were some of the sweetest photos ever taken in their family. The joy and blush on his face and the way Morgan seemed to be looking right at him. Their mother had it blown up to eleven by seventeen and framed it. People always asked her which studio had done the portrait. *I took it*, Eva would say with pride. *Those are my grandbabies.* They played together beautifully at family get-togethers, always happy to play cards or checkers or build a fort. Like siblings almost, and that was part of the reason Hannah wanted to live close to her sister. So the kids would have each other. So if they ended up only children, as it looked they might, they wouldn't *feel* like only children.

But as Hannah headed toward her son's room, shielding Morgan behind her, she felt full-on dread. Was she being paranoid or pragmatic? She loved her son, but having an adolescent boy, to someone who'd only had a sister, was like having an alien down the hall.

She was worried every time she saw an animal now, even on the damned wallpaper. She was worried when he offered to slice carrots for dinner and complained that the knife was dull. How the hell did he know the difference between a dull and a sharp knife?

She swallowed hard, then opened the door.

Miles was on his knees, putting shirts in drawers as he'd been told to the night before, and Morgan leapt onto his back, tickling him. "Surprise!" she cried, and he laughed, falling over.

"I got you good, admit it," she said.

"Dude, you attacked me from behind like a coward!"

"Like a ninja, you mean!"

Hannah let the relief wash over her. Miles was so much bigger, yet he was delicate with Morgan, faux wrestling, swatting the air. All these years when he had let her win their thumb wars, their races for who got to go first. And he was patient, too, spending hours teaching her how to shuffle cards. And when she was better than him at something—cartwheels, dance moves, her effortless somersaults into her backyard pool—he seemed interested in learning even when Hannah knew he wasn't. Usually, Ben would come and rescue him, proclaiming it was "man time!" just to drive Morgan crazy and make Miles happy. Mike didn't do that; Ben did. She'd come into the room and think her husband didn't even know his own son.

So she didn't intervene, didn't tell him to finish unpacking, didn't say anything at all. She was needlessly worried, and she needed to get over herself. She left them alone, let them laugh themselves silly, while she went through the email chains with Sarah Harper from Boxt. Yes, there was a cancellation fee stated in the agreement letter, she was sure she'd negotiated that. She found Sarah's profile had changed on LinkedIn, announcing her new job at a start-up in Boston. She sent her a carefully worded breezy message, containing her fury because, well, start-ups needed writers and had a lot of funding. And because guilt was a powerful motivator. Then she wrote a terse three-line email to the accounting department at Boxt, reminding them of her two-month cancellation fee, sharing the email trail.

They all walked back to Hillary's house together and sat in the kitchen. Morgan told Miles what to expect the first day of school and which teachers were supposedly nice and which were supposedly mean and what the best day to eat in the cafeteria was (Tuesday, pizza pita day).

Ben took his headphones off his neck, lending them to Miles to hear his favorite playlist on Spotify. It was Ben who'd gotten the kids into the *Hamilton* soundtrack, Ben who'd insisted John Legend was the Sinatra of their time. She was grateful Ben's music was going into her son's ears and not just Mike's classic rock. Glad she would never have to get into Mike's truck and hear Kid Rock blasting ever again.

It was only on the way home, bellies full, content, that she stopped just short of the porch and suddenly sniffed, alert, like a dog. There it was. The smell of death.

The memory of Hillary's expensive coffee in her nose was suddenly gone. She turned to Miles; he looked away too quickly. His hair fell across his eyes like a veil, and instead of flicking his head like he usually did, he let it stay. Let it shield him. He was only half an inch shorter than Hannah now, but he hunched down next to her, folding his shoulders in as if trying to be invisible.

She remembered the half nest, the wisps of hair on the porch. Damn it, she should have listened harder to her intuition. Then she thought of the calls she'd have to make, to his father, his therapist. She thought of the punishment she'd have to mete out. She thought about how badly she didn't want to do any of those things.

"Miles," she said, "tell me what happened."

The therapist had said she should be careful about asking questions, giving choices. With this issue, with boundaries and limits, statements were clearer.

He didn't answer, and in that space, she wavered—could she be wrong? They lived in the woods now, near a creek, close to farmland. Things passed through; creatures lived and died. They were not in a village with sidewalks anymore. They were on the edge of suburbia, but it was more like the country than anywhere else they'd lived. They were part of the natural world. This made things better. Then she realized, just as sharply, that it could make them worse. There was more death around them, not less.

"I didn't mean to."

Wasn't that the very definition of a compulsion? Wasn't that the precise point that the psychiatrist she couldn't afford had explained to her so carefully?

She took a deep breath. "Oh my God, the box cutter. Did you—"

"What? Mom, no. I swear, I—"

"Did you…leave it in the woods? Bury it? Where is it?"

The questions flew out of her mouth; she couldn't help it. The statements were gone, evaporated.

She grabbed his arm—too hard, she'd think later—and spun him to face her. It took far more effort than she expected. Her arm ached with force and regret.

"Tell me where it is," she declared.

"I hid it."

"Get the shovel," she said.

He glanced nervously up the hill toward Hillary's.

"Can we wait till it's dark?"

Of course that was the reasonable choice. He didn't want to risk anyone seeing him, didn't want his beloved cousin next door to know. And she, of course, the keeper of his secret, didn't either. Doing it was one thing. Being bullied about it was another. But she didn't know, couldn't know, how much she'd regret saying yes. Yes, he could wait.

It was only after they'd finished unpacking—when dusk fell and Miles put on the headlamp and started digging out back, the small grave for the fox corpse he claimed he'd found dead, claimed he hadn't killed, and Hannah had nudged with her toe, looking at the fur, checking for wounds or blood, trying to prove him right or wrong and coming up empty—that she heard the faint chorus from the opposite side of her street, down the gully, near the creek, calling out one word over and over, a chant. *Liza. Liza. Liza.* Hannah thought, *What a strange name for a dog.* She left him to work in the low light and was about to call Mike and leave a message for the therapist.

Then, the text from her sister.

Because a six-year-old girl named Liza, who lived in the house across the street, the shrouded house with the weather vane and the couple on maybe their third marriage, had gone down to the creek to look for frogs and hadn't come back.

Hannah's hand went up to cover her face. Dear God. She'd already felt a vein of affection for that house, the dark greens and grays, the possibilities it held. Already the neighborhood had managed to change shape, to scare them, disappoint them.

In that suspended moment, as she breathed by the low light of her phone, a flash of recognition ran through her. She couldn't see through the glossy leaves, but it was as if she saw that little girl. Another child drawn to animals, and animals had led her to something sinister. Hannah could picture the crayon drawings of frogs and deer and squirrels dotting their fridge, the animal books that lined their shelves. A girl who fearlessly nestled her rosy cheeks into the dusty fur of strangers' dogs and begged her mother for a rabbit on top of their house.

She knew that kind of kid. She had that kind of kid.

four

EVA

They found her bucket. That bothered me tremendously, that tidbit, whispered to me by Hillary as we stood together in a line outside the Harris family's guest cottage, serving as search party headquarters, waiting for instructions. *A symbol of innocence, wrenched from her tiny hands!* I shuddered. I also nosed around the guest cottage, wondering if they had two lots and would ever spin it off as a separate property or even rent with the option to buy. (That's what Margot had told me she was searching for.) Oh, I was becoming a regular Harriet the Realtor Spy instead of focusing on the tragedy at hand. *Shame on you, Eva.*

I'd pictured that bucket as red plastic, light and childlike, bobbing in the overflowing creek. All that rain, rushing by. Was she swept away? The news reports said the water in Tamsen Creek was nearly ten inches higher than normal; it had spread out in a monstrous pattern, it seemed to me, pouring over rocks and moss and spent leaves that usually provided picturesque natural margins. Now it was just wet grass along the sides and gray, churning water rushing through. Uglier than I'd ever seen it, a molten, throbbing slash.

As we got through the line and entered the mudroom of the guest-house, which probably doubled as their pool house, given its proximity, I was surprised to find it quite orderly and large. There were cubbies and benches, a stacked washer and dryer, the kind I hated, and a tiled dog bath, replete with hanging collar, leash, and chew toys.

We were handed flyers with the girl's photo and specific information about what little Liza was wearing and carrying and where she was headed. To the creek to catch frogs was what she'd told her mother. Something she did nearly every afternoon, like clockwork. The mother said she was shy and didn't have many friends at school or in the neighborhood but loved to explore, so she'd let her. We work so hard as parents to keep kids to a schedule, and look how it comes back to haunt us. Why, anyone in the neighborhood could have known the girl had a pattern, as regular as a snack.

In the close-up photo, she was missing two teeth in the front, showing off her checkerboard smile proudly. The photo had an informal, silly quality to it that made me wonder why the family had chosen it. I couldn't say for certain if it was the same girl I'd glimpsed the other night; that child had seemed a good deal younger than six, with longer, wilder-looking hair. On the flyer, it said she was carrying a house key on a white lanyard, a bucket, and possibly a mug. They'd found the bucket but not the lanyard or mug. It tore at me inexplicably, on another level, when I read that the bucket was white enamel, monogrammed, and oversize, used to fill the dog's water bowl.

They wouldn't ordinarily tell anyone this level of detail, I was certain, except they were also looking for a matching enamel mug. The scoop for the dog's dry food. The child would use it, I supposed, to capture frogs and ferry them to the bucket. White enamel. Black monogram. I looked around. Perhaps in these tall cabinets, there were matching black-and-white monogrammed dog towels? (The girl herself was wearing green wellies, paisley leggings, and a pink pullover with a drawstring hood. That bothered me too, the drawstring.)

I cleared my throat, projected. "Is the monogram the dog's initials?"

The friend or relative coordinating things, the man in dark-gray leggings and black half-zip—how I hate to see a man's scrawny limbs in leggings, so emasculating—blinked hard at me instead of answering. His mouth opened slightly, as if he had to pull in oxygen to fuel an answer. I was certain that after a few seconds, he wished he'd ignored me and not looked right at me.

Because he didn't just say a quick *yes*, or *I don't know*, or for God's sake even offer a laugh. The question hung in the air a long time, long enough for the rest of the group, numbering thirty or forty, to repeat it down the line.

"I don't think that's relevant," he said.

I shrugged. "You just told us to notice everything, even if it seems random."

"In the woods, I meant. As you fan out."

"Oh. Okay." I rolled my eyes at Hannah and Hillary, who whispered to me to behave. These were her neighbors, *their* neighbors now, and it wouldn't do for an outsider to embarrass them. Never mind that I was technically a neighbor, too, lived so close I occasionally walked over here, cutting through the gulch of another neighborhood, or did until things got so damned slippery and wet with this September rain.

There were mostly women in the group, a few teenagers, only a couple of men. Morgan and Miles had begged to come, claimed other kids were doing it (which was correct, but they were seventeen and eighteen), and the girls, with a look of horror on their faces, had said absolutely not. Under no circumstances. And Morgan's chorus of *why not, we want to help, we can look, we're brave* was met with no excuses or reasons. As it should have been. God knows I didn't always agree with their parenting advice—I was at odds with the way Hillary overscheduled Morgan's summers, and don't get me started on Miles's hair, which Hannah and Mike never forced him to cut and which always fell in his face, like a sporty British girl. Like an unkempt Princess Di, he was with that hair— horrifying. As if the boy didn't have enough to worry about, with his slender body and bookish ways. To add feminine hair on top of the equation struck me as madness. But keeping them home today? Absolutely.

Hillary knew several of the neighbors of course and introduced us. We shook hands as we signed in and picked up our maps from the volunteer table on the patio. If you looked down the sloping property, the creek was not only visible, swollen with rain, but audible. Even over the chitchat, you could hear the water churning, almost riverine as it leapt and fell over the rocks and logs. It was inescapable; it beckoned. Oh, to a child, the magnetic sound of water, rushing, babbling, breaking against rock, seeping into tide pools of treasures. Poor child, I thought. How could she have had any other fate? The creek called, loudly, to anyone who set foot in that backyard.

One of the women, Susan, who I felt was a bit overdressed for searching crime scenes in the woods, in her turtleneck and Barbour coat and suede boots, said that Hannah should think about joining the neighborhood book club. She said they read a variety of books, and there were lots of smart women in it, as if she had to emphasize and overcompensate somehow for this new neighbor who was a writer. She said this directly to Hannah and didn't include me in the invitation, even though I was standing right next to her, obvious as a bump on a log. Older ladies who don't live at old lady homes don't get invited to things much unless we offer some kind of useful skill that is becoming fetishized by the young. Pottery. Quilting. Magic loop knitting. I suppose if I start gathering plants and making my own cocktail bitters or sustainable fabric dyes, I can become popular again. Maybe Morgan could put me in one of her videos dancing to rap, and I'd rise from my early crypt and enjoy relevance once again!

Oh well, who needs 'em. Overdressed, underfed women discussing books to make themselves feel like they were back at college. Who wanted to go back to college and write papers again? Not me. Just let me enjoy the damned book!

I thought I might meet some nice retired male searchers, someone in a yellow vest and hiking boots and a sensible hat. Someone like that would be nice to have coffee with. But Tamsen Creek was the land of the stay-at-home mom. The men had important jobs, meetings in other cities, traveling even over the weekend. They'd chosen this neighborhood partly because of its proximity to the highway that zipped down to the Philadelphia airport, as well as the less obvious but unspoken nearness to the county airport where private jets took off and landed. Depending on what client Ben was serving, he utilized them both, and so, too, did many of his neighbors. Ben certainly was gone on business well over half the time. Hillary pretended she didn't care, because she was busy and independent and did everything in the household anyway, but I knew she did. Wasn't that why you got married, so you could share in the triumphs and tragedies of communities? Now, the husbands would hear about this hubbub not over dinner but over text message between their surgeries or presentations. They'd feel terrible, of course, remind their wives to set the alarms and not let their children wander off. How awful that I went immediately to stereotype. But if this wasn't a stereotypical place, what was? As far as I could ascertain, none of these women held paying jobs except Hannah.

It was only later, when I asked Hillary where Ben was off to, that I would learn many of the men had stayed home, still badly hungover and exhausted from their monthly neighborhood poker game on Friday, and behind on everything else because of it. Hannah said that Mike had offered to come and help but that she'd told him no. I suppose she thought he was just trying to worm his way back into his ex-wife's and child's hearts, because when I commented that Mike probably would have been the only person with backcountry skills, the only useful person on the search, she'd glared at me.

"What?" I'd said. "He's camped outdoors his whole life. He's tracked animals, hidden from them in stands or dens or whatever you call them. I think it's fair to say Mike would be an asset."

And the two of them had stared at me, ganging up the way they still do, two against one, and said that anyone observant and capable of walking in the woods could be helpful! Anyone with a good eye! There was no need for tracking scat or carving a path! And I suppose I was being sexist and stereotypical. And I dared to support someone they'd already cast out.

What was I supposed to do? Just because Hannah said they'd grown apart and had nothing to say to one another, were we to pretend we didn't like him anymore? Should I forget that Mike was kind to me and had some good qualities I wish I possessed?

As we walked for several hours, adjacent to the creek, heads bent, the sun rose steadily over my left shoulder and landed over my right, so I knew I was at least staying in a straight line. It was boring work, and I had trouble concentrating on what to look for, what was important. Weren't all the weeds bent? Wasn't all the earth trampled? Still, I didn't see any cigarette butts, threads from clothing, buttons, anything remotely human. Someone in another line had a metal detector, and I guess he was looking for shotgun shells or maybe some old heiress's jewelry, who knew.

All I could think as we continued going single file, walking within three feet of one another, as synchronized as chorus girls, was about the family. Where were they while we were searching? The mother, the father, the siblings? Was someone investigating them? Why couldn't we be told what kind of family had lost this child?

What kind of people could own this grand and glorious house and have seen fit to give their dog a special bucket? And not their little girl?

And what kind of husband needed to stay home all weekend nursing a hangover?

Well, the answer to that I certainly knew all too well.

five

HANNAH

That first day of school, Hannah tried not to obsess about her son or her lack of regular work and failed at both. She sent out exploratory emails to contacts at other pharma companies and messaged former clients letting them know she was available. Ben would certainly follow up on that meeting about his client, but she didn't want to pressure him. Then, she settled down at her kitchen table to focus on finishing her final edit of a history professor's essays about his time in the Peace Corps so she could bill him as soon as possible. But oh, how she'd hated this project. She'd run out of constructive ways to tell him how to make a sentence come alive. *Write better!* she'd wanted to scream.

The final proofread was endless and tedious, and she was constantly interrupted with thoughts of her son and the realization that her jaw was tense, her neck, her breathing shallow. She kept getting up to pace and refill her water glass and eat half a banana and then, ten minutes later, the other half.

Drop-off at school had gone smoothly, but she kept picturing all the boys lingering outside on the grass, bent over their phones. A variety of sizes, the way boys were at this age. Some as tall and muscled as men, the others half their height and weight. Miles had agreed to be driven to school but insisted on taking the bus home, because Morgan had told him that Hillary was wrong—lots of the boys rode the bus home but the girls not so much. Dirty, smelly, what? She wondered why, but he wanted to belong, so Hannah didn't question it. One day. One bus ride home. *We will see how it goes*, she'd thought as she dropped him off and drove through the winding path through campus. With fifteen hundred students, the buildings were sprawling and multistoried, with a pool, sports complex, and climbing wall. The scale of the campus alone would certainly worry some parents. But Miles liked to explore and had a great sense of direction, like his dad. Once, when he was six, he'd wandered from their campsite and gotten lost for almost an hour, the worst hour of Hannah's life. Mike kept saying that Miles would know to follow the river back. And sure enough, that was exactly what had happened. Mike had been proud: a free-range, capable kid who could navigate the outdoors.

Then she got home and couldn't stop thinking about all those new boys. Would Miles get lost not on the grounds but in the personalities, the types? Were they friendly? Were they cruel? Or were they that confusing in-between, like girls could be? She shuddered to consider what they were looking at on their phones. Porn? Other kids in this neighborhood got phones at ten, eleven, twelve, she knew. Because Miles didn't go to sports practices or after-school activities, because he had access to some video games and her iPad and computer in a limited way, she'd always thought thirteen, which was a few months away, but didn't want him to feel left out. Was she an overprotective, idealistic, screen-time-nagging idiot? Should she have gotten him a phone even though he didn't need it and it would ruin his brain?

Hannah stood up to drink her third glass of water and eat another handful of cashews from her stash in the cupboard, and almost as quickly as the thoughts came to her, guilt washed over her, too. That little girl across the street, Liza Harris, was still missing, and she, Hannah, knew exactly where her son was. She'd been more calm walking through the woods with her mother and sister than she was waiting here, safe in her kitchen, thinking of Miles at school. Jesus, what was wrong with her?

She came back to her computer, but the alien sound of a helicopter overhead rattled the windows, startled her. The family had suspended the volunteer search across the wooded paths and short brush throughout the hills of their neighborhood, but helicopters, here, in the suburbs? Had they paid for these, or the police? There were dense, sloping stands of trees ringing the neighborhood, separating it from the old Tamsen farm. Woods too thick for ordinary volunteers. Did they know something was down there? Or were they just too lazy to search?

The next one swooped loud and low to the east, too close. Was it over Hillary's house?

She stood up to look out the kitchen window when a sharp knock on the front door shook the floorboards. The house was old, but at that moment, it felt downright flimsy, like it couldn't hold her.

Two men stood on her porch, looking around in a way that reminded her of home buyers, surveying the land, construction, looking for peeling paint. They were about the same age, both with brown hair, but one was sturdy and muscular, the other taller, lanky, a little gray in the front of his hair. Their rayon pants and button-down shirts made her think they were with a church group. She sighed deeply and prepared her standard line about being on deadline and wondered if they'd say that deadlines wouldn't matter when the rapture came. She'd heard that one before. But as she approached the door, they both held up badges to the windowpane.

Again, guilt flooded her chest. How could she keep forgetting what was going on around her? *That's what being a writer will do to you*, she thought. A deep dive that can carry you away from almost anything on the surface, even someone's darkest tragedy.

"Afternoon," the shorter one said. "We're canvassing all the neighbors about the Liza Harris case."

"Of course," Hannah said and invited them in. They introduced themselves as Detectives Carelli and Thompson. Up close, she could see more differences in their hair, skin, faces. Carelli, the shorter one, was tan and dark-eyed. Thompson was pale, and his eyes were hazel. The sprout of gray in his cowlick threw a little bit of light in his serious face, but not much. He would have been handsome, perhaps, if he smiled or got some sun on his face. Neither of them smiled, so she didn't either.

They looked around at a few remaining boxes and not-hung pictures.

"Just moved in," Thompson said.

Not a question, but she answered by nodding.

"Where's your son today?"

"He's at school." She frowned. "Wait, how—"

"You look a bit like your sister. I bet you get that a lot."

She blinked. "No, actually. Not anymore."

They asked her when she had arrived, if she'd noticed anything amiss. On moving day or before. No. Did she ever walk on the trails through the woods. No. Not yet. Anything she could think of that she'd observed across the street? Even the smallest detail that might have meaning? From any time?

"There were balloons," she said dumbly.

"Balloons?"

"Tied to the mailbox. The day of my walk-through on the house."

"For a party."

"Yes, I assume. But—"

"But what?"

"There were no cars."

"I'm sorry, no cars?" Thompson's neutral face had moved into a full frown. He was older than she'd originally estimated.

"I was here most of the evening, here and at my sister's. And there were no cars for the party. I left around seven, seven thirty."

"Maybe the party was later?"

"For a six-year-old? Doubtful," she said.

"And this struck you as odd."

"Just this moment," she said. "I'm realizing this right now."

"Okay. Well, maybe the party was the day before."

"I don't think so," she said. "The balloons hadn't lost air. They were fresh balloons, not limp like they are the next day."

The two men blinked at her, sizing her up.

"It's a mom thing," she said dumbly, but it was true, and they nodded. "So maybe no one came to her party," she continued. "Which would be traumatizing."

She could have kept going on this topic, shared the stories of moms on social media who railed against kids who RSVPed yes and then didn't show. They posted photos with the birthday boy alone in a party hat, and strangers made it go viral, sending cards and presents and prayers to this poor lonely kid. It happened. She could certainly imagine that little girl having her heart broken, running into the woods in tears, too broken up to notice she'd wandered into something dangerous.

But their blank expressions told her to stop. They either cared or didn't care, but at least she had come up with *something* to tell them. She was proud of her powers of observation, even if they weren't. They asked her what day this was, if she was certain it was Wednesday, and she looked in her phone and told them. A Wednesday, yes.

She offered them coffee or tea, gesturing toward the kitchen.

"How about a glass of water?" Carelli said.

"Yes. Of course. Water."

She poured from a Brita in the fridge. They thanked her and raised their glasses as if toasting her new home.

"*Nostrovia*," she said, then instantly regretted it. Why she'd done that, she couldn't say. Would they ascribe meaning to that? Would they walk away thinking she wasn't a teetotaler but a Russian alcoholic who drank vodka on a Tuesday?

"So your son," the taller one said slowly, setting his glass down on the narrow dining-room table, drawing out the pause as if she might fill in the blank, blurt something out. He swallowed and frowned, considering his next words—or hers. But she waited, raising her eyes in anticipation.

"He's coming home on the bus, is that right?"

She was annoyed they knew this but quickly realized they had probably just assumed. Since she clearly wasn't leaving to pick him up and was here, working.

"Yes."

"He was with you this weekend?"

"Yes."

"Not with his father, here?"

Now it was her turn to take a deep breath. What the hell had Hillary told them? That she was divorced, that she had a kid, what else? They'd obviously interviewed her sister earlier, and she felt once again the second born's annoyance. The older sister always went first, always had power over her. Could she have given her a few minutes' heads-up, at least?

"Yes."

"He didn't leave for any sports practice or go to a friend's house?"

"No."

"No hikes in the woods?"

"No," she said firmly, her face reddening. Jesus, they had a lot of nerve!

"You're sure?"

"Yes, I'm sure. We were unpacking, not…perambulating."

They exchanged a glance.

"It means strolling," she said quietly.

"We know what it means," Thompson said.

"I have a lot of work to do," she said. Which was exactly what she would have said to the Jehovah's Witnesses or to the kid from the Clean Air Committee or anyone else who'd knocked at her door. She told herself she was not being uncooperative, just practical.

"Before he gets home," Carelli said.

"What?"

"You want to finish your work before your son gets home."

"Yes, yes I do."

They finished their water and took a final sweep of her living room.

"Do your bedrooms face west or…south or north?"

"I beg your pardon?"

"Your bedrooms. Are the windows only to the west? Or is there a corner window? Just so we understand the configuration here," Carelli said.

She blinked.

"Configuration means the layout of the house," Thompson said, barely containing the smallest smile.

"We just moved in," she said, setting down her glass. "All we've seen were some balloons. Now if you'll excuse me, I'm on deadline."

"Journalist?"

"Depends on the day."

"Gig economy, amirite?" Carelli said.

Ah, an attempt to cozy up to her, understand her predicament. If it had come from a person at a coffee shop or bus stop, it would have meant one thing: commiseration. But what did it mean coming from a cop? That she was underpaid, desperate? That some days she would do anything for money?

She forced her lips into a weak smile that she hoped made her look friendly enough but not desperate. And not stupid, not lonely, not any of the things that would make a divorced woman confide in a cop about her financial instability.

They walked to the front door, and she stood back, watching them open it and step onto the porch.

Thompson looked at her through the screen, cocked his head.

"Just to be clear," he said, "the Harris family didn't come over and welcome you to the neighborhood? The little girl didn't run over to see if someone her age moved in?"

"No," she said.

"What about the other neighbors? Anyone bring cookies or—"

"No."

"Wow," Carelli said. "Not very friendly."

"Or maybe they're all on deadline," Thompson said.

They gave her a business card and said to call if she remembered anything else, even small, like the balloons, and she nodded. She stood at the door and made sure their car turned around and drove away, made sure they didn't wait to see her son. They'd probably started at the top of the street and worked their way down. There was only one more property below her, before the main road. She hadn't met that family yet, but Hannah had said they were quiet and kept to themselves. Which was exactly what everyone in the world said when their neighbor went to prison. *Go talk to them*, she thought. *Go have a drink of water with the quiet people, not here with the loud, angry, busy people.*

It was only when she sat back down at her computer that she found even more sting in what they'd said. Did they think she was faking being on deadline? Did they think she was an idiot for mentioning the balloons?

Or did they merely want to rub it in that dozens of people had seen a moving truck unloading and hadn't bothered to come up and say hello to her and her son?

She thought of her old neighborhood in Narberth, twenty minutes away, but it couldn't have been more different. The parade of neighbors the day they'd moved in. Casseroles, bottles of wine, cookies. She thought of how close the school had been, how the kids walked there in clusters. Now she'd moved to a place where the kids ghosted another kid on her birthday. And no one welcomed the new kid either. The crimes against kids were adding up daily.

As she settled down to work, she remembered, suddenly, sharply, that Miles had gone outside the night they'd moved in, walked down to look at the swollen creek. He'd been gone, what, five minutes? Seven? But that could hardly be called a walk. That was more of a glance. And it was Friday, not Saturday. They wanted to know about Saturday. She continued working for an hour or more and then looked at her watch.

The bus was late. One day, and their little system was already unreliable.

six

EVA

Should I take it as a snub that once again, I wasn't invited to the neighborhood book club? That my own daughters didn't think to ask if their mother could attend?

I suppose not. After all, I don't read that much, never have. The girls both know that. Seems wasteful somehow, my hands too idle. I'd rather knit or play cards. And besides, if I started socializing as much as they did, who would babysit? Hannah had been included after being in the neighborhood only a week, so that boded well for her fitting in. I was happy for her.

I came at the appointed hour—six. Hillary and Hannah had agreed that the kids would stay at Hillary's because she had the elaborate finished basement with video games, Ping-Pong, air hockey. Sometimes I wondered if they weren't more for Ben and his poker buddies than Morgan. And of course there was the pool, but the evenings were getting too cool for that. And the kids were at an age when they still did kid things with their grandmother. They'd bake cookies; they'd play a few rounds of kings in the corner. They'd show me cat videos they found amusing. Adolescence hadn't hit them full force yet, but it was coming, and my daughters weren't ready.

Case in point. Miles was twelve years old and couldn't stay at home for a few hours when his mother was down the street with the neighbors? When I was younger than he, I sold doll clothes door to door, babysat at night, and walked the two blocks home in the dark without a single thought. I know Hannah worries about boys on the bus—and she should, given what he's been through—but I thought she was perhaps overreacting to the little girl's disappearance. Yes, a small child had wandered off, but at the press conference on TV, the police insisted there was no evidence of foul play. No reason for panic or worry to spread throughout the neighborhood. Little ones can tumble down a hillside or drown in an inch of water after all. A tragedy, but singular to their size and vulnerability. So was this any reason to never let her nearly grown son out of her sight? There was a huge difference between the fear you felt for a boy of twelve and a little girl of six. Wasn't she going to scare him more by overprotecting him? I know, I know, middle school is a tricky time. When some boys are still tender and soft, and some rise up out of their sneakers, vines grown into trees. And Miles, still in the muddy middle. Tall but reedy.

As soon as my girls had walked out the door, I went into Hillary's large pantry and brought out flour, sugar, cinnamon, and butter and assembled a batch of snickerdoodles. Big ones, too, none of those little thumbprints. I baked them and called the kids to help sprinkle cinnamon sugar on top while they were still warm. And then I watched Miles sit at the island and eat six cookies. Six! Yes, I let him. I confess I wanted him to like me, to draw himself closer. I thought perhaps that would work better, bringing him to me rather than the other way around. He looked at me, straight in the eye, as he took his fourth cookie, and I gave him a small nod. I refilled his milk glass to offer even greater encouragement. *Dunk away! Wash 'em down!* The coded signals between us. The hint of a smile. Progress! Maybe we could be better friends after all this time. He was certainly a boy who could use a friend. Morgan had one cookie that took her as long to nibble as it did for Miles to gulp down three. She waited patiently while he ate cookies four, five, and six, dangling her feet, picking up sugar particles from her plate with one finger, then carrying the plates to the sink. *Good girl*, I said.

Afterward, the two of them went downstairs, and I picked up my knitting—a jaunty beret—and wondered how things were going over at the neighbors' she shed. That's where the book club was being held, in Susan Somebody or Other's charming backyard structure that probably cost more than Hannah's little spring house, a structure a rich woman erected out of protest against the above-garage man cave. Hillary had told me the story of their renovation one-upmanship a year or so ago, and I'd found it amusing. Susan and…oh, I can't remember, Sam or Steve or something. He had his man cave, and now Susan had her she shed. Couldn't she have just called it a bungalow and called it a day? Oh, everyone had an outbuilding now, didn't they? Tree houses for the children, caves for the men, sheds for the women, cottages for the pool, or in the case of the Harrises, separate baths for the dog.

Dear God, whatever happened to a hammock?

Downstairs, the slide and thrust of a fast-paced air hockey game came up through the vents. Small shouts and groans to punctuate the clicks of the lunges and parries and requisite disappointments. Did Morgan even watch the Philadelphia Flyers, follow the team, care about this sport? I didn't know. Her father seemed to like all sports, unable to choose. Mike had been the same way when he was living with Miles and Hannah. So many holidays spent with those two men sneaking off to the television, groaning over bad plays, and cheering so loudly over good ones they rattled the china in the cabinet.

Going all in on all sports seemed a bit reckless to me, like liking all animals or all men. Best to be specific, not to generalize.

I was grateful that air hockey sounded different from Ping-Pong or computer games. Once when I babysat, the two of them had played Ping-Pong all night, and the tap-tapping had lodged in my head, entered my dreams like an inane pop song. The next time I came over, I hid the balls in my pockets and professed ignorance when they asked where they were.

Anyway, I digress. They'd been outside earlier in the afternoon, running around doing who knows what, but they were downstairs, playing air hockey, when the commotion began outside. They ran to the top of the stairs, or Miles did, leading, and he was leaping up them, based on his thuds, two at a time. He'd heard something the rest of us did not, like a dog's whistle.

Only as he headed for the door, his cousin in tow, did I hear it, too: sirens. Multiple. Rounding the corner. Were they coming this way? Did he know they were?

"What's going on?" I asked dumbly, as if they had a police scanner. As if they knew any more than I did. Even the internet isn't that fast or accurate. You can't know everything all the time, despite your desire to. No.

They opened the door, and I expected them to stand on the steps, to wait. But that was what an adult would do, not a child. They rushed down the steps, hurtling down the lawn, drawn by the lights and sound.

Who could blame them? I let them go, didn't hold them back. The night was cool but pleasant, and I was struck as I looked at the yards and houses, the way the lights had just begun to dance off green bushes and brick archways, some nestled at the base of mature trees, that this was the only time of the year when homes are truly themselves. Not embellished and decorated for seasons or holidays. Not stripped bare and admonished by winter or swollen and colored by spring. No, these were the real homes. A rare moment, I thought, and I wondered if I had ever really noticed it before. Oh, the things you see when life slows down. The time you wasted all these years when you weren't looking properly.

I sensed the children would stop at the street and watch, and that they did, at first. But whatever was happening just kept happening. A parade of multiple police cars, an ambulance, a fire truck. The whole township emergency force, it seemed, was on our street, headed up and over. But we were the only ones who stood outside.

A thought seized me suddenly—the book club. The lane above Hillary's house, where the she shed overlooks the gully on the other side of the hill. And I swear, the moment it hit me was the moment it hit Miles. He started running. Morgan looked back at me, torn. And then I heard the screech of brakes and a thud. Not a loud one, more a glancing blow. But Miles, Miles was so thin.

We ran down together, Morgan and I, and were met with a police officer holding up his hand.

"We'll need you to stay back, ma'am. There's a fluid investigation going on."

I despised the use of the word *fluid* this way, but there was no time to argue with him over vocabulary words.

"But I heard a crash, and my grandson—"

"Police car hit a deer coming down the hill, that's all."

"Are you sure it was a deer, bec—"

"Yes. One hundred percent."

"Did you see a boy? Did you—"

"Ma'am, no. Go back to your homes. We're cordoning off the area, but you're safe."

"But my grandson—"

"It was a deer, ma'am."

In the shadows below us, I saw a figure crouching between the bushes of the neighbor's house. As the candy lights flashed nearby, they briefly illuminated a lock of his hair, the set of his chin. Miles. Hiding from them? Or from me?

"You should tell us more about what's happening. This is our neighborhood," I said huffily. "These are our children."

"Ma'am, I know you're all on high alert because of the child missing, but there is simply a fire in a playhouse at the end of the street—that's all I can say."

"Are you sure it's a playhouse? And not a shed?"

He didn't answer me. He just gave me the kind of look you give a naughty child and turned away. I thought I saw him shaking his head, as if I had been making a joke and wasn't perfectly, deadly serious.

"My daughters are in that she shed down the street," I screamed. "Twenty women are there, in the she shed!"

"It's a *playhouse*," he called over his shoulder. "An empty playhouse."

I told Morgan to go home and to text her mother's cell phone and make sure she was all right. She said no, she wanted to stay with me. No, I insisted. I told her I'd be back in a minute.

The lawn was wet and uneven near the street, full of pocked, sloping indents, soupy, like it wanted to be a stream and a landscaper had refused to let it happen. I stepped slowly, grateful I had on sneakers. Surely, Miles heard me coming or knew I would be, but he waited until the cars were past us. Their lights took them elsewhere, past the book club house, all the way to the end of the street.

I was about to bend the bushes, to whisper his name, when he stood up.

He held something in his arms, bigger than a baby, smaller than a person. He started to walk the opposite way, toward the neighbors' house, as if I wasn't there.

"Miles!" I said it sharply, necessarily, I thought.

As he turned, I saw the shape of the fawn in his arms.

I felt my breath traveling the length of my throat, down my body.

"We can't take it home," I said.

"I know."

"You have to leave it here," I said.

"But it's not dead yet." His voice was cold and matter-of-fact, a mile from tender.

"The vet won't take a wild animal, Miles. It could be sick. It could make you—"

I saw the arguments not adding up in front of him. His rejection, his lack of belief in everything I was saying. He lived in a different world from mine.

"It can't die alone."

My breath again. What did that mean? Was he planning to kill it? Put it out of its misery? Did he expect me to, like his father would, in a heartbeat? A sturdy rock, a glancing blow. A twist of the neck like Mike did with a bird in the field? His father would not hesitate. Had he taught him these skills? At his age, some young boys in Pennsylvania killed and gutted deer without blinking an eye. Others brought home the wounded to feed and tend and refused to eat meat. Which side was he on? Why couldn't I tell?

"Miles," I said evenly, "you have to leave it here, for its mother. The mother will come if you leave it."

It was the best argument I could offer. But I did not want to witness his choice. I decided to trust him, because I had to. If he was going to kill it, if there was a knife in his pocket or a garrote up his sleeve, anything that justified the chill running up my spine, I didn't see it. Before I turned, a plume of smoke rose in the air above our heads, darkening the sky. The first smell of something burning, comforting as camp. But then the next breaths came, singeing us with threats. I coughed and told him we needed to go back now.

I didn't wait. I left it in his hands. But he did not come back to the house.

seven

HANNAH

T he fire didn't put an end to book club. No, it just added some fuel to it. Secrecy, gossip, and something to watch from the large patio connecting the main house and so-called shed while everyone drank their champagne and sauvignon blanc. That seemed to be the prevailing attitude—that it was there for their entertainment and speculation.

"Probably torched it for the insurance money," a woman named Anne said. Her hair was blond and thick, her sunglasses pushed into it, holding it back, like a hasty headband. She wore no makeup, had a normal number of wrinkles but was still very pretty, with large brown eyes and expansive white teeth. Naturally white, not that electric white that looked as if it might glow in the dark. If she hadn't just accused her neighbors of being criminals, Hannah might have thought at first glance they could be friends.

"Is that a mob joke? Just because they're Italian," Hillary said. "Cut them a break."

"Half Italian," someone added. "He's Italian, not her."

"She's Venezuelan."

"Oh, she looks Italian."

"Who cares what they are? They're my neighbors. They're my friends. God, you guys," a woman named Monica said. "I hope it's wet enough from all the rain that the fire doesn't spread. So many leaves and branches this time of year." Monica picked up her phone and called her caretaker, who was still at her house and assured her that all was safe.

Hannah couldn't remember her name, the allegedly Venezuelan neighbor, which didn't seem important at the time. She couldn't be expected to learn who everyone was right away.

Susan was the woman hosting, a small woman with a head slightly too big for her body, like someone who'd shrunk everywhere she could. She had on a chunky sweater with suede boots and large mesh earrings, everything textured and designed to be noticed or touched. She reminded Hannah of a girl in college who told her sorority sisters she always wore cashmere or angora because it made her boyfriend want to cuddle, like a blanket. Susan made up for her size by making big sweeping gestures with her hands and face, proudly showing off her new shed, which was almost as large as Hannah's house and had nicer appliances and several arrangements of fresh flowers that matched the cover of the book they'd read—peach and green.

Hillary had told Hannah there was no need to bring anything, and she quickly found out why—Susan had the event catered, with tuna sushi sandwiches and radishes and pea pods wrapped in spring lettuce and the smallest desserts Hannah had ever seen, truly bite-sized. Beautiful, delicious, fancier than the word *shed* would lead you to believe. And small. The real estate was large, but everything else, including most of the women, was small.

Only a few women wanted to talk about the book, an Auschwitz love story Hannah had skimmed the night before so she wouldn't feel left out. As they stood watching the smoke above the hill, listening to the sirens, Anne sighed and told Hannah she was "done with the Holocaust." *Strike two*, Hannah thought. Still, there was something useful about a woman who said out loud what merely skittered through others' thoughts. Anne was probably an old-fashioned bigot, but at least she was honest.

Another woman, so short she was child-sized, Tara, with pin-straight red hair, offered a vape pen, and Hannah shook her head.

"I know vaping's controversial now, but if you ever need edibles, let me know."

Hannah smiled and said she wasn't into that, especially with a middle schooler at home. The woman looked at her oddly, head cocked, as if she didn't quite see her point. Some moms secretly smoked pot in Hannah's old neighborhood, giggling around the fire pits when the kids weren't home, but she hadn't expected it here, out in the open, where people were more proper and had more money.

Hillary hadn't mentioned pot when she'd described the ladies in book club. She'd mentioned kids' ages, hair color, hobbies, husbands' jobs. Hannah had asked if any of the women worked, and Hillary had sighed and said they all did volunteer work, which was really, truly a lot of work. Hannah had nodded; she'd heard that familiar refrain but didn't know firsthand. She'd never had the luxury of being that kind of busy. But they hadn't gone over their addictions. Pot? Adderall? Alcohol? Vicodin?

Oh well, she supposed. Plenty of time for that.

The emergency response to the fire a few properties away had been robust. No one at book club seemed particularly worried about it; there was no talk of walking down to see if their neighbors were okay. Gone were the days of bringing blankets and buckets of water, but still. Maybe they didn't know their half-Italian neighbors. Maybe they knew they were away. Maybe they were just leaving things to the professionals. Of course, you couldn't go down there with a vape pen, could you?

Hannah spoke to Hillary, not the group.

"Shouldn't we maybe go see if anyone needs help?"

"Help?"

"I don't know, if they have to go to the hospital for smoke inhalation, if they might need their kids picked up somewhere or their dog fed or—"

"Wow, you really are a writer."

"Fire is no joke."

"No, of course, but it's just a playhouse, Han."

"That's even worse. There's kids, there's toys—"

"They don't have any kids. The previous owners built it. They were gonna tear it down. Plus there's professionals swarming it. I'm sure it's fine."

So it wasn't the fire exactly that brought the evening to a close but a call from Hannah's mother. Hannah took the call and hurried to the edge of the deck, away from the chittering women, so she could hear. Still, hearing didn't matter much; she could make out her mother's words but didn't quite understand what she was saying. She knew her mother's tone of voice. Better safe than sorry. She'd always suspected her mother was a little wary of boys and their style of play and speech. She'd raised girls after all.

Hannah told Hillary that Miles was acting out and she had to go home.

"Acting out?" Hillary said.

"Yes."

"That's what she said?"

"Yes," Hannah replied with emphasis and annoyance, grabbing her sweater off the chair, heading for the driveway. It was an old-fashioned phrase, vague enough to mean a million different things. Maybe he had snuck a cookie when she had told him no. Maybe he was teaching Morgan the lyrics to a song that had swear words in it. Who knew?

"I'll come with you," Hillary said.

"No, don't be silly. Stay with your friends."

Hillary blinked. Hannah knew her sister well enough to know what she was considering in the moment. If there was something left out, a detail in the margins being overlooked. What had their mother actually said? What was going on with their kids, at her house? Subtext—she was scanning for it in the air. Mother's intuition? No. Hillary had a particularly fine-tuned bullshit detector and knew her sister like the back of her hand. Hannah hadn't lied to her, but Hillary knew, intuitively, something was off. And every molecule of her being was wondering why. *Why, why, why?*

"They're not my friends," Hillary stage-whispered with a smile, and she linked arms with her sister.

"Wait," Susan called as she saw them leaving. "Where are you going?"

"Babysitter called," Hillary said. "Sorry!"

"But you didn't sign up for the fall festival yet," she said, brandishing a list on a bright red clipboard. "We still need a few people to help with pumpkin carving and the cocktail station. Ice, napkins, etc. The food and music are all taken care of."

Hillary had mentioned the fall festival and summer block party to

Hannah when she'd seen the house. Cited it as an example of neighborhood togetherness, and she'd liked the sound of it. And she certainly appreciated the value of any drinking activity that took cars out of the equation. People were so stupid around alcohol in the suburbs.

"We'll do cocktails," Hillary said. "And napkins. Put us both down for that."

Hannah bristled. Why did the nondrinker always have to bring drinks? Why, whenever Hillary told her what to bring to dinner, did she always ask Hannah to bring wine?

"Okay, will do. But…we have to vote on the next book! It's the last meeting before January, remember?" Susan called out as they walked down the driveway.

"Whatever book you want is fine with us," Hillary replied.

"Well, Anne's turning everyone against my new Holocaust pick," Susan said. She pouted at them broadly, animating her face again in a way that was almost hideous in contrast to the rest of her but wasn't. *Jolie laide*, Hannah thought suddenly. A French word from her old word list. Pretty but ugly.

"Susan," Hillary said, "don't listen to her. Vote your heart."

They walked back together, not discussing the smoke in the air, the police and fire trucks, the lack of intellectual rigor of the book club, or their mother's babysitting deficiencies. They didn't discuss the weather, the week ahead, or any number of things they might have on another evening. Hannah was worried, and her sister knew it, so she kept her mouth shut.

"Wait, did you actually tell her to *vote her heart*?" Hannah said suddenly, laughing, as they got to the bottom of Susan's long driveway. "Do you maybe have a brain tumor?"

"I just needed to shut her up and let us leave. I mean really. I thought I was at a political rally for a second there. Sign up for this, vote on that."

As they started to walk down the hill, a blue sedan with Lyft and Uber signs in its window pulled up to the curb. A woman exited. She was tall with dark hair. Not a hint of a smile as she nodded hello to Hillary.

"Evening," Hillary said. She didn't introduce her sister, and the woman started walking up the long driveway. "Uber drivers hate long driveways, have you noticed that?" Hillary said as they walked. "It's really absurd. I mean, what's the point of paying if you have to walk?"

Something about the tall woman's gait, slow and methodical, like an adolescent boy's, made Hannah turn and watch her.

"Who's that?"

"Someone late for book club who's going to get yelled at for not reading the book."

Hillary's studied breeziness and lack of introduction hung in the air. Along with the way the woman walked. So familiar, it made Hannah shiver.

"Wait, is that…is that her sist—Is that Marisa Gothie? From high school?"

She stopped and watched her walking, and Hillary pulled her arm.

"I thought the Gothies moved," Hannah whispered.

"Well, people move back. As you should know."

"Jesus, Hillary, does Marisa live here, in the neighborhood? Does she come to the book club?"

"No! She lives somewhere, I don't know. West of here. And yes. Sometimes. Once in a while. She's friends with Monica. But not her sister."

"Why the hell didn't you tell me?"

"Because it's been twenty years, and it doesn't matter."

"It matters to me," Hannah said. "Great, well, I guess I can't be in the book club."

"Stop it, Han," Hillary said. "Let it go once and for all."

Another fire truck and an ambulance approached them and passed from the Gotham Road side. Without flashing lights and sirens, they were just lumbering beasts, moving slowly, too large for their narrow, winding street.

"Weird that they're leaving but the police aren't leaving, too," Hannah said.

"I guess."

Hannah stopped and turned back, as if she wanted to snapshot the moment, capture it to understand it better.

"I think there's lights from three police cars down there."

"It's probably just the ornamental lights of their landscaping on the trees or something."

"Red lights?"

"Okay, I don't know. But you're on edge now, so just stop worrying. And please don't buy into that whole bullshit arson situation. Anne is a fucking racist."

"I'm not buying into anything," she replied. "But three police cars?"

"I would normally say they're bored and looking for excitement. But they have a kid to find now, so there goes that theory."

"Maybe these two things are related. The fire and the missing girl."

The idea was suspended between them now, and Hillary shuddered. "Jesus, I hope not." She crossed herself quickly, as she'd done since childhood, looked at her sister, and stared, until she did the same.

Hannah thought of her father, who used to take them to church so their mother could sleep in. Her father had taught them how to cross themselves, how to throw salt over their shoulder, how to blow on dice and wish for snake eyes. He'd also taught them how to put out a grease fire, with baking soda and a rug. A grease fire he started once or twice a month by falling asleep drunk while cooking. There were a lot of ways, she knew, to start a fire.

But only a few to extinguish one.

eight

EVA

I watched through the window, waiting, hoping to catch Hannah before she got inside. I saw them walk up the driveway together and sighed. Of course, the two of them coming back together. I hadn't counted on that. That complicated things, of course. How could I win in this situation? Both grandchildren mad at me, and soon, if I didn't choose my words carefully, both daughters, too.

Oh well. You don't become a mother to make friends, do you?

Above me, I heard Morgan stomping around in her room. Cleaning it up, allegedly. Throwing clothes into the hamper, toys into her baskets and cubbies. Thud, thud, thud. All the money they'd spent on this house, and how the sounds still carried! No soundproofing! I'd sent her there when she'd tried to run down the driveway toward Miles. Grabbed her little arm when she didn't pay heed. And the look on her face! The shock of betrayal! Fun Grandma turned into stern Grandma! But I knew I was throwing right thing after wrong.

I should have grabbed Miles's arm, too. Should have yanked him away, let the animal fall, endured the screams from both of them. Was that what Hannah would have done? I don't know. It certainly was what Hillary would have done. No nonsense, fast-acting Hillary. But Hannah would have wanted the story, the reasons. Would she have stayed down there, waited with him, reassured him somehow even though there was another child alone up the hill? Would she have worried, as I did for a moment, what exactly he planned to do with that animal if I left him alone?

I'd left him there a few minutes to make up his own mind. Then, when he hadn't returned, I'd gone halfway down. I told him I'd called animal control and they were on their way.

"No, Grandma! They'll kill her!"

"Miles, they are the experts. You are not. If she can be saved, they'll save her."

That had always worked with my girls. Research, expertise. *It's not up to us. Let's turn to the authorities.* But they weren't rebellious. Wise and crafty, but not rebels. Miles was another story altogether.

"No!"

"Miles," I said, "you have to leave it in case you are seen…tampering with an animal. They may think you've hurt it! What would happen then? Do you want to go to prison? Now get up here right now!"

Oh, later I would beat myself up about those words, my haste, my choices. The empty threats turned full. But it seemed perfectly reasonable at the time. Not prescient. Not prescient at all.

And so he started his slow walk up that hill of grass. So artificially green, still, devoid of clippings, mulch, or errant leaves thanks to the trucks that arrived every other day and tended it.

I sent him into the living room, the boring, dull living room, with no television, no toys or games. Just a silver bowl and a book of Avedon photographs. Not even a candy dish. Not even a magazine he could thumb through.

Unlike Morgan, he was silent. Sat still and fumed.

I didn't tell him I'd called his mother. I didn't really want that on me as well.

I stood in the foyer, planning my careful speech as the girls walked in. And then I began.

I'm so sorry, but the kids weren't listening.

The police cars were whizzing down the street, and there was an injured f—

But there was no need to continue or explain. The look on Hannah's face, eyes widening, cautioning me as clear as a traffic signal, stopped me cold the moment she heard the word *fawn* coming out of my mouth.

nine

HANNAH

Her son in the living room, head down, feet up on the glass coffee table, reflecting himself back. Double-long floppy hair, double-huge white sneakers. At this age, sometimes boys were all top and bottom regardless of what was in between. She said nothing and didn't need to. She immediately recognized the look on his face when he glanced up.

Miles had always known what he was doing was wrong, and he did it anyway. Did the knowledge make him a better kid or a worse one? That, Hannah did not know. That was the problem with only having one. That was the problem with him not having close friends. That was the problem with her having no brother or husband to bounce things off of. She had no focus group, no baseline.

"Let's go," Hannah said. "Apologize to your grandmother."

He lifted his head and muttered sorry.

Eva nodded and sighed.

"Where's Morgan?" Hillary interjected. "What did she do, Mom?"

Eva started to answer then held her breath, waiting for Miles and Hannah to make their way to the door. Hannah opened the door and turned back to her mother, shooting her a look of warning. A stern one, she hoped.

They walked home quietly, Miles in front, Hannah behind. She steeled herself for another conversation, another punishment, another call to his father, his therapist. A team, a squadron, a platoon of discussion. All for what, really? Because at the end of the day, at the bottom of the barrel, that was the problem, wasn't it? No one understood why he did this or what it might mean or how it might escalate. In this case, the animal was injured already. But did they know if the other animals were dying because of Miles or in spite of him? No one was there and knew where the blood had come from. We're in uncharted territory, the therapist had said. And Hannah had translated: No one knew if it all meant he was going to become a veterinarian or a serial killer.

They cut through the side yard, approaching from the west. It was almost completely dark now, and she'd left a light on in the kitchen but no lights on outside. Hannah made a mental note to get lights on timers, maybe some stepping stones, with solar-powered lights on the path. She let her mind be temporarily diverted by thoughts of nesting, settling. She thought of the Home Depot as she approached the porch, which added to the shock of seeing two men sitting on it.

"Miles, get back," she whispered, gripping her son in one hand and her phone instinctively in the other.

"Sorry to bother you again," one man said, standing up. When the other stood and she saw their height and weight differences in shadow, she should have breathed a sigh of relief but didn't. Carelli and Thompson.

"Hello, gentlemen," she said evenly, scrupulously avoiding the word *officers* so as not to upset her son. "Miles, go in and do your homework."

She turned on the small porch light and pulled a third chair out of the kitchen. Wooden back, woven seat, it looked wrong on the porch next to the low-slung Adirondack chairs, but she didn't want to stand up. She was suddenly exhausted. She leaned one hip on it and gestured to the other chairs, but they didn't sit back down. She hoped that was a sign of a quick visit. In and out. No coming in for drinks and niceties, no.

"Out for a walk?"

"Just coming back from my sister's."

"For dinner?"

"May I ask why you're here?"

"We're canvassing the neighbors with an additional ask as the scene is secured."

"The scene?" She wasn't familiar with the language, the subtleties, or the not-so-subtleties. To her, *scene* was a theater word. *Ask* was a corporate word.

"The crime scene."

"You mean the fire *was* arson?"

She was shocked, absolutely shocked, that the gossiping women had been correct. In her experience, that *never* happened. That was why gossip was so delicious; it was usually completely detached from reality.

The two men glanced at each other.

"I guess news doesn't travel that fast after all," Thompson said.

"What news?"

"A body was found nearby. A young girl."

"Oh no. The girl—"

"We don't know. We're still awaiting confirmation. You'll see all this on the news later anyway, so…"

"Oh my God," she said. "A neighbor did this? Is that what you're thinking?" She felt her cheeks flush in the low light. As if they would tell her that. Or anything.

"Have you met the family who lives at the fire location?"

"No. All I know is—" She hesitated. "They're, um, Italian."

They looked at her oddly.

"There were mob jokes," she said. "At book club."

They blinked again. She realized with horror that Carelli was probably an Italian name.

"It doesn't mean anything."

"We heard you left the book club meeting early," he said. "When you saw the fire."

She took a deep breath. Already they were telling on her, gossiping? She'd met them once! How had that come up, exactly? What on earth did it matter?

"That's not why I left," she said huffily.

"Okay. Why then?"

"My mother was babysitting and asked us to come back."

"Because?"

"The kids were a bit of a handful. Too much…sugar."

These statements, she knew, were not really lies. And if she knew anything about her mother, it was that she wouldn't air the family's dirty laundry in front of strangers. She'd even been careful in front of Hillary, to protect Hannah.

She took a deep breath and hoped it wasn't audible. God only knew what they would make of a deep breath. But her head was reeling now, ideas about her new neighbors and their kids and their husbands and the people who came and went from their homes, the gardeners, the dog walkers, the installers of custom closets and remote-controlled blinds radiating in all directions, like the paths connecting their homes.

"I'm sorry," she said, fearing her panic was visible and open to interpretation. "This is just overwhelming. As a parent, as someone who just moved in." She trailed off and rubbed her hands across her eyes. "I mean, I thought it was a safe neighborhood, and now an abduction, a fire, a death. Jesus."

"Yeah, and right after you got here," Carelli added.

She looked down for a second and willed her blood to stop boiling.

"Did anything seem off to you at the book club meeting?" Thompson continued.

"Off?"

"Unusual."

Where to begin? she thought. The fact that it was catered and people were dressed like they were going to an expensive restaurant, for starters, instead of walking on a wooded path between their houses. That there were people who vaped and offered gummies, that there were racists and sign-up sheets for neighborhood events? That was all totally unusual to her, but not to them. Not to them at all.

"Well, I don't know anyone, so I don't know how they usually act."

"But nothing stood out as strange?"

"No."

"Your sister seemed like her usual self?"

"Yes," she said firmly, knowing Hillary would say the same of her, no matter what she thought. She knew she could at least count on that.

Finally, they wrapped up their circular line of questioning, and they stepped away from the porch. But Carelli turned back suddenly, his finger in the air.

"I think I know the answer to this, but you don't have a security camera on your house anywhere, do you? One of those apps?"

She hesitated, not because it was difficult to answer but because she wanted to know more.

"We're collecting footage from the cameras of your neighbors," Thompson explained.

"From Hillary?"

"Yes. The whole street. And then the neighbors in the back."

The back. The neighbor through the trees? She could barely see the house through the trees. She knew it was bigger, fancier than hers. And bigger and fancier usually meant security cameras. She felt the smallest frisson of fear creep up her neck. *Night. Fox. Son. Shovel.* But as she finally shook her head no, answering the question they already knew the answer to, and they said their goodbyes and walked back toward their patrol car, she stood a long time on her porch before she went inside.

Up the hill to the right, around the curve of the road before it dipped, there was a moment that afforded a view not only of trees and houses but the expanse of the farmland estate beyond. She'd driven there on the first day, and her breath had caught in her throat. Like something out of a movie. So many acres, rolling through the edge of the suburbs. The green, the hills, the split-rail fence. The horses grazing. It seemed to go on forever until it dropped out of sight as the road tucked itself in and wound through the trees again. If she and Hillary had walked a bit farther beyond Susan's house, they would have seen it again. But from the vantage of her porch, looking up the hill, she saw only the gray and brown shadows of police flashlights bobbing and sweeping in the low fog.

Her son crept up behind her, startling her, asking if she was okay. She said nothing. There were words still waiting to be chosen, floating in her. He was at the age when she could lose him, lose him so easily, if she said or did the wrong thing.

They stood together for just a moment, till a dog bayed in the distance, a police dog, she supposed. She thought she could hear her son's heart racing, keeping time, keeping up, with the animals, always.

"It has to stop, Miles," she said quietly.

"I know," he said.

"Forget what's happening to the animals. You are hurting yourself by not staying away. Do you see that? Do you?"

He stood next to her, his body language not gesturing yes, not seizing into no.

Closing the door, locking the last open window against the first evidence of autumn's chill, she decided to leave it at that. To not press the matter any further, to leave it to his therapist, who she'd call in the morning. She crawled into bed with her laptop, thinking she could do a little work.

But the detective's words kept coming back to her and interrupting her own, dangling themselves in front of her computer screen. Not about the security camera, not about her neighbor in the back, not about her son and a shovel and a shallow grave.

But about her sister.

Had Hillary seemed her normal self?

She lay there and wondered not whether she'd answered correctly but remembering how he'd said it, how offhand, how nonchalant. As if there wasn't a reason, a dark reason, they'd asked her at all.

ten

EVA

I was almost out the door when the police showed up. They didn't ask me to stay—which I found fascinating, relieving, and yet irritating—but of course I did. I wasn't about to leave just as things were getting interesting!

Moments before, I'd just shrugged off Hillary's nosy questions, told her that Miles was concerned about a wounded animal, fascinated by the fire, and wouldn't come back when called, and I told her I didn't want Morgan dragged into it. Rabies, distemper, wasting disease, blood, guts. It was an easy enough leap to make. She seemed satisfied with that, but I wasn't, of course. I knew it was more complicated, that this was part of the story, the secret, that Hannah was keeping.

So I lied to one child in service of the other. These are the things mothers do, whether they admit it or not.

Morgan came down and apologized, which was really unnecessary, but it was so like Morgan to try to keep us all tethered and sane. Who would think that the youngest of us could prove to be the axis, the ground wire? That of all the combinations of DNA, Morgan's would be the one we all revolved around?

Hillary made coffee, because police always want coffee, don't they? But I saw the way they surveyed the foyer, living room, kitchen. I knew that a request for coffee just gave them more free time to look around, to notice, to ponder. Coffee was just a stalling tactic! It took quite a few minutes to brew coffee. Oh, the things you learn late in life. Never too late to be fooled. Never too late to come out on top either.

They asked me polite questions about having my family all living nearby, how long I'd been in the area, if I worked or volunteered. They weren't writing anything down. They weren't considering me a witness or a suspect or a useful nosy neighbor. No. They weren't really even looking at me. I was just something to work around while they waited for the coffee and silently assessed the value of Hillary's modern art, custom furniture, hand-blown glassware, and coffee mugs thrown by a potter in upstate New York. Everything in that house was distinctive and original, signed by someone. Whether you recognized the name or not, it didn't matter. That the items were subtle and neutral, hardly overtly artsy, nothing like the funky colorful vases I'd collected from students at the Wayne Art Center, didn't matter either. That wasn't really the point.

Hillary told people she lived to support the arts in every form. But when I was feeling the most cynical, I thought it was because she couldn't bear to have the same things other people had. She'd always shared with her sister growing up: mascara and a curling iron and even a hairbrush and one single oversize chenille robe. After all, they were never both in the shower at the same time, so why not? They'd almost shared a single personality when it served them. But now, she didn't want to share with the world. She wanted to be different, to stand out, in her own way.

Finally, the coffee was ready and Morgan sent off to fold her laundry, the endless pile from camp that Hillary had threatened to throw away instead of wash. They had two washers and two dryers, but that didn't mean anyone in that house enjoyed using them.

The two men sipped politely, and one took a macaron from the plate Hillary had set out. But really, why the pretense? Did the police have to sip coffee and eat snacks at every house on the street? Was investigating anything like trick-or-treating for detectives? Or were they lingering for a reason? Was there perhaps more to this than a fire?

At last, the tall one put his mug on the counter and got to the point. Video. They'd noticed cameras at the front door, aimed at the street, and were asking every neighbor with them to have a look.

"Because of the fire?" I asked.

"Because a body was found," he said.

My hand flew up to my mouth when I heard the word *body*, but Hillary kept her cool.

I'd been with Hillary the evening the cameras had been installed; Morgan and I had taken turns posing on the front steps, pretending to be burglars, just to test it. It had been fun but surprising to see how spooky we both looked. Nothing looked innocent in the murky black-and-white of night vision, not even a little girl and an old lady. Especially an old lady.

Hillary explained politely that they could only watch in real time on her phone, that the footage wasn't saved.

Oops. I suddenly had a deep interest in my nails and cuticles.

"There should be a thirty-day history saved to the cloud," Carelli said. As if he was reading from a manual. As if he'd looked it up. As if people tried to weasel their way out of this every damned day, and he had it memorized.

Oh, how that term annoyed me—cloud. But I supposed, given how unreliable and fleeting it could be, there wasn't really a better word.

"Is there?" Hillary replied quietly in an offhand tone. She glanced at me briefly, probably because I couldn't help looking at her. We both knew that she knew about the saved history. We'd discussed it in detail with Morgan the night of the installation! We'd gone back an hour later and looked at ourselves at the front door and laughed. History. Cloud. Laughter. That night, they all mingled together as one.

Hillary logged on to her account and went back to the Saturday before Labor Day, the day the little girl had been reported missing. I looked over their shoulders, trying to be inconspicuous. Trying to be incurious. Three in the afternoon to midnight, they skipped through in fifteen-minute increments, the light changing ever so slightly frame to frame, like jump cuts. Streetlights, motion timer lights, one car's headlights. One car they watched backward and forward until I was dizzy, determining color and make (BMW, gray or blue). It seemed odd to me that there was only one car, going in one direction, in nine hours of footage. It was the weekend!

And yes, the weather had been bad, rainy, awful, but still. But they said nothing, and I knew better than to open my mouth and make a random comment.

They skipped through past midnight, 1:00 a.m., 2:00 a.m., nothing. All the way to morning.

Carelli sniffed loudly and rolled his head to one side, which made his neck crack. That's how close we were all standing; I heard the sickening crack of the man's bones.

"Sorry we couldn't be more help," Hillary said breezily, as if I was somehow part of the equation. "More coffee?" she offered.

"Maybe a splash," Thompson said, and Hillary made that tight smile, the one that kept her from frowning. But I knew it was as good as a frown. She couldn't keep that from me. She went to the pot, poured him more, then returned it to its base. She turned it off with a flourishing click, as if that was the end of that.

We watched him sip, and Carelli took another macaron, chewed. They said nothing; we said nothing. Hillary took a breath, trying to keep her annoyance in and failing.

"Aren't they delicious macarons?" I said.

"So good," Carelli said.

"I'm partial to the strawberry. You must have a long night ahead of you," I added, trying to help the cause.

"Yes, you should take a few with you for fuel," Hillary said. "I'll wrap them for you now."

"Before you do that," Thompson said, "could we scroll back, please, to Friday afternoon and evening?"

Hillary blinked. She asked what the date would be, as if she couldn't subtract one day from another. As if she couldn't remember what date Saturday had been. As if she hadn't been a math minor. As if she didn't know that was the night before the girl went missing. She did as she was told.

I was slightly at an angle behind her; I could see the curve of her jaw, her cheekbone, lit by the harsh light of her screen. And there, at 8:00 p.m., a figure approaching the door. Frame by frame, in shadow. I kept waiting for the shadow to grow in height, but it didn't. The size remained small, so small, as the girl with the blond hair stepped up on tiptoe to ring the doorbell. A dress, not a nightgown. White lanyard around her neck. The tiny holes of her missing teeth. It broke my heart, that incomplete set of teeth. That she hadn't lived to know the joy of them growing back in. And then, the front door opening, closing, the light sweeping out and back. Ten minutes passing as they clicked through them, as if ten minutes were nothing. As if ten minutes couldn't mean the world. Then, at last, footage of her leaving. Her small frame hopping down the steps as if she didn't have a care in the world. We watched as she grew fuzzy, out of focus, blurred into the foreground of the yard until finally, she was erased into gray. I felt Hillary's shoulders move down into her ribs, as if she was safe. But the tiny hairs on my arms stood upright, vibrating their antennae warning.

"Probably selling candy for camp or something," Hillary said dismissively.

No one said her hands were empty. Or that it was awfully late for a six-year-old to be out.

The detectives didn't look at each other or at her or at me. They just stared straight ahead at the screen.

"Camps are usually finished by now," the taller one said quietly, but Hillary said nothing.

"When we didn't answer, she probably came in and looked around. Kids. Curiosity."

"And no one around here locks their doors," I added sunnily, though I doubted it was true. Back in my day, certainly. But now? Why would someone go to the trouble of an elaborate alarm system with cameras and notifications and then not lock their doors?

"No internal cameras?"

"What? No."

"No nanny cam?"

"No nanny or cam."

"Had she ever been to your house before? If we download all your footage from this summer, would we see her?"

This shocked me. I felt like they were anticipating us, asking us basically if we would lie to them. Entrapment!

"I don't believe so. I only know her in passing, waving to her mother in the yard."

"We will need to understand your family's whereabouts that night."

"Morgan was at camp in Vermont," she said quickly. "I believe we were en route to get her."

"We?"

They looked at me, and my hands immediately, instinctively went up in protest. *Don't drag me into this*, my body said with every molecule.

"Well, me and my friend Jane. Our kids were there together, so we drove up."

"And she can corroborate this?"

"What?"

"Provide an alibi?"

I'll admit these were upsetting turns of phrase. *Corroborate. Alibi.* They stopped me in my tracks, too. I thought of all the technology available to people now, these apps and cameras and devices worn flapping on people's wrists. Someday, the police will not need lie detection tests; they'll know our blood pressure, our heart rate rising and falling, while standing next to us.

"Yes, of course. Jane Tartan. She lives in Wayne."

"And where was your husband?"

She thought a long time before she answered. As if there wasn't an enormous family calendar in the kitchen screaming the answer to part of that question.

Camp pickup, color coded in pink.

Poker night, color coded in blue, for Ben.

eleven

HANNAH

The week went smoothly for Miles, and because of that, it went smoothly for Hannah. She hadn't realized how linked her moods were to his, that last year when he hadn't wanted to go to school and begged to stay home, feeling ill, she had felt queasy, too. Now he woke up without being told, got dressed, poured his own cereal, sliced his own fruit. He told her she didn't need to make him lunch anymore, that the food at school was "decent" and that only kids with allergies brown-bagged. He did not want to be seen as a kid with allergies. And Hannah knew, at this tender age, in eighth grade, that even an allergy could make you be bullied. God forbid you were weak. God forbid you were human, that food was your kryptonite. She was grateful that he was growing, that he wouldn't be small, that he didn't have acne, and now, that he didn't have food allergies. He wasn't perfect; he had his quirks, but he could pass for normal, and that was all that mattered. Normal. He bounded out the door a shade early each day, without prodding, and waited for the bus with Morgan with what Hannah supposed was a normal amount of excitement.

On Friday, she watched them from the porch for just a moment before going back inside. His small, awkward movements, shrugging his book bag off at the curb, gesturing as he spoke with his hand but not his arm, as if animating anything more was too much work. And Morgan, a bundle of energy in contrast. Covering her eyes dramatically, touching his arm, dancing a bit with her shoulders. Whatever she was telling him about apparently required movement. A TikTok video? A YouTube show? He didn't watch those things regularly, preferring to use his screen time on video games, but Morgan did. She had her own iPad and laptop, and although they were supposed to charge at the charging station in the butler's pantry and not in her room, she was known to sneak them in and devour her favorites. Hillary had told Hannah this in frustration. Miles had even told Hannah this when begging for a relaxation of the rules. Hannah felt a new surge of love for her son, for the way he tolerated whatever girly thing Morgan was sharing, for listening to her when he probably had no interest whatsoever. He was polite. He was openhearted. He was good. He loved his cousin.

Hannah went inside, got dressed in a white button-down, cardigan, and black jeans, and drove to Malvern for her meeting with Ben. She'd been to his finance office once before, for a party of some kind, when Hillary had insisted it would be fun, and of course it wasn't. When your expectation was fun, there was never any fun.

The building was a midrise of steel and glass in a new office park on the side of the highway but not far from the small downtown, which was getting rehabbed and discovered by brewpubs, vegan restaurants, coffee shops. If it weren't so removed from every place else, it would be a cute place to live or work.

In the conference room, Ben's admin, Lauren, had laid out copies of a PowerPoint deck along with pens and a pitcher of water and tumblers. Old-school Ben. How many people came in with their own water bottles, prepared to take notes on their phone or laptop? He also refused to have music playing in the offices and hated the trend of colorful socks with crazy prints. Ben never even wore socks unless it was snowing.

Hannah shrugged off her coat, sat down, and had to force herself not to open the deck. He was probably old-school about that, too, and didn't want her to page ahead until he could explain.

He walked by the door with a headset on, holding up his finger to signal he needed a minute. Then he made an exasperated face and a *wrap it up* sign, or maybe it was a *this person is batshit crazy* sign—they looked the same. Still, she smiled at his performance framed by the door. She missed having coworkers.

"Finally," he said, coming in with a smile. "There should be a law that conference calls only last half an hour."

"What about meetings? What's the rule on that?"

"Forty-five minutes," he said quickly, then laughed. "No, seriously, do you want to have lunch after?"

She thanked him but said she had a conference call with the Philanthropist, and it would last significantly longer than half an hour. The woman was too scattered to put any of her thoughts in writing. She just wanted to blather on the phone and expected Hannah to write it down, shape it into something.

"Sometimes being a ghostwriter feels like half typist, half therapist," she said.

"Well, I promise you this client will be easier than that."

"Ben, if Hillary overstepped about connecting us, I want to be sure that—"

"Don't be crazy. Of course, a nonprofit's budget can't compare to pharma companies, and some of their projects are tiny, but I bet they'll find you perfect for it, really. They'd be lucky to have you if you can make the numbers work. And this backgrounder will give you a leg up." He turned the first page to reveal the logo—me3.

She frowned a little; it was a strange name, a little blind.

"Me three? Or me to the third power?"

"Me three."

"So you said they're linked to high schools?"

"Yes, they have a loose partnership with the #MeToo movement. They offer support and peer mentorship to girls who've been sexually harassed by their classmates."

He went on to describe their grassroots work, their board of prestigious therapists and educators and scientists, how they'd started in Pittsburgh, then moved into Philadelphia and were about to open in DC and Boston, and how the director was smart, dynamic, and media savvy.

But she felt the noise of the office air-conditioning buzzing, tinny in her ears. She thought she might faint and didn't think water was going to help.

Fucking Hillary. She was the only person who knew how to help her and hurt her at the same damned time.

twelve

EVA

When I was married, which seems an eternity ago, no detectives ever came to my door at night and asked where my husband was. Which I suppose is some kind of cold comfort.

But then in those early days, before he died, I never knew where he was. Even when I thought I did, I didn't. Only afterward, when the autopsy blamed his liver and his heart, did I realize what he was actually doing when I thought he was working late. Drinking and watching sports with his cronies. The drink was always the same: whiskey chased with beer. But the sports and the bars changed with the season. I found all those specifics out later, after his funeral, when his friends and coworkers told me things that confused me, that didn't make sense, didn't add up. I pieced it all together and surveyed it like a thin, mismatched quilt. And I knew suddenly that even though he was a football player in college, it wasn't his passion for sports that had driven the behavior but his passion for drinking.

I would have welcomed the company of policemen on some of those dark nights. I would have let them have pot after pot of fresh coffee if they liked. In the early years of my marriage, I became a good cook; I took it seriously, like it was part of my job. There would have been homemade coffee cake or banana bread iced and waiting for the morning. I would have been their favorite informant, I'm sure. Of course they would have pegged me for exactly what I was: a lonely, bored housewife. They didn't need footage from a security camera to know that.

Oh, if she needed help or someone to count on, that little girl had chosen the wrong house! I was always home, always available. What did she need? What did she want? The way Hillary had suggested she'd been selling cookies, so dismissive. As if any child's errand would be of no importance. Hillary, who had been the fiercest, smartest, most enterprising child of them all! How her fifth-grade teacher had said that she'd made up "pre-tests" for her and her sister to study, then tried to sell them to the rest of the class. How, even younger, she'd approached the boys in the neighborhood with a plan to market lawn services—she would do the flyers and ads, and they would do the labor.

Hillary's answer had been reflexive, defensive, weak. Did the police think she was covering up? There were no boxes of candies or forms in the child's hands. The police weren't stupid. How would they peg her? These police who stereotype people at first glance, not just because it's quicker, because it's easier, but because if you asked, any one of them would say they were right nine times out of ten. Nine times out of ten, a stereotype holds. *She was lonely. He was stepping out. It's always the husband. Kids go door to door selling stuff.*

Now, my tremendous relief at having raised two girls who don't seem to have their dead father's addictive tendencies had dissipated. There were new things to worry about. New secrets to keep.

When the detectives left, Hillary had said, "Let's keep this between us."

"Well, I'm not going to hold a press conference," I'd huffed.

"You know what I mean."

"Hillary," I had said. It always came out like a sigh, those names with *H*'s that I'd chosen. It always sounded dramatic even when I didn't mean it to. But this time, I'd meant it.

"I just feel terrible, like I—" She had stopped.

I'd finished.

"Like you convinced her to move to a murderous neighborhood where everyone is under scrutiny?"

"Yes. Basically."

"Well, why should you feel guilty? You didn't kill the child."

"Jesus, Mom, do you have to be so blunt?"

"It's what old age does to you. It shortens your time and therefore your sentences."

"Well, I'll shorten mine. Don't tell Hannah."

"I'll let you tell her."

"Mom."

"Your sister would be the last person to think any of this was your fault."

That had been my final word on the topic, and I'd raised my eyes for emphasis. She'd said nothing, but the look on her face said way too much. Hillary is a beautiful woman, but her face is capable of every shade of ugliness. When I think back and consider everything in that look and all that was packed inside as she bade me goodbye, I saw the world in it. I saw pity—pity for her clueless mother who stupidly thought the best of her daughters. I saw fear, competition, envy. I saw the huge house and the handsome husband and the beautiful daughter and the home-cooked, from-scratch, all-organic meals. I saw her whole universe compacted into her narrow eyes. All that she had at stake.

Was I wrong? Would Hannah judge Hillary for having more, for having it all? Admiration, wistfulness, hope, even envy perhaps. But would it really mix together and turn into judgment?

Still, when I got home that night, I confess I locked all my doors and kept the outside lights burning and lay awake in bed, wide awake, listening and ruminating a long time. I had too many secrets in my head. Like a therapist or a priest, I knew too much, and I couldn't hold it all. It burst the seams of my brain, leading me to other moments, other arguments between my girls, other tensions I'd noticed but hadn't excavated. A night in high school when one had come home later than the other, their voices rising from their room, waking me a second time after the door opened at two in the morning. Fighting over a boy? Or the curfew? What? Other places I probably needed to go but didn't want to visit.

I thought of everything the security footage didn't show. All the things the police were looking for. Like which way the little girl walked as she went down the driveway. If she was going up and down the block, which neighbor she sought out next.

Had she wandered down to say hello to my other daughter, my grandson? Had she gone to see the boy obsessed with dead things?

thirteen

HANNAH

When Hannah got home, she sent the director of me3, Cat Saunders, a note with links to some of her relevant work. Their website and social media feeds were great, and the TEDx talks were compelling. There was no sense turning down money just because Ben had been reluctant and because she might feel a teeny bit of PTSD over something stupid that had happened twenty years ago. *Grow up, Hannah*, she told herself.

Over the years, she'd found writing to be a clean, detached way to contribute to causes. She didn't have to hold hands and wipe tears. She just had to create content that made other people feel things. And Cat seemed, well, for lack of a better word, cool. Like Hannah might actually like her instead of want to strangle her. So email sent. *Fine*, she thought. *We'll see what happens.* She got an autoreply that said Cat was currently in a two o'clock meeting but would reply soon.

Next up, the Philanthropist. Hannah had gently suggested to the Philanthropist that they organize their process, but gentle didn't seem to work with her. Hannah had sent a rough outline, timeline, and guided questions to help discuss her life chronologically the week before and had been rewarded with a FaceTime call insisting she preferred to operate free-form. "I'm at my best off the cuff," she had said, as if she'd been told she was a natural storyteller, a true raconteur.

Hannah had worked with a few truly charming people over the years with great stories to tell. She'd made her reputation as a ghostwriter with people like that, translating their spoken stories onto the page.

But this woman was a different story. Everything she said sounded like a diary entry mixed with name dropping. "I had tea with Desi before he got on the *QE2*. We went to the most marvelous fundraiser for the Bidens, and they served lamb chop lollipops." Hannah was going to have to start poking in the tender parts to get anything out of her. When she began asking pointed questions, when she asked to speak to her relatives and friends, the Philanthropist was going to dig in her heels. Maybe she knew there was nothing to tell, or maybe she had secrets. Who knew? But whatever the case, Hannah wanted to write a deep story. The Philanthropist thought the glossy surface was fascinating.

Hannah sighed and changed into leggings and sneakers. She sat in her living room, in the white canvas chair near the fireplace, and put up her feet. She kept a bowl of cashews next to her and allowed herself to eat three at fifteen-minute intervals as a reward for listening to the Philanthropist drone on. After an hour, she'd endured three unconnected stories, about her current neighbor's dog (small but vicious), her sorority's pledge week (drunk but harmless), and her second husband's first wife (a showgirl), and the cashews were long gone.

She stood up, went outside. Time for a walk. Running might be too aggressive if it was still wet, but she'd see what the terrain was like. Other than walking to book club, lifting boxes, and hanging a few pictures, she hadn't exercised since the move. It had been weeks, and her body felt tense from leaning over to unpack and hunching over her laptop. She stretched on the porch and tried to decide between the high road, which went past Hillary's, or the low trails, which went past Liza Harris's house.

There had been police vans parked in the Harrises' driveway for several days earlier in the week, with techs around the house, doing something in the soil, around the windows. Once, she glanced out and saw them carrying bags out of the house. One day, there was a police dog in a neon vest circling the property, sniffing at the edge of the creek. *Action News* and *Eyewitness News* had done live reports from the street several times, their cameras pointed toward the creek and trees.

She'd avoided the paths and street, stayed inside. She worried the news vans might come early, when the kids were waiting for the bus, but they didn't. She supposed interviewing minors was not exactly ethical. On television the night before, after the police had verified the cause of death as strangulation with an unknown implement, she'd seen a spokesperson for the Harris family, the same man who'd organized the search, saying they hoped for new leads, that someone had to know something or have seen something, and he urged them to come forward. Carelli and Thompson stood behind him, faces stony, as if embarrassed someone had to help them do their job.

That day, though, the coast was clear, and she was eager to stretch and work her muscles. She chose to walk the lower trails, and in her mind, she only did this for novelty, because she'd already been on the street and upper trails on their way to book club.

The path down to the wood-chipped trail from Brindle Lane was slippery with muddy rocks and roots, and she couldn't help thinking of how much more nimble and goatlike kids were, navigating obstacles with smaller feet and lower centers of gravity. She thought of the little girl skipping down there alone, weightless, her bucket only full of possibility. Looking for frogs, they'd said the day of the search. But had she found any? And where had she gone to look?

She looked back at the Harris house from this low angle. Every week that passed approaching October, every leaf that fell, would offer a clearer view of who these people were and how they lived. The pool house and pool. The sloping yard with stepping stones leading to the path, easier to navigate from their home than the road. The woodpile in a lean-to near the pool house, stacked and ready for the cold weather ahead. As a child, Hannah had watched the woodpile behind her own house grow smaller and more uneven every year after her father's death, down to nothing. She could picture her father, hungover, she knew now, Saturday morning, chopping wood, her mother worrying as she watched out the window. Never letting her daughters go near him, never letting them learn that task.

Would this family keep chopping wood? Would they rake their leaves, change the flowers in their oversized pots, or let it all go downhill? Would they stay in this house? Would they put it on the market? And how would a new buyer feel, given the terrible story they inherited?

She squinted as if she could see in the windows, doors. She could not. The shades weren't drawn, and the curtains weren't pulled, that much she could tell. If someone was home, they were awake, dressed. Was their extended family assembled? Or had they fled the home and its memories? Any other option struck Hannah as cruel. To be a mother, alone, grieving. And then, just as quickly, the thought pierced her heart. *That would be her.* If something happened to Miles, she would be alone. She *was* alone. She shuddered, put it out of her mind. Her sister was next door! Her mother was around the corner!

"Where are the binoculars when you need them?"

She jumped at the sound of his voice.

"Ben," she said, her hand up to her heart. "Where did you come from?"

"From the path below."

"Not from home?" The path heading down was steep, through the woods to another development.

"No. I, uh, had a lunch. I mean a meeting."

She screwed up her face. "Sounds like you don't know what you had," she said, laughing.

"You know, lunch plus a meeting equals a leeting," he said. "I love a good leeting."

"Yeah, uh-huh." She glanced down the hill. "Looks slippery down there."

"Only in parts."

Sweat glistened on her brother-in-law's neck and face and dotted through part of his blue T-shirt, which made his navy eyes look even larger. Ben almost always wore blue clothing, she realized suddenly, as if he knew this was to his advantage. Had she ever seen him in black, gray, tan?

"I didn't know you ran."

"I am a man of many talents, Ms. Sawyer."

"That I do not doubt."

"So you're snooping, right? Thinking about taking up investigative journalism instead of writing content?"

"Stop. I guess it looks bad, but I was just wondering about the family. If they were home, if—"

"If they needed anything?"

"I suppose."

"Anything they need they can get delivered."

She blinked. "I wasn't just thinking of food."

"Neither was I."

That seemed like an awfully cold, pragmatic response, but she supposed he was right. Masseuses came to the house, therapists were online, Uber Eats brought anything you wanted. So much for the need for neighborly niceties.

She glanced at her watch, and as if reading her mind, Ben said he had to get going; he had to shower and take Morgan to dance class, because he'd promised.

"Sometimes I wish I could work from home so I could take her to dance more often," he said.

"I bet you do," Hannah replied.

"But working at home for hours feels weird. Gets claustrophobic."

She tried to imagine feeling claustrophobic in a house as large as his. Hannah remembered going over once and asking if Ben was home and her sister looking around quizzically and then saying she didn't actually know. She had texted him to find out.

A person could get lost in one of these houses.

"Well, thanks again for today. And have fun dancing with the girls," she said, turning to go.

He struck a ridiculous dance pose, half twerk, and she laughed.

She walked down fifteen feet, then twenty, and when she turned back, she wasn't certain why she felt a need to see Ben's feet hit the street, to make sure he was going where he said he was going. She glanced back one more time at the Harrises' house. The windows, the French doors, all that glass. Did they think about their child's death all the time? Did they look out their windows and worry that death was everywhere? Her breath caught, thinking of that. Wasn't that how Miles saw the world, too? Worried about creatures and death?

A slight movement at the edge of the house drew her eye. A small camera rotating. There were more, too, she saw now, the eyes of a house, radiating out. Blinking at her, at them, at the world.

There were cameras, she supposed, everywhere.

She raised her hand, stupidly, and waved.

fourteen

EVA

Margot's voicemail hadn't said she had something important to discuss but that she had something *interesting* to discuss. And for a certain kind of person, that was even more motivating, wasn't it?

She was stuck at an open house in Gladwyne until four, so I decided to drive over there. Maybe I'd stumble upon some cottages for sale as I drove the back way through the winding roads behind Bryn Mawr. There was one small stone house I'd always rather admired, and there it was, set on a hillside, flower boxes dripping with seasonal blooms, flag waving as I drove past. No sale sign. Oh well. It was one of those houses that looked small and probably wasn't. I remembered the words of the two agents I'd interviewed before I'd spoken to Margot: "Are you sure you wouldn't be happier looking for a condo?" Ugh, a condo. Show me a gardener who was happier in a soulless condo and I'll show you a penthouse with a rooftop garden.

Margot's open house was a low-slung contemporary made out of what looked like concrete to my eye, but what did I know. I found it hideous, but again, I knew, there tended to be a lid for every pot.

I walked in and immediately wished I'd brought sunglasses. All those windows, all that light.

Margot called out that she was writing up a sale and to come to the den.

After I stepped down into the living room, the choices were right or left, with a staircase on either side. I turned right and was rewarded. Margot sat behind a desk made of clear plastic or polymer or who knew what all. When I sat down in the matching chair opposite it, I was worried I would crack it in half like old Tupperware.

"I'm just finishing up in a sec."

"Take your time."

"Isn't this place just awful?" she whispered, as if she were being recorded.

"Yes, actually, it is."

"But I got an offer on it from a very handsome Phillies player today, so there you go."

"There's no accounting for taste."

"Ugh, I think he was twelve. Didn't know better. I kind of feel bad."

"Really?"

"Nah," she said, laughing, waving her hand in front of her face. "He was happy." She closed her computer and put it into her leather bag. "So, Eva," Margot said conspiratorially, "are you ready?"

Margot was a darling girl, but she always sprinkled that phrase into her speech, as if she thought heightening suspense would make people listen to her more carefully.

"Yes, Margot," I sighed. "I'm ready for my interesting news."

Margot walked around to the front of the plastic desk and leaned against it so she could be closer to me. Since we were alone, I wasn't sure why this was necessary, but I do remember thinking that perhaps Margot had been a drama major.

"The carriage house," she said breathlessly. "I just heard from another agent who heard at a cocktail party why the owners took Hannah's offer and didn't call us."

"Because...they forgot we existed."

"No."

"Because they hate you."

She cocked her head and gave me a look that said *Impossible. You know everyone loves me.*

"Wrong. Because they were paid $300,000 over asking."

I frowned. "But you looked up the transaction. You saw the price, $385,000. We know Hannah is struggling—"

"That's just it. The couple got $300,000 separate from the house transaction and down payment. In cash."

"But the house is only worth $400,000 at the outset," Eva said. "Right?"

"For sure."

"Hannah does not have that kind of money."

"I believe you. But someone she knows must."

"It…it sounds so…shady," I said.

"Yes, it's shady all right. It's also straight up illegal, Eva. It's tax fraud."

"But why would they do it? Did the owners demand it, or—"

"No. I think whoever did it knew there was competition. Whoever did it knew you were waiting in the wings."

"Hannah didn't know. And Hannah doesn't have that kind of money," I repeated dumbly.

"But Hillary does," she said. "And Hillary could have seen you. Or the owners could have said something, even though they are not supposed to."

"Is that what the person at the cocktail party said?"

"No, that's what I said."

"Maybe she knew about the offer but didn't know it was me," I said.

"Well, that's the most hopeful takeaway, isn't it?" Margot said and sighed.

"Well, my daughter and I aren't enemies."

"Well," Margot said, "maybe not now. But if that ever changes? Now you at least have something on her."

As I pulled out of the parking lot, I thought long and hard about the phrase *waiting in the wings*. That's what most of my life has felt like as a parent, just holding back and waiting until I have to swoop in.

fifteen

HANNAH

She and her sister had walked part of the upper path when they went to book club, but Hillary had been leading. Hillary had known the way, didn't hesitate once, even as it grew dark, and Hannah hadn't been paying attention. Now, she tried to retrace her steps up the hill, from creek to road to lane, to see the damage from the fire, but she'd clearly turned the wrong way. She stopped, annoyed with herself. You were supposed to get lost in the dark, not the light.

Stands of trees encircled her, their green mixed with a few golden leaves. Just enough coverage still to block her view. To shroud the sounds from the houses, the road. She didn't remember this spot or this feeling of being deep inside the trees. For a long stretch, she actually couldn't see anything. Not the creek, not the streets, which had to be there, one above, one below. Not the houses with their blinking cameras and their shrieking alarms and their close-to-the-house landscaping, pointy and sharp, boxwood and holly, that warned you not to get too close to the windows. All that receded, and now, she could be anywhere. Lost in the woods, the vague scent of damp pine and grass in the air.

She couldn't see the book club's pool house ahead, the neighboring house, the scorched grass and trees. She couldn't see Susan's house, perched below it, either. But as she kept going, she knew she was going in the right direction, because she could smell it slightly, invading the cleanness of the pine. Ash mixed in, duskier now. A bonfire smell. An autumn smell from childhood. Would it really linger that long? Or had there been another fire in a fire pit, something else?

She kept walking up, up, slipping a little on the leaves and wood chips, leaning down with her hands to climb up part of it, scrabbling really, until she stood at the crest of the hill. The trees thinner and less solid there, no oaks or sycamores, thin birches, tall lindens. The evergreens on the edges of properties, planted as a dark green fence, a perimeter, to keep people from wandering off the path. Did it work? Or did living along a path ensure that people wandered in, like architectural tourists, like sneakered anthropologists, wondering how folks in McMansions lived?

There were a series of right and left turns on the path, forks she could have taken and didn't, and unlike in a park or on a mountain, they weren't marked. She smiled wryly at this thought and at what the trails would be called—*Book Club Pass. Missing Girl Gulch.* The wood-chip floor and low branches, the wooden planks set over the muddiest, rootiest parts—these were all known to residents and maintained by someone, but who? The neighborhood association? A team of volunteers with what, machetes and mallets? She shuddered. She realized how little she knew about the neighborhood, let alone the neighbors. *My sister is here! It's a good school district! I can afford it!* That was the sum total of her thought process.

Finally, she came around a bend and entered a clearing in the trees, off to the right. She heard a car through the trees. Was it the street where the book club had been? Susan's house? Above Rose Lane, it was Linden Lane. Linden Lane, which dipped down to Ford Gulch, then the covered bridge over to Tamsen Farm Road. Had to be. She was about to go through the trees to the street, to save time, when she heard a sound ahead.

A small gasp, then a rustle.

She kept walking slowly toward it, as if she knew the sound was too soft to be dangerous.

The path split, and on the right-hand fork, a woman stood, blowing her nose. Petite. Blond. When she looked at Hannah, her eyes were rimmed in red, as if she'd been crying for days. On TV, the Harris girl's mother looked more composed, as if she'd marshaled her strength. Now, that strength was gone.

"Are you all right?" Hannah asked and immediately wanted to kick herself.

"No."

"Should I call someone for you?"

"You're my neighbor," she said, half questioning.

"Oh," Hannah said. "Um, yes, I'm new. Just moved here. Hannah."

"You waved at my house, the camera."

"Oh, God, how embarra—"

"I liked it," she said and smiled, a small, tight smile. She slipped her Kleenex in the pocket of her turquoise down jacket and held out her hand. "You're Hannah Sawyer. I'm Kendra."

Kendra's smile didn't get any bigger as they shook hands. She provided a few awkward pleasantries about the neighborhood. About people being nice, generally, and quiet. As if she was apologizing for the hubbub, the flashing lights, the badges tapping on windows.

Hannah breathed in deeply, trying not to study her but being unable to stop noticing. Her hand was thin, almost weightless. Everything about her was diminutive. Her mouth, her seashell ears. Her feet swallowed by her running shoes. Hannah felt large and ungainly next to her, but also, it had to be said, powerful and healthy in contrast. Had Kendra's daughter been that small and vulnerable, too?

"I'm so sorry about your daughter," she said. "I was part of the search party."

"I know."

"Oh?"

"I wasn't there, as you probably know, but the police make a list of volunteers. Then they kind of hover. They love those search parties. I think they enjoy luring people in and watching to see if anyone behaves oddly. Not that anyone did. Or anyone they told me about anyway."

Hannah hadn't thought of that. How awful that this woman knew that anyone there to help could be a criminal. Right outside her windows. In the pool house. All over her yard. Had they told her this, or had she surmised?

"So…does hiking help you take your mind off things at all? Not that anything could help."

"It does, a little. Partly because Liza loved these woods and paths. She was a little explorer. Always wanted to be outside."

"Free range," Hannah said.

"Yes. Which is why part of me is grateful she was found so soon. And wasn't, you know, kidnapped and kept somewhere in a shed or something. I'm awful to think of that and compare, I know. But at least she was running free and happy."

"I don't think you're awful."

"Well, you haven't seen me in the middle of the night, freaking out, blaming her father, blaming myself," she said. That small smile again.

"Your husband is home?"

"Yes, and my son, for now."

"Oh, I didn't realize you had a son. I—"

"He's in college. He took a leave."

Hannah shouldn't have been surprised by this, but she was. She should be accustomed to women who looked too young to have grown adult children. The Main Line was full of them. The world was full of them. Moms proud to get asked "What's your major?" when they dropped their kids off at college.

"The police went all the way up to Colby to interview him, too, can you believe that? As if he could magically, invisibly have flown home and strangled his sister."

Hannah startled a bit at the words Kendra used: *kidnapped, strangled.* They flew out of her mouth naturally, as if they were just other verbs. She supposed if you heard them often enough, they could be.

"Are you a runner?"

"Sometimes. But I'm not really exercising per se, just clearing my head. I wanted to see the area where they found her," Kendra said, "but it's still cordoned off. I just came back. Is that where you're headed, too?"

"Um, not rea—"

"It's okay if you are. Everyone's curious. I saw your brother-in-law there last week, just staring at it in the middle of his run."

Hannah opened her mouth in surprise, tried to speak, but could think of nothing to say.

"It doesn't mean anything. Despite what the cops tell you, it doesn't. He was watching the fire cleanup like a little boy with a Tonka truck watching construction."

"That does sound like Ben," Hannah said.

The wind picked up a bit, and they both reached for their hoods at the same time, which made them both smile. Kendra's shiny blue hood was rimmed in coral, and it was pretty against her skin and her eyes, even after crying. It made Hannah want to throw away her black jacket and get something brighter, happier.

"I was just walking. Just wandering, really. Thinking about running, but it's slippery. I got totally turned around for a while."

"Try it in the dark."

"I don't think so."

"We hung lanterns for a while. Solar ones. The neighborhood association. Then kids started stealing them, throwing rocks."

"That's terrible. Kids from somewhere else?"

"Hard to know. Friends of kids, who knows. They were on foot though, so…"

"Lanterns would be pretty."

"Yes. Now we only have them for the fall festival. They're still planning on having it, you know. Susan came and asked me if it was okay, and of course I said yes. Just because a killer is roaming free, we shouldn't stop the kids' fun. Oh, that sounded terrible, didn't it?"

"No," Hannah said. "You shouldn't have to watch what you say in your own backyard on top of everything else you're going through."

They walked for a while in silence, making their way slowly, hands in their pockets, hoods muffling the babble of the creek and the rustle of squirrels, the last calls of the geese overhead.

"Kendra," Hannah said as they approached her house, "if you need anything, please don't hesitate. Even if you need someone to…I don't know, drive you to get a root canal, I'm there."

Kendra laughed, her mouth finally stretching open. "Well, that's a first. Usually people offer chopped salad or chicken quesadillas. But thank you. And you know what? I'd rather have a root canal, to be honest."

"I bet you would," Hannah said, smiling.

"Maybe we could walk sometime," Kendra said. "Some morning."

"I'd like that."

Kendra looked off into the trees, then closed her eyes briefly, like she was meditating.

Hannah took that as a cue. "I'm going to head back. Cross the street. Hit the computer again."

"Great. I'll come over one of these mornings," Kendra said wistfully. "Perhaps we can keep each other from getting lost."

"Anytime," Hannah replied.

Hannah cut through the thin brush to the road, then dusted off her pants. The walk had been mostly downhill, and her shins protested a little. Crossing the street, she saw it coming up the road. One of those conspicuous cars that don't belong in the neighborhood. The detectives' car. Heading to her house. Almost as if they'd known who she had been walking with and talking to.

sixteen

EVA

I'm not used to seeing my children rattled. They're strong girls by nature, yes, but they're also accustomed to hiding their issues from me, a holdover from my days as a grieving widow. Has this made them come across to the world as secretive or reticent? Probably. They certainly both carry themselves that way, inscrutable, unflappable. Hillary even more so than Hannah, due to a false chipper veneer layered on top. But Hannah just had a quiet kind of rectitude. Like she was preserving her energy and words for something else.

So when I turned onto Brindle Lane, just to say hello, I confess I wasn't surprised the detectives were on the street first. I was, however, surprised to see them not at Hillary's but on Hannah's porch. As I pulled up closer, I was even more surprised by the high color in Hannah's cheeks and her hands gesturing, flailing in the air as she spoke to them.

So I kept on driving. If they glanced in my direction, noticed my dull gray car moving up the street, I didn't see or care. I went to the top of the street and turned around. I pulled in and parked in the circle at Hillary's house, as if that was my intention all along. Morgan was at school. Hillary and Ben were clearly both gone, their cars missing from the garage. The blinds were at noncommittal half-mast, and token lights illuminated half the living room as well as the kitchen sink. The whole house had that tight look as if it had nothing to say. I suppose I should have been a burglar myself with insights like these, but a life of crime had never occurred to me. I was one of those people who couldn't pass off bakery-bought cupcakes as my own. I could barely tell a white lie to my daughters when they asked me what I thought of their hair or clothes or why I'd called them back from a book club meeting.

I knew the code to the house alarm and also knew Hillary would want me to go in and make myself at home. Her voice was in my head, saying *Go inside, Mom!* When had that happened? I could hear her questioning me, asking why on earth I'd sit in the car and wait. Saying that was silly. And it *was* silly. But that's part of the joy of being old—you can justify silly, lazy, or anything you want. I sat outside her house and listened to her admonish me for sitting outside her house as if she were there beside me. This was how people spoke to the dead, but this was also how people listened to the loud and the large, the biggest personalities in the room.

Did my daughters ever carry my voice in their heads? Was I ever their guidepost or even their woodpecker, their tape playing on repeat? I didn't think so. If that was a failure of my youthful parenting or my grief or my lack of traditional rules, I couldn't say. And perhaps I was wrong. Perhaps they carried me around, too. But I believed, more than ever, they carried around each other.

I sat there until I drowned out the voice. I sat there until I admitted to myself the real reason I wouldn't go inside and make myself at home. The truth was I couldn't stop thinking of that camera trained on the door. How everything looked different through that lens. Filmy. Suspicious. Guilty. I did not want anyone to know I was those things, too.

Which is why I punched the code into the garage instead, where there was no camera. Not to make myself at home amid the bikes and tools but to see if the binoculars were still hanging on the pegboard near the wellies and the wheelbarrow and the rake. So I could focus in and lip-read what was happening at my other daughter's house and try to figure out all the things she wasn't telling me.

They were there all right. Hanging next to a butterfly net and a nylon kite. I pulled them off and was about to leave when I noticed something odd. The gunmetal tray in front of the cubbies, the one that always held the family's muddy wellies, boots never allowed inside the house or car. It was so very like Hillary to own something fancy to hold something plain, a tray perfectly sized to hold three pairs of green boots, lined up according to size. But now there were two pairs, just two. The smaller two.

seventeen

HANNAH

Hannah had moved to the neighborhood for a lot of reasons, but one of them was to stave off the feeling, post-divorce, of always being the only one alone. Her old house had been a twin, and the yards were all nestled close together, so yes, if she screamed in the middle of the night, someone would hear her. She had neighbors close by, and that was worth something.

But everyone around her was a couple and knew Mike. And going to their potlucks and block parties without her husband and seeing them all gathered there, around the microbrews in the silver tubs, taking turns at the grills set up in a row, so many of them, all belonging to someone else—and all of them buddies of Mike's—that somehow sharpened her loss. Whereas Hillary had said that her street was all women, all the time, because half of them were divorced, and the other half were married to men who traveled internationally for their jobs or worked insane hours in New York and commuted. She'd made it sound almost like a sorority but with lots and lots of money. What she'd failed to mention was how busy stay-at-home moms could be. Had her neighbor Kendra felt that, too? She'd seemed lonely, not just grief-stricken on the path.

But as Hannah walked up to her house, where the detectives were waiting for her, she felt more alone than ever. Two against one. Men against women. Logic against intuition. They would have all the facts now, and she knew it.

"Good morning," Thompson said with his small, careful smile. Carelli stood behind him, not making eye contact, scratching at a spot on his face as if he'd just found a spent cornflake crumb there.

Good cop, bad cop, Hannah thought immediately, then reversed herself. *That's what they want me to think. Stay open, Han. Stay open.*

"How can I help you?"

"Is your son home?"

"Um, he's at school," she said slowly. "By law. In the state of Pennsylvania."

"No need to get testy," Carelli said. He was moving his tongue around in his mouth now, and Hannah wanted to scream at him to wash his face. To brush his teeth. Grow the fuck up and learn some basic manners.

"Well, it's a somewhat ridiculous question. You already know he's there," she said. "You both know perfectly well where he is."

"He might've stayed home sick," Carelli said. "Or faked being sick."

She gritted her teeth but did not respond and did not invite them in. There would be no offerings of beverages, no niceties. They were beyond that now, she saw.

Thompson looked down at his feet, and she had a good view of the back of his neck. From that angle, he looked vulnerable, thin, his ears turning red at the tips in the cold. Beneath the layers of his rayon suit, she saw his rib cage expanding as he took several deep breaths before he spoke. Hannah recognized that move. It was what she did when she was scared. When she had to summon strength. When she had to rise up to the challenge. Now, was she the challenge?

"Ms. Sawyer, we need you to go pick up Miles and bring him down to the precinct for an interview," he said. Softly but firmly. He continued to look at his feet, not meeting her eyes.

"What? No. What for? No. No, we are not doing that. I am not doing that!"

"You can stay with him, since he's a minor," Thompson added, as if softening his original blow. As if she didn't know her son's age. As if she didn't know she had every right to be present.

"No!"

"So," Carelli said, "just so I'm clear, you're refusing to cooperate? You're withholding information that could help in the inve—"

"No, I'm refusing having a couple of grown men try to…manipulate a child who has done nothing, absolutely nothing, wrong."

"If he's done nothing wrong, you have nothing to worry about."

She almost laughed out loud. How stupid did they actually think she was?

"I have work to do, and you have no right to be here."

"We have *cause* to be here, ma'am." Thompson reached out his hand as if he was going to touch her, pat her on the arm, but stopped. A reflex he had to curtail, his hand flailing midair. But he was looking at her directly now as he attempted to land the word *cause*. Aiming it, burying it, letting it go deep.

"Cause? Do you have a warrant?"

"No," Thompson said with an exhalation, "but we have surveillance video that implicates your son."

She kept her lips as still as she could, refusing to let words she'd regret fly out of her mouth. But they churned inside her, and she was certain they were all but visible on her face.

"No, you don't."

"The neighbors provided surveillance video from their homes," Thompson said.

"Without a warrant," Carelli added. "Because they want to help their neighbors get justice for their child. Unlike some people."

"Leave," she said. "Now."

"He killed and buried an animal in your backyard. That's how it starts, isn't it? When he was a toddler, he pulled wings off flies, didn't he? And then he works his way up to worms, to—" Carelli was punching the air now with his hands, his face starting to turn crimson, his cheeks ombre and turning. Her porch an interrogation chamber with its spotlight the hidden, waiting moon.

"No!" she cried. "He did nothing! He found it!"

"Why didn't you call animal control? Why didn't you call your brother-in-law, your sister? Or, better yet, your ex-husband, the hunter?

Why did the kids at his former school think he was offing animals behind the playground, huh? If it was all innocent, Hannah, why—"

"That proves nothing! You need to leave! Now!" She pointed to the street stupidly, for emphasis. As if they didn't know where their car was and where they needed to go. She held her hand in the air a long time, achingly long, before she lowered it to her side. The blood pulsed back in as if she was wounded.

"What if we told you we had evidence linking the girl to your house?"

"I'd say you were lying," she said. "I'd say prove it."

Her heart pounded inside her chest. She thought of what she'd seen in the binoculars that first night, the ghostly edge of what had looked like a wing. Was that a little girl, wearing wings, running between the houses? Or an owl, a wild turkey? And would that show up on a camera, too?

"Is this what you want? Your son dragged out of soccer practice in handcuffs? Without us hearing his side of the story?"

"You don't know anything," she said.

Carelli stifled a chuckle, and she thought she saw Thompson shoot him the smallest of warning glances.

"My son," she said firmly, "does not fucking play soccer."

eighteen

EVA

So this was what the world had come to: surveillance. Other grandmas stayed home and started baking their Thanksgiving pies early, picked out knitting patterns for all the Christmas socks they were going to make, then met their friends for a lunch of tea sandwiches. I, on the other hand, had opened someone else's garage, picked up a pair of high-powered binoculars, and joined the world of police stakeouts, of front porch cameras, of backyard motion-sensitive lights, of neighbors not trusting neighbors. I was crouched out of sight of one daughter's fancy mounted camera, eyes trained on the other one. Slightly more exciting than baking or playing canasta at the Saturday Club, but shameful nonetheless.

And to make it all worse, I was rewarded for it doubly.

I wondered why Hannah was so upset, talking to those two detectives, and at first, I was just foolish enough to believe it was connected to her sister and brother-in-law. To poker night, the little girl at the door, and the missing boots. You didn't have to be a brain surgeon to add those things up.

Two neighbors' SUVs drove past Hannah's slowly, noticing the police car. Probably taking photos on their damned phones. How many times had the detectives visited her? Three? Four? And Hillary's, just once.

I suppose the police knew more than anyone and were just trying to play all the angles. But if they expected my girls to turn on each other, they had another thing coming. Hannah had sent them on their way with an angry flourish. How I wished I could read lips! But I could read body language. One detective meaner than the other, louder. She had told them both to go to hell, one way or another. She would not implicate her sister. No.

I watched her go inside, and I swear I heard the dead bolt click in the door. The men walked back to their car, a slow stroll down the hill as if they were looking for something else along the way. They sat there longer than I would have thought. To rattle her? To scheme? Two more cars drove by, slowed down, took note.

How long before this news spread around the street, the book club, the poker night? How long before people put this other equation together, that the second a new boy appeared, a girl disappeared?

It occurred to me as they pulled away, heading west up the street, that they could be coming to Hillary's next. Why not? Two birds, one stone. We'd made it all very convenient for them, hadn't we, with my two girls living next door to each other? But they kept going. I waited five minutes, ten, and was planning to leave. How much more information could I hold in my head anyway? Miles and his dying deer. A girl waving goodbye to Miles. Hillary and her front door with the girl. Ben and his missing boots. And on top of it, a shady real estate transaction. Dear God, I had a lot to think about!

Then suddenly, Hannah's door opened. She walked down the porch and around the side yard, and I froze, put the binoculars down for a second, believing she was looking up the hill, coming for me.

But no. She walked to her small backyard. She traced her toe in the dirt, outlining something. She brought her hand to her mouth. Was she stifling a yawn? Or a sob? I got my answer when I saw her wipe a lone tear off her cheek.

And then, she turned to the back woods and held her middle finger into the air for a good five seconds, until she dropped it and went inside.

Here only a week, and already she hated a neighbor? What did that neighbor know?

I watched her as she went back inside, but something made me look closer at the small patch of yard. Zero in. Change the focus. And see the shovel, leaned up against the door.

And I knew for certain she wasn't protecting her sister but her son. Her dead-animal-carrying son.

nineteen

HANNAH

The day after she'd moved in, a welcome wagon basket had appeared on her porch, seemingly overnight. As she'd stepped out to retrieve it at 6:00 a.m., wiping dew off the plastic cover, it bothered her to think of who had delivered it and when. An innocent volunteer, a woman probably, if those committees were anything like they were in Narberth, but it was still unsettling. That she was alone and slept so deeply she hadn't heard someone step onto her porch, so near the vulnerable divided light windowpanes, delicate as candy.

The basket contained a tin of tea, jam, a box of crackers, coupons to local restaurants. No wine. No Xanax. Nothing useful to a stressed-out mom. Rolled up and secured with ribbon were two flimsy, laminated placemats dotted with ads for local lawn services, nearby dentists, and vets.

She'd put the ugly placemats under the kitchen sink as liners, and after the detectives left her house and sat outside in their damned car for no good reason other than trying to rattle her and make her crazy, she fished them out, laid them across her table, and surveyed all the listings.

There were no ads for local criminal attorneys. Of course not. Where was the *emergency* welcome kit? The bail bondsman. The all-night drugstore. The closest sporting goods store that sold ammunition. She sat at her computer and rubbed her eyes. She would not call her ex-husband, who would say she was overreacting. And she would not call her sister, the person who would know the most, would know exactly who to call and how to get an appointment. No. The secret was too deep and too fraught to explain to someone like Hillary, who thought in black-and-white terms. Hannah realized with a start that Hillary thought a lot like Mike, just a Mike who held things behind a calmer reserve. Ugh, how had she gone through couples therapy and not realized this before? That she'd sort of married her sister? And lastly, she couldn't call her mother, who might understand, simply because she wouldn't be able to help.

So she did what she always did. She went online, researched a few names, and then got on with the day. She made it all the way through another conference call with the Philanthropist, managing to make all the notes, complimenting the older woman on her memory and recall of small, inane details—which was extraordinary, she had to give her that—and at the end of the call, almost on a lark, she asked the woman if she happened to know the lawyer at the top of her list. The one who was so wealthy and yet still so principled he could afford to take certain cases pro bono.

"Of course I do," she responded. "I bought a table and made a huge donation at his foundation dinner last month."

And just like that, she had an introduction. She'd told her it was for "research" on "another project," and there was no questioning, no delving further. But before they'd hung up, Hannah thought she heard a ripple of excitement in the woman's voice. Either she got off on helping people or she loved being so close to intrigue—and potential gossip—that she could almost taste it.

Hannah did not really want to know which it was.

She called Jay DeSanto's law office, dropped the Philanthropist's name, and got an appointment.

twenty

EVA

The question everyone would ask me later was "Didn't you think about going to the police?" And I say, with what? A child crying over a deer, a girl waving to a new neighbor, a pair of missing boots, and a shovel? I could almost see their faces as I shared these non-events with them. You get to be my age, and you're familiar with those looks from men. They want bold headlines, black-and-white, shouting. They don't do subtle, gray whispers. Even I, with my many years of parenting and observing and consoling and retreating—even I didn't understand fully what I'd seen. How could I expect them to?

I remember that year after my husband died, the dog growled one night at three in the morning, waking me. I checked to make sure the girls were in their beds, and then I opened the front door a few inches, peering out. I smelled lime in the air, like the lingering cologne of someone passing by. I called the police, and they repeated what I said back to me until I understood, finally, exactly what it sounded like. How flimsy and bendable. Ethereal as a dandelion.

"You sensed someone in your yard? You smelled traces of lime?" Hearing your words like that, repeated but differently stated, with emphasis on the laziest verbs, was like hearing yourself in some other realm, another planet. Yes, I kept saying. The dog only growls at men, I added. But I couldn't say what they wanted: *I saw a man, and here is what he looked like. I heard him walking through the trees, and here are his footprints in the dirt.* That is evidence. Everything else is just a floater, a dream.

So police could have hunches, but women could not have intuition or sense memories. And there's a reason they call something "eyewitness," because that's the only witnessing they want. As if eyesight were infallible! As if people weren't color-blind! But no, sight weighs more than sound. Listening can be counted on more than sniffing. And goose bumps that ride up your arms as you look out into a foggy night? That just means you are cold.

And how would that tip the balance anyway? The police already had the front-door footage of the girl visiting Ben, and the shovel certainly led me to believe something was clearly buried in Miles's backyard. They were already sniffing in two directions. My non-information times two wouldn't change the score at all. When you added it all together, it just made me more confused. It just showed how something could be nothing, because obviously my grandson and my son-in-law could not both be guilty, could they? Dear God, the thought of that! Colluding! One covering for the other! No. Impossible. Maybe for father and son, but not for uncle and nephew. So wasn't it entirely possible that neither of them was guilty? Couldn't I just decide that and act accordingly?

I felt unbearably full with the information I possessed. I could only imagine how my daughters felt. The girls were used to bearing their load together, not apart.

And so I found myself waiting at the middle school, behind the buses, sitting on a bench. School was probably the only place an old woman could loiter without anyone thinking she was homeless or suicidal or lost. An old man? Absolutely not. An old woman? As long as she was clean, no problem.

Miles saw me before I saw him, however, and to his credit, he didn't duck away.

"Grandma? What are you doing here? Is something wrong?"

"Well," I replied with a sigh, "yes and no."

"Is Mom okay?"

"Again, that answer could go either way, but let's just say yes. But we need to talk." I dangled my keys and pointed to the car.

"Aren't we waiting for Morgan?"

I blinked and looked at him. His eyes, so long-lashed, wide open, innocent. The eyes girls would fall in love with someday, if he ever outgrew his awkwardness, his oddities. I said a prayer that he would keep some of his thoughtfulness along with his lashes.

Of course this thoughtful boy would think of his cousin, and this idiotic grandmother wouldn't. Not only were we *not* going to wait for Morgan, we were going to hustle our buns out of there before she saw us. Damn it, I'd forgotten about Morgan! Here I'd been sitting on a bench out in the open, like I had nothing to hide. *Good God, I'm bad at surveillance,* I thought. *Earlier today was clearly a fluke.*

"Not this time," I said simply and picked up my pace walking.

I asked him if he wanted a milkshake, and he looked at me strangely before saying sure. I know what he was thinking—that he wasn't allowed ice cream on weekdays. Or wait—were those Hillary's rules for Morgan? Probably. Hannah was more relaxed about food and rules, but I sometimes got them all switched up. Especially when I babysat them both and merely imposed "Grandma's rules." Grandma didn't have many rules, that was for certain.

There were quite a few options for ice cream in Wayne, but I knew the best place with the most flavors was on the edge of town, so we drove farther out and waited in line in the gravel parking lot, then sat at the picnic table.

"We should probably text your mother that you'll be late."

"No, the bus takes, like, forever."

"Okay, then."

I ordered strawberry, and he had chocolate. I wanted to tell him to mix it up, try one of their crazier flavors, go wild! But maybe he felt the same way I did about ice cream—it's not meant to have bits in it, combos of things you have to stop and chew. It's a beverage, not trail mix, for God's sake.

We sat at the picnic table and sipped. Mine was thick and needed to melt. I couldn't get it through the straw, but Miles managed fine. Stronger, I supposed. I was losing strength everywhere, even my mouth. And paper straws? Oh, I know the environment, the oceans, but that was a trend I despised. They melted before I could get anything through.

"Miles," I said slowly, "about the thing that happened the other night."

"Jeez, Grandma, please don't tell my mom."

"Well, I haven't. Really. So far. But you know that puts me in an awkward position. Extremely awkward. But even worse, well, Miles, I saw something else. Something that could put me in an awkward position, perhaps, with the police."

"The police?"

Dear God, the look on his face. He had never considered that the judgment of his family, his so-called peers at school, and the look on the face of his therapist wouldn't be the sum total of his punishments.

"What do the police have to do with anything?"

I felt bad for him, as I often did. Tall as he was, there was a softness to him that made you want to gather him in your arms and pet him.

"Miles, I saw you with a little girl the night you moved in. I stopped by to bring brownies, remember? When I left, I saw her waving to you."

He stopped drinking. "Wait, what? I don't even know her."

"Well, I think that was her. The girl."

"No."

"I think so."

"I didn't touch her. I didn't even talk to her. I only said hi."

This struck me as odd, that he immediately said *touch*. Was this just a coincidence?

"Did she say anything to you?"

"She came out as I was walking toward the street and asked if I liked frogs, and I said yeah. And she said me too."

"That's it?"

"Yeah, I swear. She waved goodbye, I guess."

I took a deep breath. "Miles, they don't know about you meeting her or the deer the other night. But I suspect they know that something is buried in your backyard. What would happen if they added those things together? Are there other animals, Miles? Is there a secret that I don't know?"

His face suddenly went vanilla white. Even the soft sprinkle of freckles seemed to pale. He looked like one of those inflatable bendy men outside car dealerships, capable of collapse at any moment.

"Is that…against the law? Because, you know, animals die all the time. Like, weekly. Probably daily. Or even hourly."

"I know. And I don't think it is, actually. But it doesn't matter what's legal and what isn't. What matters is how it looks and what it means. And it looks bad. And with a death in the neighborhood, the police are searching for anything that is unusual, you know? And that is highly unusual."

"But it doesn't mean anything."

"So you say."

"You don't believe me?"

I shrugged slowly, dramatically. Older people are world-class shruggers, our faces and bodies rubbery and loose, moving in slow motion already. I felt my face and body curl into such stagey animation, it was almost grotesque. But he got the point. Oh yes. I heard his breathing quicken, felt the fear growing inside him while I posed.

"Miles, if you're killing animals, it's not that great a leap to say—"

"Grandma! I am not killing animals! I love animals!"

His voice was a stage whisper, but the color was back in his face.

"You love them," I repeated.

He nodded, sniffed.

I didn't want to ask what that meant. I feared what that meant. He was a boy, going through adolescence, at an age when no girl was ready for him, with no father at home to guide him and too much freedom within his household. A boy who had been bullied over something at his former school and was in therapy. A boy who cradled a dying deer like a lover. Dear God, who was he? *What* was he?

I took a deep breath. I wanted to believe the best of him, I did. But I knew too much about the world. I knew children raised with the internet had access to every terrible act the world had ever dreamed up. Every sick obsession or fetish. When a boy facing manhood used the word *love*, was it a euphemism?

"I'm not doing anything wrong," he said. "I'm trying to do everything right, and it's hard."

"Okay," I said. "Your secret is safe."

"Thank you."

"However, I need you to do something for me."

"What?" He slurped up the last dregs of his milkshake.

"If you see anything else or hear anything? Will you come to me? And let me figure out what we should do next?"

"Okay, Grandma," he said, and he waited patiently while I finished my milkshake.

twenty-one

HANNAH

C at Saunders wasn't one to beat around the bush. In one brief phone call a few days after her email, she had told Hannah she needed someone on board immediately, that if Ben liked her, that was all she needed to know, and could she start by attending their regional meeting at the Marriott in a few days? There would be a select group of high school girls speaking briefly about their experiences with the program, and Hannah could interview them afterward with a videographer.

And that was how Hannah found herself ushered by an event coordinator to the back of a small corporate auditorium with a cameraman named Justin, who had his feet up on the chair in front of him and looked like he might be about to take a much-needed nap. They were there to listen to the program but also to await being told where they were supposed to set up after the presentations. Justin was mildly annoyed, since he had two bags of equipment and needed time to assess the space and the light. But Hannah found the presentations helpful for background, and the girls' brief speeches gave her a few additional ideas for questions. She hadn't spoken to Cat yet in person; she was acting as an emcee on stage, introducing, cajoling, encouraging laughter and applause as needed, all in a vibrant red jumpsuit. Her hair was a little tousled and her makeup subdued, as if not to distract from her fire engine of an outfit. Hannah remembered reading somewhere that men loved the color red, and she was surprised to note that most of the people in the audience were men, maybe seventy percent. She'd thought there were more female teachers and school administrators, but maybe these were businesspeople, venture capitalists. Maybe she considered this more of a fundraiser and photo op than a meeting, which would explain why Ben was there, sitting on the aisle in the tenth row with a few other men he seemed to know well.

As she passed by him, he reached out and grabbed her hand, then stood up and gathered her into a hug.

"You're here!" he said.

"Observant as always," she said with a smile.

"I knew you and Cat would like each other," he said. "Two powerhouses."

"Well, one."

He frowned while he smiled, a particularly Ben kind of face that was impossible for anyone else to make.

"Don't hide your light, Hannah," he said. "I think I'll embroider that on a pillow and give it to you for Christmas."

"I'd like to see you with a needle and thread," she said.

"Let's catch up later," he said. "I know you've got work to do."

He nodded to the coordinator, who smiled back appreciatively, and they continued to their seats.

After the final speech, Cat said something about refreshments followed by breakout groups, and the coordinator appeared by Justin's elbow and said they had secured a room for them, a suite.

They set up on the fourth floor, in a suite with a large common area. The coordinator said she'd bring all the girls back in an hour, and Hannah told her no, she wanted to meet with each of them alone, in twenty- or maybe thirty-minute shifts.

"But that's…more work," the coordinator said.

"Yes, but it will result in much better interviews," Hannah replied. "We don't want them distracted."

"Yeah, plus we need it quiet when we're rolling sound. We can't have a bunch of talking in the room," Justin said.

"Okay," the coordinator sighed. "I'll bring you the first girl and hold the rest in room 405, and you can just walk them back and get the next girl."

"Great," Hannah said.

The windows faced south, and Justin grumbled about the light, taped up filters, and rearranged the furniture. Instead of the sofa and upholstered chairs, he brought over two barstools from the kitchenette to face each other.

The first girl, Sami, a thin, olive-skinned brunette, had not spoken on stage. She seemed especially nervous, biting her fingernails, sniffing compulsively. When Justin's explanation of how to thread the microphone cord through the back of her sweater confused her and he moved toward her to show her, she stood up quickly and said no, not to touch her.

"It's okay," Hannah said. "He's just trying to help."

They finally got her situated and started to record, but Sami wasn't very talkative and kept glancing over at Justin when she was supposed to be looking at Hannah.

"Can you tell us a little bit about the afternoon you were attacked?"

"No, because there's a lawsuit. My lawyer says I can't discuss it."

Hannah bit her lip. Why had they put Sami in the mix if she couldn't speak to her experiences? She shifted gears to the last questions on her list, asking her about how me3 had helped her, and she answered all those questions readily.

"Circling back now, I know you can't talk about the facts of the case, but can you describe how you were feeling that day?"

"I was feeling hopeful. I had a biology test, and I had studied really hard, and I thought I was going to get a good grade on it."

"So you were having a pretty good day?"

"Yeah."

"Anything else you remember about feeling good?"

"I had lunch with my friends outside because it was sunny. It was the first sunny day in a long time."

"And after the attack, which we won't get into, what was the first thing you did that made you feel better?"

"I called my sister," she said.

Those words rang in Hannah's ears, staying, vibrating, taking up space. Because she'd done the same thing, hadn't she? All the air in the room seemed to evaporate. Hannah put her hand on her throat, willing herself to swallow, breathe, feel grounded again. It had been a long time since she'd had a panic attack about those boys in high school. Images of that night suddenly swam in front of her eyes. The pale flesh of a bare, numb foot. Then, just as suddenly, the paw of a fox, the hoof of a deer. She shook her head slightly, erasing them, trying to center herself again.

Finally, the air started to come back to her lungs. She didn't faint. She didn't throw up. It was entirely possibly no one had even noticed what was going on inside the theater of her own head.

She was able to form a few more questions about the organization and the help of peers and wrapped up the interview a little too quickly, perhaps, but professionally. Sami left, and Hannah went to the bathroom, blew her nose, put eye drops in her eyes, which always had a way of waking her up, setting her straight, and went out into the corridor to retrieve the next girl. *Please*, she thought, *let this girl have a different story, one that doesn't mirror my own.*

As Hannah walked down the soft blue-and-gray carpet toward the descending numbers, closer to the elevator and the middle of the building, she was almost to 405 when a door opened at the far opposite end of the hallway, toward the exit stairs. The other suite, on the corner, she supposed. A flash of red caught her eye, and she realized it was Cat Saunders exiting. She swiped her key card in the room directly across and went inside. They probably had a whole bank of rooms on the fourth floor, and Hannah wouldn't have thought anything of it if Cat hadn't been barefoot.

Hannah stood outside 405 now, quietly, waiting, not knocking, expecting something else to happen, and it did.

Another person came out of the suite, one of the high school students who'd spoken earlier. Carly something, last name started with a W. Wendell? Wentworth? She'd have to check her notes. Blond and curvy. She was laughing a little, and she reached back inside the door and pulled out someone else playfully before they both knocked on Cat's door.

Ben. She saw him for just a second before she turned her back, tried to be invisible at the opposite end of the hall. But she'd seen enough. She'd seen his hand on the young woman's back, guiding her across the hall.

twenty-two

HANNAH

As Hannah walked to her car to drive to the appointment with the lawyer, she recognized a few women from book club at the head of the path across the street. Tara and Susan. Not walking, just standing. At the sound of Hannah's boots on the pavement, they turned and waved, and she waved perfunctorily back.

"Hannah!" Susan said, starting to walk over. "Where have you been hiding?"

"Just working," she said. "Not hiding."

"Well," Susan said, "I think I'd hide under a rock if the police were at my house as much as they're at yours."

Hannah blinked twice. "They're just, you know, doing their job."

"Well, they seem awfully laser focused, don't you think? I mean, how many times have they been there, interviewing you? Or, you know, your son?"

"I…live the closest to the Harrises," Hannah said.

"Yeah, that's probably why," Tara said, pulling slightly on Susan's arm.

"But they didn't interview all the kids, you know," Susan said. "There were other boys they didn't ask."

"They didn't interview Miles," Hannah said firmly.

"I understand you want to protect your son, but I mean, come on. It's not exactly a coincidence, is it?"

"Look, I don't know what you're talking about," Hannah said. "And I'm late for an appointment."

"Let's go, Susan," Tara said, and Susan shrugged off Tara's hand violently, shot her a look.

"Come on, Hannah. Your son moves in, and suddenly this happens? I mean, you can't keep your head in the sand."

Hannah pushed past her, got in the car, and slammed the door so hard both women jumped. Tara's face was white with shame as Hannah pulled away. Or maybe Tara the vaper was just high and pale.

Well, Hannah thought as she pulled away, *so much for book club*.

The last time Hannah saw a lawyer had been for her divorce, and that woman's office was in a strip mall a few miles away. She knew Jay DeSanto's office would be in the city, but she was unprepared for the penthouse views and his glamorous receptionist and spent the first few minutes trying to figure out how high his hourly rate could possibly be. The first meeting was a favor—but what about the rest?

She had her answer in the first sixty seconds. He breezed in and told her he'd give her some advice because she was a friend of a friend but that representation required a $50,000 retainer for the first two months.

"Wow," she said.

"That's always the first question, so I like to get it out of the way."

"Do you ever waive that fee for an interesting case?"

"Sometimes," he said and smiled. "Make me interested."

She told him the story—at least everything she knew.

"The police have been over asking questions multiple times."

"How many?"

"Four, I think. And the last time, they demanded to interview Miles."

"Have they been on your property at all when you're not home?"

"Not that I know of. And they know my son buried an animal in the backyard because of a neighbor's video camera. They claimed to have other evidence but didn't tell me what it was."

"They were probably bluffing. If they had more, they might do more."

"Like what?"

"Like get a search warrant. Or demand your son's DNA."

"This is ridiculous," she said. "We've never even met this girl. They should be focused on someone who knew her and, you know, watched her, someone obsessed or something."

"Do you know if there are any other suspects? Seen them interviewing anyone else who did anything strange?"

She thought sharply, suddenly, of Ben and his behavior at the Marriott. "I, uh, don't know."

He leaned back in his chair and didn't interrupt the rest of her story, about how she'd met the mother, how she felt sorry for her, how she thought that because she lived the closest to the Harrises, she'd been targeted or something. He didn't ask any more questions, just listened, and she liked that about him. She'd thought of lawyers as being all talk, and he looked as if he'd be that way, with his air of confidence and his perfectly fitted suit. But he wasn't.

He paused after she finished and took a deep breath as if considering everything, adding it up.

"Look," he said, "you did all the right things. You didn't take your son down to the station. You didn't let the cops look at your property without a warrant. I sense they have nothing on you or your boy. They're just trying to put two and two together and make it a hundred. They're fishing and hoping. If there hadn't been a dead child involved, none of your neighbors would have even ponied up their surveillance footage. It's too personal. No one wants anyone to know that they order cake in the middle of the night or an escort service or whatever it is."

"Escort service?"

"Hey, it happens. Especially when money is no object, like in a neighborhood like yours. People tend to be very private and skeptical. Frankly, I'm surprised anyone gave up that footage. Very surprised. And for the record, burying a dead fox on your property is not a crime. Killing it isn't either, technically, but it has to be reported to the game commission."

"He didn't kill it."

"Did you?"

"No!"

"Why did your son bury it then? If he didn't kill it?"

"It was…a kind of punishment. He isn't allowed to be near wild animals."

"Because of rabies."

"No."

"No?"

"Well, yes, but…"

"What's the but?"

"Can I tell you this without paying you $50,000?"

"Yes."

"But it's still privileged information?"

"Yes. Privilege has nothing to do with payment."

"He has a…comforting compulsion."

"What?"

She felt the bubbles of sweat starting to dot the nape of her neck and the red flush that spread along the ridge of her ears.

"I don't know any other way to describe it. When he sees an animal in pain or near death, he…needs to be…he has to be…close to it."

"Close to it?"

"Yes. That's what the therapist said."

"And there's nothing more to it? Nothing, uh, violent or…kinky? Or—"

"We don't think so, no."

She felt her legs drop down, settling into the velvet upholstery of her chair now that she'd told him. Her shoulders moved back down into their sockets, and her jaw unclenched. *This is why people tell the truth*, she said to herself. *Because the weight of it becomes unbearable, and the release feels so good.*

"Hannah, that is some seriously strange shit."

"I know."

His face was full of concern, as if he were a teacher or a relative. Or a friend, she'd think later. Almost like a friend.

"Who knows about this besides you and his therapist?"

"No one."

"No one?"

"Well, his dad."

"Your ex."

"Yes."

"On good terms with him? He's not out to ruin you or get custody?"

"No. But he's in denial, thinks it's more of a…bird-dog quality."

He laughed, said he was sorry, that he couldn't help himself sometimes. The things he heard. The rationales some people made.

She smiled. She had to smile back, because she understood. It *was* ridiculous on some level. Her son and her husband, both of them.

It was one thing for people to ascribe human qualities to animals, but when they started doing the reverse? Making animal behavior equivalencies? That usually got people into trouble. True or not true. Monkeys running. Dogs fetching. Birds pecking at you. Normal people don't want to be animals, no matter how in tune with them they are. She remembered asking Miles that first morning after: *Do you want to be a fox?* And the look he shot her, face twisted just shy of cruelty, actually made her feel so much better. *No. Jeez, Mom, no.*

"Other family know?"

"No. We haven't told anyone."

"Friends?"

"Some boys at school bullied him about liking animals instead of girls, made up stories about him with animals at the edge of the woods, but it was all bullshit. They don't really know the gist of it. They don't know."

"Are you sure? Maybe a best friend, and that friend tells a parent—"

"No, I don't think so."

"A school counselor?"

"No. Just the specialist."

"Okay. Look, you don't really need me, at least not yet. They have nothing. But what you might need is a private investigator."

"Why?"

"Because someone else is guilty, and they're wasting time on your son while a killer runs free in your neighborhood."

"Jesus." Such a stark way to put it. She was suddenly vividly aware of her neighbors, encased in secure houses, with alarms on their windows and doors. She thought of her thin windows, her tiny dead bolt. She calculated how much she remembered from self-defense classes in college. It added up to very, very little. Still, she couldn't help thinking of who else was out there. And she couldn't help thinking of her brother-in-law, his weird behavior at the offsite meeting and on the path. He had seemed, well, guilty.

"PIs aren't nearly as expensive as lawyers," he added. "Some of them cost less per hour than a spin class."

Then he smiled and paused, and she took that as her cue to leave. He probably thought she knew what spin classes cost or what ex-cops were paid per hour to dig up information, but she was more aware of what plumbers made per hour, and movers and babysitters. And now, expensive defensive attorneys.

He walked her to the door and out to the lobby. He told her that if the police asked for another interview or for DNA, to say no and call him immediately. If Miles sensed he was being followed—around school, at the mall, anywhere—he was to throw nothing he'd eaten away. Not gum, not a straw, nothing. He even told her she had to drive her own garbage to the dump, not to leave it at the curb, ever.

"Police can take anything you throw away and test it for DNA. Legally."

She took this information in slowly, with a sick feeling in her stomach. This was real. This was forensics. This was science, up against good or bad parenting.

He said nothing more about money. "I'll give you my cell number," he said. She entered it into her phone as he repeated the numbers. "Even if it's the middle of the night, call."

She nodded, and they shook hands. His palm was warm, and hers was damp, she knew. She hoped he'd seen that before, didn't hold it against her. She took the elevator forty floors down to the lobby, and it shook a little on the last ten, made her heart race. How long had it been since she'd ridden an elevator in a skyscraper? Writer's questions.

At the traffic light, waiting for the walk signal, she looked at her watch. She had to run to catch the next train, and there wasn't another one for an hour. When she got to the platform, she was sweating, breathing heavily, and she felt a little stupid. She had four minutes to spare; she could have used those to walk and calm down.

She had a full day's work to get in before her son got home. She was scared by what Jay DeSanto had told her, yes, but she also felt buoyed, reassured. By the time she got off the train and walked to her car, her sweat had cooled, and she felt ready to tackle the tangle of the Philanthropist's book. But as she turned onto Brindle Lane, she saw that would be impossible.

She parked her car on the street and strode up to the door.

"You think you can just come here every day and bully me into bringing my son to you? Get off my property!"

She thought of her trash cans in the back, and her breath seized in her chest. Where was Carelli? Was he going through her plastic bags at that very moment, one step ahead, looking for soda cans, just as Jay had warned her? He said it would happen at the curb though, hadn't he? Otherwise, was it illegal?

Carelli came around the side of her house slowly, phone to his ear, gesturing. No gloves on his hands, no baggie. *Okay*, she thought. *Okay for now.*

"Ms. Sawyer," Detective Thompson said, "calm down. We're not here to talk about your son, I promise."

"Oh, so you think I'm guilty now? Leave. Unless you have a warrant, leave."

"We have a warrant."

Her face fell. She could actually feel it dropping, skin, muscle, the heaviness of blood. It went along, in synch, with her stomach, everything soft and liquid falling, settling deep into her bones. *Fear, this is what true fear feels like*, she thought. She had never felt it before. She thought she'd known it when she went into labor, when Mike left their house for the last time, when Miles was found with his first animal. But no, that was warm-up. This was the real thing. Her knees might actually buckle; she bent them as if to protect her balance and stood on her lawn with nothing to hang on to but her purse. *Stay upright*, she told herself. *Do not go down. Do not close your eyes for one second.*

"No," she said.

"It's for your sister's house," Carelli said. "Any idea where Hillary or Ben is?"

Hannah thought of her brother-in-law, where he might be, where he could be, and felt sick. The last time she'd seen him, the way he'd touched that young girl. So strange to witness in that dark hallway.

She shook her head, like she didn't really know him at all.

twenty-three

EVA

The day I'd brought Miles home from school, I'd asked him if he knew how to play poker. I had this cockamamie idea that with his help, I could infiltrate the next monthly poker night and find out where all those men had been. But Miles didn't know any more about the game than I did. He also told me he didn't think I'd like going anyway, because they drank and smoked cigars and "other stuff." I was right and truly appalled by the "other stuff," and he just shrugged and said Morgan told him some of his classmates' dads smoked pot, did edibles, or worse. Worse? Cocaine and stuff, he said. Stuff? I don't know, he said, just stuff. And after I resisted the motherly impulse (which never goes away, I am here to tell you) to take names and phone the authorities, I felt a kind of joy spreading through my chest. Miles had just told me something very, very secret! Something he could never trust his mother to know. But he trusted me!

I'd told him that men need to blow off steam and stress just like kids do at recess. Poker night was just a kind of recess for dads. That was why men paid to go drink beer and throw axes at targets (I'd seen this on the television news) and why they went to the garage and pounded nails and went out into the yard and chainsawed limbs that brushed against the house.

"Is that why they kill deer?" he'd said.

Oh goodness. He was thinking of his father, of course, and of himself, his interests. But again with the deer?

"Well, I think most people kill animals to eat them, Miles. As your father does."

We'd all made a little pact to never disparage Mike, and I had given myself a little check mark for remembering. And it was true; Mike had always said it proudly, that he ate whatever he killed. Miles had shuddered visibly when I said the word *eat*. Miles was no Jeffrey Dahmer; he was an inch away from being a vegetarian, that much was certain.

The next time I swung by Hannah's house, a few days later, I thought it was to check on Miles, to make sure he was okay. But when I pulled up, Hannah was walking between the yards, heading, it appeared, to Hillary's driveway. She was striding with a kind of purpose, her phone pressed to her ear. When she got to the circle, she stopped and started gesturing animatedly into her phone.

I rolled down my window. Her voice didn't carry far enough for me to hear exactly what she was saying, but she was yelling. Yelling loud enough that anyone could hear an occasional word. Like *Hillary*. Like *Ben*. Like *goddamn it all, listen to me*.

Yelling in a way she couldn't yell in her own home, where Miles might hear her. Where Miles might look up from whatever he was doing, his homework, his video games, or his deer videos. Good God, who knew.

twenty-four

HANNAH

She'd run out of the house before she had a chance to think or grab a coat, and now she was a little chilly standing in the circle, deciding whether she should just go inside Hillary's where it was warm. Of course she should. But somehow, that felt wrong now. Were the police somewhere watching? Would they check the cameras, know if she touched or took anything? Good God. No, she waited. She did a few jumping jacks to keep warm, then felt ridiculous when she realized it would be captured on camera and stopped. She sat on the macadam—another word from her youthful list, she thought—near the garage, out of the camera's view, feeling stupid. Why did she even need to be there to make sure the police didn't disobey? Wasn't that Hillary's problem, not hers?

The next car that came up the driveway wasn't her sister's but her mother's. Hannah's heart sank. Maybe Hillary hadn't understood the import of what she'd said. That she or Ben had exactly two hours to get home before the police executed the search by breaking down the door. It was a courtesy, made to the more expensive homes, Hannah supposed, to wait until the homeowner was there. They could avoid lawsuits and problems replacing the expensive mahogany doors and imported glass windows was what she originally guessed. But Thompson and Carelli were sneaky, watchful. At least Carelli was. These guys didn't care about things, money, lawsuits. She imagined there was probably some other reason they waited for the homeowner. A psychological reason, a cop trick.

Extending a courtesy created trust. And trust made people relax, let down their guard. Maybe they could glean cues from people's body language about where to start searching? Wasn't that perhaps why they'd told her first? Not to find out where her sister was but to find out how she'd react? And now, she'd played right into their hands. Rushing up here! Protecting her sister! Doing fucking calisthenics instead of going inside. What the hell would they make of her?

But now she had to marshal even more strength. Bad enough that she had to argue with Hillary—now she had to lie to Eva. She took a deep breath and decided to pretend that everything was fine. She'd been fine when she left the lawyer, and she'd be fine now. She just had to summon that feeling.

"You look upset," Eva said as she climbed out of the car, more slowly than usual. Eva had always been thin and spry, the spring of an athlete in her movements, but she was slowing down. Inevitable, but it made her daughters worry. One of the functions of having only one parent; you noticed and worried twice as much.

"Me? No. Just surprised. I was expecting Hillary."

"Well, you know the code. Why are you waiting outside?"

"Oh, you know, just, enjoying the day."

"I think we should go in, don't you?"

Hannah glanced at her watch. Almost five. The day nearly gone. Hillary was certainly taking her sweet fucking time. The police would be back soon, and then her mother would know. Hillary's last words had been not to tell her. Hannah had assumed it was out of embarrassment or not wanting to worry her. The same reasons Hannah hadn't told her about Miles.

But now, Eva had that look in her eye, the look she'd had in high school when Hannah had come home late or hidden beer bottles in the bottom of the recycling bin. That look, that "I know something is up with you two" look. The last time she'd seen it junior year of high school, she and Hillary had held firm. They hadn't told her a thing. Some secrets simply had to be kept forever. Because there were no statutes of limitation on breaking a mother's heart.

"Why don't we go down to my house and have some tea? We'll come back later when Hillary's home."

"Hillary has tea."

It wasn't particularly cold, but it was breezy. She felt it every time in the narrow ledge between her pants and her short boots. Or maybe all her nerves were simply on fire.

"Well, I have a bit of work to do though. On my computer."

"Then you go work, honey. I'll go in and wait for Hillary."

Hannah's jaw felt tight. She ran a hand across it, trying to loosen it. "No."

"No?"

"I can't let you do that."

"Hannah, what on earth is going on?"

Hannah didn't answer.

"Has Hillary changed the code? Has there been a burglary, or…"

"No, Mom. I, uh, I think you should go home."

Eva's eyes turned to steel. Hannah knew telling her mother this was futile. She had no agency over her sister's home, after all. She could tell her mother to leave her own property but not Hillary's. And Eva was not easily dismissed. She was one of those older women who had been dismissed one time too many and had vowed not to take it anymore. And who could blame her? But still, what bad luck for her to show up at the exact moment when the shit hit the fan.

Too late.

The police came up the driveway first.

Hannah's eyes met her mother's, and she couldn't hide her anxiety and fear.

"Oh, no," Eva said. "Is this about the front door footage?"

"What front door footage?" Hannah asked. For a brief second, she allowed herself to think her mother could be talking about her jumping jacks, no more, no less. Then she came to her senses.

twenty-five

EVA

Hillary's black SUV came roaring up the driveway not long after the police. What a difference in their approaches. The police, stealthy, crawling. Hillary, gunning it, breaking laws even on her own street. She left her car door ajar, alert beeping, as she strode up the walk and grabbed the search warrant from the shorter policeman. Her green eyes turned murky and dark when she was angry. I wonder if she knew that. That she could never play poker with her husband, because she had a pronounced tell.

I turned off her car with that silly button all the cars have now, closed her car door gently, and tried to stay out of the way. The police walked inside, not taking off their coats, not stopping to remove their muddy shoes the way Hillary preferred. Oh, that was a portent, wasn't it? That they would ruin things before they began.

Hannah coaxed her sister away from the door, trying to calm her down. She took her by the hand, but Hillary yanked hers away roughly. By the time they reached me, she was practically foaming at the mouth.

"You want some kind of medal for giving me a heads-up? For being cozy with them?" Hillary spat.

"What? I'm not cozy with anyone!" Hannah said.

"And you," she said, addressing me. "Were you...lurking here, too? Did you tell them something?"

I thought suddenly of the boots in the garage. Of the lack of boots in the garage. Would Hillary have seen those, too? Did she know even more? What was she worried about me finding?

"What is wrong with you?" Hannah asked.

"What is wrong with me, Hannah? Well, how about you tell me," she whispered roughly, "why, when I called the best fucking criminal lawyer in town, he told me he couldn't represent Ben because he had a conflict of interest in the case?"

"Hillary, I—"

"Did your shit ex-husband manage to kill a kid while he was out hunting deer?"

"No!"

"Well, what then?"

Hannah was taller and heavier than her sister, but she looked smaller now, folded up. She was so unaccustomed to being teamed up against her. It was always those two against me, against the world.

"What? What is it then?"

Hannah looked at me, the smallest of glances, but I knew what it meant. She couldn't bear to say it. It was my signal, the parent bat phone, to step in. Maybe she knew I knew. Maybe she didn't. But I intercepted it, and I acted to the best of my ability with what I had.

"Hillary," I said softly, "I believe they're also investigating Miles."

"Wait, what?"

"Yes."

Hillary's eyes narrowed. She glanced toward the door, put her hands on her hips. She shifted from foot to foot as if testing her balance, preparing, coiling to pounce. She had on dark-green leggings and a black fleece jacket, and she started zipping her zipper up and down an inch or two, back and forth. It looked like a ritual a baseball player might go through before he stepped into the batter's box. That or she was trying to buy time to figure out what the hell was actually going on. Or maybe, just maybe, for the second or third time in her life, she was nervous.

"So," she said, turning back, "is that why they're in my house? Not because of Ben but Miles? They think he hid something somewhere? He's over here all the time, I mean—"

"No," Hannah said.

"How do you know?"

"Because they told me."

"Police don't tell you anything that's true, Hannah. They tell you things to…to throw you off. Especially when you're a suspect, too."

"Not always," I said.

Hillary's look sliced right through me.

"And you? What did you know?"

I held up my hands. She had a lot of nerve, really, when she'd all but asked me to keep her secret about the front door! Really, Hillary, this was beyond the pale. This was what stress could do to you—you couldn't keep your secrets straight, let alone safe!

She stepped toward us.

"Both of you have been hiding stuff about my nephew being a suspect in a murder of a little girl? When he's here all the time and plays with my daughter, who is half his size? Huh?"

"Miles wouldn't hurt anyone or anything."

"Well, of course you would defend him. You're his mother."

"Hillary, this isn't about Miles! Your husband is a suspect! The two-hundred-pound man who cuddles my son and ruffles his hair! And you didn't tell me anything!"

"There's nothing to tell!"

"They wouldn't be here if they didn't have a reason! And Mom—Mom wasn't even surprised! Didn't register a drop of shock. So you two kept something from me, is that it? Ben did something, didn't he?"

Neither of us had the courage to speak, to tell her what we knew or didn't know. But if I knew anything, I knew this much. Hannah already had suspicions, too. It showed in her face, in the fierceness of her argument.

I turned to say something to her, something loving, something to help these girls forgive each other. They always did; they just needed a nudge. But the simple words stuck in my throat. Not because I didn't care or I couldn't form them.

But because a backhoe was crawling up the street slowly, as if the day wasn't almost over, as if it had all the time in the world.

twenty-six

HANNAH

Detective Thompson covered the space between the sisters' houses at approximately the same speed that the backhoe traversed Hannah's driveway. Slow, plodding, careful. Hannah couldn't tell if he was walking at his normal speed or drawing it out, wishing he didn't have to deal with her. She had the impression both detectives were growing tired of all the women they had to talk to on this case. The prospect of having two male suspects must be a relief to them. She'd seen on television the empathy cops showed when interrogating guilty men. They probably preferred fucked-up male suspects to ordinary female witnesses. Harsh but true. Easier to relate to a criminal surging with testosterone than a woman trying to describe what she saw and remember what time it was.

The only thing in Hannah's eye line moving swiftly were a couple of neighbors, drawn down the hill by the flashing lights. Not Susan and Tara this time but a man and woman Hannah didn't recognize. They lifted their phones as if they were about to take video, and Hannah wanted to scream, run to them, throw their phones to the ground. But how would that look? Who exactly would that help?

She took a deep breath and met Thompson near the backhoe. He was calm enough, showing her the paperwork, explaining they were digging a few places where they'd found evidence.

"A dead animal is not evidence of a crime."

"So you say," he said. "But as we said earlier, we found more linking her here, so we have to look further."

"What do you mean, you found more?"

"We found the girl's necklace with her key ring."

"What? Where?"

"On the edge of your property."

"No," she said.

"I'm afraid so."

"How do you know someone didn't plant it there?"

"With all due respect," he said with a sigh, "how do you know someone did?"

He went on to explain that they were digging everywhere they'd found evidence of note, not just her yard. He was watching her face to see whether she was surprised or not surprised. Whether she would say in response, "You mean there's other places?" or to whether she'd simply be nonchalant and accepting. How should she behave? She had no clue. And the thought of not only Carelli but her sister watching this from their perch on the hill made her crazy. *Are you happy now, Hillary?*

"So this is what, a dirt-only warrant?" As she said it, she was suddenly aware of the symbolism, the double meaning.

"One thing at a time."

She almost laughed. Was he warning her? That soon they'd be inside her house, too?

They stood on her porch, facing off, in the very place where she'd imagined so many lovely moments. Gin and tonics with her sister as they sat in the waning light. Looking at the fall decorations, the pumpkins and hay bales and mums, enjoying and maybe comparing. So what? Comparing was part of life. Watching people she would meet someday walk their dogs, their clothing changing slightly with the seasons, the gloves and hats added, the small clouds of frost escaping from their mouths as they spoke the quiet, ghostlike hellos of people just getting to recognize each other.

Would that never come now? Were all her porch dreams—of raising her kid next to her sister's kid, the cousins running between houses like it was a lush college campus, like the world belonged to them—were they all gone?

"Isn't there someone else on your radar?" she asked suddenly.

"Not sure what you mean."

"Besides these two houses, besides someone connected to these two particularly, spectacularly unlucky sisters."

"Are you saying your sister is unlucky? Is there—"

"No! No, goddamn it. My sister and I are fine. Normal, upstanding citizens. People who pay their taxes and don't run red lights, okay? So I am wondering if you don't have someone else you are looking at, Detective. Someone whose background would actually indicate they have a problem? Instead of maybe tangentially, oddly, circuitously connecting the dots, how about actual fucking dots?"

He didn't answer, and she wanted to shake him. Of course he couldn't tell her; of course there were rules. Rules that he broke when he wanted to and rules that he stood by when it suited him. He turned suddenly, and she stared at the nape of his neck, his modern haircut, and was angry, furious at herself for noticing how youthful that part of him seemed. Like you could see the boy still within him, the one who believed in fighting crime, who thought he was after the bad guys after all. Where was that part of him? The part that wasn't beaten down with cynicism, the part that believed in innocence? The innocence of boyhood, when had he lost that?

"Well?" she asked, but he didn't answer. She followed his gaze and saw a woman standing in her driveway as if she were waiting. She was just a dot of blond.

"Hey," Kendra said, waving a hand.

"Do you need me, Mrs. Harris?" Thompson called down to her.

"Oh, no. I…do not."

"She's here for me," Hannah said, waving and walking down.

"You two are friends?"

Hannah ignored him. "Give me a second to change," she said. "I'll be right down!"

Thompson shook his head and went back to Hillary's.

She went inside, pulled on sweatpants and a long-sleeved T-shirt.

"Miles," she said, "stay inside and do your homework, okay? I'm locking the door while I go for a walk."

He stood in front of his window watching the backhoe turn over the earth.

"Have you ever been in one of those?"

"No," she said. "Did you hear me? Stay inside. And don't go to the door. You can play a video game when you're done."

"Okay." He nodded and she set off across the street, toward the path.

"I figured you might need a walk today," Kendra said.

"Yes, about that—"

"You don't need to explain."

"Oh, I think I do."

"No," Kendra said, stepping nimbly off the street onto the path, "I know it's not your son."

"What? How—"

"I've seen him," she said. "On my walks. Seen him watching butterflies landing on his wrist, letting caterpillars crawl up his arm."

"He loves animals."

"I can tell. I can also tell he's gentle."

"He is. But how…I mean, I hate to say this, but shouldn't you suspect everyone? How can you not?"

Kendra stopped, ran a hand across her mouth. Hannah couldn't help thinking that she was an example of the phrase *small but mighty*. There was a force field around her, a kind of armor. As if she'd grown a protective shield simply because of her size, her blond hair, all the things about her that made people underestimate her. It saddened Hannah to think of Kendra's little girl, too young to have grown the armor, that she couldn't protect herself. Hannah felt tears starting to pool in her eyes and blinked them back.

"Because if I did, I would be filled with rage. I am incapable of believing the whole world is evil. I can't do it. I just can't. I've already lost my daughter. I can't lose all of humanity, you know?"

Hannah nodded. "Yes, I guess so. Yes." She tried to imagine walking through the world suspecting everyone was evil. That was like living in a hell, a prison. How could you even sleep at night?

"It's a man, not a boy. And half the men around here are gone all the time, so that narrows things down. They should be on to someone else soon, let your boy off the hook. Besides, they're digging up every time capsule and Barbie doll any kid has ever buried under a pile of leaves. They'll find something else to fixate on besides some pet hamster."

"I hope so."

She wanted to tell Kendra more, that it wasn't a pet hamster, that it was both better and worse than that, but she knew she couldn't go that far. It was too dangerous to tell anyone too much, but especially her. Hannah liked her, but she couldn't lose her head.

They walked down along the creek, partly in silence, listening to the water rise and fall over rocks and branches, changing direction, gathering speed. It had finally receded a bit after the rain. It wasn't that deep, and she supposed after a few frosty nights, it would freeze; there'd be a crackling layer of ice trapping all the tadpoles and frogs. She'd never considered that thought before, and she realized with a kind of horror that it was something that Miles would think of and be upset by. That it would keep him up at night, worrying.

They started the gradual rise, headed to the highest point, where the light hung in golden ribbons between the trees.

"I wonder what it was like when this was all one property," Hannah mused. "To have all of this as your view."

"Yes, our street was just the driveway, I think."

"Really? All those twists and turns?"

"They did it intentionally, to keep people away. I'd heard the family preferred horses, hated cars. That for a long time before it was subdivided, they'd just show up in downtown Wayne and hitch them to a parking meter."

"No."

"Yes, there are pictures at the library, 1945, '46, something like that."

"That's hilarious."

"There's a boy at Haverford School, one of their descendants, who still does it."

"You're kidding me."

"Nope."

"What does the horse do while he's at school?"

"The janitor built him a little lean-to."

"Jesus."

"Yeah, literally. It's kind of manger-y."

"I bet."

"My daughter used to beg to go see it." Kendra paused and picked up a stick, tossed it off the path. "She wanted to ride horses. We were just waiting for her to be big enough. She loved animals, too. Like your son."

"They might have been friends."

"Yes. But—they weren't, were they?" She looked at Hannah with a searching sadness. Trying not to be too vulnerable, to make a mistake. Hoping against hope, Hannah supposed, that the world hadn't punished her daughter again. For having trusted one person. For having made one single friend and believing her son was not someone she should fear.

"No. He doesn't know anyone in the neighborhood except his cousin."

"Who's that?"

"My sister's daughter, Morgan. Next door."

"Oh, I didn't realize," Kendra said, trailing off. "We love Morgan. She was kind to Liza. We were hoping…"

Hannah waited, wondered, but didn't ask.

"Hoping," Kendra continued, taking a breath, "that she'd be old enough to babysit someday."

Hannah nodded in agreement. They stood at the highest point of their walk, looking over the farmland stretching out in all directions, the split-rail fence, the mature trees spilling leaves. The gift of a stone house at the end of the path, a portrait of what used to be. When people valued land over houses. When people didn't need a slew of extra rooms for their offices, their guests, and their hobbies. They were content to just let the land be enough. Who lived there now? Who were they even looking at?

"Do you know who lives there now?"

"One of the stepsons. Lives there alone, if you can believe that."

"Wow."

"You can see him riding around, repairing fences now and then."

"I guess if he's a loner, then the police have investigated him, too."

"Yeah," Kendra smiled. "He picked a terrible time to be an introvert."

As they headed back, retracing their steps, Hannah asked her a few safe questions on innocuous topics (or so she thought). If she was in the book club (no), if she was friends with any of the other neighbors (not really), and if she worked (not anymore). The clipped answers made Hannah realize that Kendra was more interested in walking than talking, so they just walked. Hannah limited her remarks to a few about the terrain, the scenery, the temperature.

"I just don't relate to the other women in the neighborhood," Kendra said suddenly. "No offense to your sister."

"None taken."

"I just don't like all the conversations about material things. What decorator you're using, where you bought your antiques, where you got that necklace, where everyone is going on spring break. It's like no one can have a real conversation."

"I hear what you're saying."

"I mean, all the shit that's going on in the world and even in the township, there should be plenty to talk about. Or kids, can't we talk about how hard it is to parent kids? Instead of how hard it is to find a cleaning person?"

She was pretty but she wasn't fancy, Hannah thought. That was probably the mistake others made. The book club, if it was indicative of the women in the neighborhood, was fancy.

When they got closer to Kendra's house, a man waved from the patio. It was the first time Hannah had seen anyone on the property since that first day, the search party day.

"Your husband?"

"Yes, my groom. We just got married. I'm divorced from Liza's father. He's been cleared as a suspect, thank God."

"Well, that's a relief, I'm sure."

"Yes. My first ex, too."

Hannah was glad the police had crossed a few people off their list, that they hadn't been idle. But why hadn't Thompson told her that when she'd pressed? Why hadn't he defended himself? Why did the mother of the victim have to be the one who filled her in?

"Are you on good terms with your exes?"

"I am now," Kendra said and smiled. "No, seriously, I am. This has been devastating for them. For everyone. All the questions. All the interviews. All the DNA. The police have been thorough, though. And oddly caring."

"Really?" Hannah tried hard not to scrunch her face in disbelief.

"One of the techs who was here told me that they had trouble weighing Liza during the…uh, autopsy. That the township has so few deaths and investigations that they didn't have a scale the right size for someone so small. He said Detective Thompson held her in a blanket and stepped onto the larger scale."

Hannah's breath caught in her chest. It reminded her suddenly, forcefully, of Miles. Miles and the animals.

"Wow," she said softly.

"So, there's that," Kendra said, wiping away a tear. "You always wonder if people, if bodies, are nothing to them, you know? If they are jaded or not. So that was…a slight counterbalance for all the annoyances, all the damage to the yard and the path and property, for all of us really. I just thought, well, it's good to know they're human, right?"

Hannah stopped, took a deep breath, and looked out over the path. Another backhoe ran below them, digging up one side of the creek. Rocks and shale and rusty red mud colored the creek water where it was digging. It looked like old blood, and Hannah had to look away, swallow hard. Everywhere in the neighborhood was touched by this investigation. How could Kendra stand to be here, to live in that house, to carry on?

"Did they…tear apart your house on top of everything else? I can't really see much from where I am."

"Oh my God, yes. Just the scraping of furniture on the wood floors alone—we have to get them resanded and sealed. And…well, everything was a disorganized mess, but that gave us something to do, to focus on."

Hannah wanted to ask her how she could stand it, how she could stay. And yet she felt so close to her now. She wanted her to stay, desperately. So she didn't broach it.

"Well, I suppose it's worth it if they find something useful."

"Yes, well, they don't know what they've found."

"How do you mean?"

"They didn't find anything they wanted, like fingerprints or hair or I don't know—mud or fibers. All they found were a couple of presents under her bed."

"Well, she just had a birthday, yes? We saw the balloons."

"Right. Well, seven girls RSVPed to her party, but none of them showed."

"That's terrible," Hannah said. Didn't say she'd known or suspected. Didn't want Kendra to think she'd been watching, even then, before anything had happened.

"Exactly. So we…have no idea where the presents came from. If she was giving them to someone or someone gave them to her. They're trying to figure that out. Not that it even matters. They don't know. Here," Kendra said, pulling out her phone. "They're wrapped badly, like a kid did it. Probably someone at school."

Hannah looked at the photo. Crinkled paper, the wide plaid ribbon not tied in a bow but a kind of off-center knot.

"What was in them?"

"Sort of cheap little stuff. Barrettes, butterfly jewelry. A little stuffed bunny. Nothing special. Like from those stores at the mall you never see adults in?"

"Well, maybe there's DNA on them."

"That's what they're waiting on. They probably asked all the kids in the neighborhood, all of her class at school. Some of the other moms told me that. And some of them felt terrible, too, you can bet that, after saying their kid was coming and then not showing up? And then my daughter dies? That's some karma right there. So I guess, you know, the police saw the balloons, figured it out."

Again, Hannah didn't mention her observation, her role. It felt intrusive suddenly, her insight. Like she was mean and judgy when she was just trying to help.

"At school, I don't think they asked Miles. None of the police asked him about the presents. Maybe they just asked at lower school."

Hannah said this proudly, as if it was the only evidence of innocence she had left and not simply her refusal to cooperate. She didn't know this woman after all. She liked her, but what did that mean? What could she feel safe sharing? Kendra could be playing her for information, just like the police. She doubted it. But still.

"Well, here, I'll send it to you. You can ask him if he knows anything."

Hannah told Kendra her phone number, and the photo showed up in her texts.

"All this—it makes you an expert, doesn't it?"

"Expert?"

"You become accidentally steeped in this, this language you never understood and never wanted to learn. Autopsies. Excavating. Interviewing witnesses, crime photos."

"Eloquently put. Yes, it's like a hobby thrust upon you. A sink or swim sort of hobby. And it's a lot. It's a lot. But it's also helpful, in a way. Distracting."

They were back at Kendra's house. She looked toward it with a kind of fondness Hannah didn't fully understand. How could she not want to flee? To run away from it? Yes, the crime happened at the creek, not the house. But still. How could you separate one thing from the other?

"Do you want to come in for a drink?" Kendra said suddenly, touching her on the arm. "Come in and meet Robert?"

"I would ordinarily say yes, I'd love to," Hannah replied, "but I don't want to leave Miles alone for too long. He might want to carjack the backhoe and go wild."

She regretted those words the minute they flew out of her mouth. As if she had no right to worry in comparison to Kendra.

"Rain check?" Hannah said quickly, lightly, she hoped.

"Yes," Kendra said.

As Hannah crossed the street, she said a silent prayer. *Please,* she thought, *let them have found nothing but one dead fox in her yard. One.* She'd just bought the house after all; who knows what else had been buried there? The one skeleton, the innocent one, the one they were expecting, died of natural causes. *Please, dear God, let that be all. Let her be the only occupant of the house, now or ever, who buried their secrets.*

Not just because of her son. But because she had a friend, and she wasn't going to let anything ruin it.

twenty-seven

EVA

The best thing about living in a small town is there aren't too many places to hide. I'd gone over to Hannah's house three mornings in a row after drop-off only to find her gone. And who could blame her? Between the police cars, the backhoes, the *Eyewitness News* reporters trolling for information, and the nosy neighbors, who would want to stay there?

From what I could see, peering through the windows of her porch, her computer was missing from her kitchen table, where she always sat and worked, so there were only a few logical places to look. A diner, a few coffee shops, but I thought those would be too noisy for her, too many people. No, I figured my girl for more of a back-corner-of-the-library girl, and as soon as I pulled in to the parking lot, I saw her car. Bingo.

Finding her inside was another story. It was one of those newfangled libraries, designed by a famous architect with lots of public spaces and corners and twists, but about ten minutes later, I walked up to a communal table where five or six people sat, staring at their computers like they couldn't bear to look at each other, and tapped her on the shoulder, and she jumped.

"Jesus, Mom. You scared me."

"Well, you look like you fell down some kind of zombie hole. What are you reading?" I squinted at her screen but couldn't see it without my cheaters.

"I'm not reading. I'm writing."

"Oh, that memoir by that awful woman?"

"Shh," she said.

"What? I didn't say her name."

Everyone around her had headphones on, so what difference did it make what I said or didn't say? They reminded me of athletes coming through the tunnels, psyching themselves up with music. That was how bad their work was—they had to play inspirational music just to force themselves to type. Was that any way to live?

"Well, I apologize for startling you," I said, attempting to sit next to her but sliding off the tiny plastic stool and nearly going onto the floor. "But you are avoiding me. Good Lord, how can you sit on this? It's the size of a tin can, and there's no back support."

"I'm not avoiding you. I'm avoiding the stupid neighbors, and I have work to do."

"Okay, whatever you say. Is there somewhere we can talk?"

"No, Mom, it's a library. They kind of frown on talking."

"Well, how about lunch then?"

She agreed to pack up her things and go with me to a new bagel place nearby. Hannah had always loved bagels; ever since she was a little girl, she'd twirl them around her finger before eating them. She was the same way with doughnuts. Her father and I used to wonder if she'd become a drum major with all that twirling and spinning, but Hannah had never gravitated toward anything that splashy. She was lovely of course—anyone with half a brain could see she had a plain beauty about her—but not destined to be a cheerleader or a pageant queen. She used her twirling hand-eye coordination and balance for sports and now, I supposed, typing and perching on stools.

We parked separately and walked in. The line was quite long, but Hannah offered to stand in it while I saved a nearby table for us. That plan suited me just fine, especially since the seats were upholstered and had backs. It also gave me a little time to line up exactly what I was going to say to her and when, so she wouldn't become enraged and do something crazy. If she asked me questions outright, I certainly couldn't lie to her. But I was hoping I wouldn't have to. I was praying her sister might have spoken to her or that, I don't know, that she might have guessed or had a vision. Something.

I was almost annoyed that the detectives didn't suspect me. I thought I could get a tidbit or two out of those boys with badges, some information I could use to clear up my family's names. But no, they had nothing to say to an old lady who didn't even live in their little enclave. As if someone from anywhere else couldn't walk right in and do whatever they pleased while that little girl was out playing in the creek alone! How short-sighted!

Hannah came back to the table with two baskets, both adorned with pickles and chips.

"Oh, my," I said. "That's a lot of food."

"It ought to be for twelve dollars."

"Twelve dollars for a bagel?"

"Yup," she replied. "Someone has to pay for this decor."

It was true that the tables and chairs were much nicer than those in a traditional deli shop. And there were two chandeliers. And a gas fireplace in the back. Yes, someone had to pay for it, and that someone was us.

"Well, live and learn," I said and took a bite. Delicious. Not twelve dollars of delicious, but very, very good. Even the pickle was delicious, crisp and garlicky. The older I got, the more I appreciated pickles. They were like a free salad on the side.

"Hannah, you can't avoid me forever," I said with my mouth full of pickle. "And neither can Hillary."

"I told you, I'm avoiding the neighbors. Pretending they are just walking by. One of them videotaped the fucking backhoe in my yard. It's probably on YouTube. And I need the library's resources."

"Okay." I struggled to get my mouth around the enormous bagel, which shut me up for a while. There may have been cream cheese and sprouts all over my face before I finally wrestled it under control. This gave Hannah an opening to shut down my premise.

"Other people work in libraries and coffee shops all the time. They find the hubbub soothing."

"Uh-huh. Well," I said, putting down the sandwich and wiping my chin, "I guess that's one solution. Because selling your house a couple of weeks after buying it in order to avoid being investigated by detectives probably isn't an option."

"Don't be crazy."

"I'm asking you not to be crazy. Not to let two cops tear apart your relationship with your sister."

"Mom, this is a little more serious than fighting over whose turn it is to wash the dishes."

I remembered vividly, suddenly, how much the girls both hated doing dishes. How they'd pretend to fall asleep, feign illness, invent homework, anything to get out of taking their turn. In most things, they were opposites, and what one hated, the other could handle. But they both hated the drudgery, the everydayness of dishes. How I used to say "Life is doing dishes," and they'd roll their eyes as if I was stupid and didn't understand their larger lives, the landscape to come. As if the world could spare them dishes!

"Well, your stubbornness strikes me as being exactly the same."

"Mom, I really think you should be talking to Hillary, not me."

"Why?"

"She's the one making wild accusations and keeping secrets. And you, for that matter."

"For the record, my dear, I believe you started first. With your son. You moved schools, and he's clearly got issues with these animals, and you haven't told your sister anything. We need to get everything out in the open."

"I can't. There's too much at stake now."

"Hannah, do you really think the police should know more than your family?"

"Mom," she said, "I love you. And I know you mean well. But this is about Miles and his safety. And I know that I have his best interests at heart. That he is my priority. And I don't...I just don't...believe that he is anyone else's priority. So I have to—"

"Lie for him?"

"Shh, Mom, no. Jesus. Protect him. Be careful. That's all."

"Even with Hillary?"

"Tell me she's not doing the same thing with Ben."

Well, she had a point there. She certainly did. But one of them had to crack first, didn't they? And it was usually Hannah. In my experience, it was usually her. Did that make Hillary stronger or just more stubborn, possessed of a blind spot, less globally smart in the long run? Hard to say. At times like these, they both reminded me of their father and the way he thought everything into submission. Did no one feel things anymore? When did everyone stop enjoying spontaneity, trusting their gut? Was everything a pro and con list to be parsed? Still, she had a point. Hillary wasn't telling me anything either. And I had to confess, all this silence irritated me. I was used to being at the center of my daughters' and grandchildren's lives. I was used to being welcome in their homes and privy to their struggles. Now I was standing off to the side, in the cold, and I had to admit, that *was part of my motivation for what I did next.* Let me in, for God's sake!

I dropped my half-eaten bagel back into the basket with a thud.

"When they were at your house digging, were they looking to excavate boot prints?"

"Boot prints?"

"You know, footprints?"

"No, they were digging for…dead animals. A fox, specifically. And other evidence, they said."

"Ahh. Of course."

"Mom, why did you say boots? Is there something happening in the investigation with boots? Did they take boots at Hillary's? What else did you see?"

Oh, I was cornered now. I felt my face flush, and it wasn't from wiping cream cheese off it with a rough biodegradable napkin.

"I, um, well, yes, they seemed to be interested. In all footwear. They took imprints, I believe, of shoes."

"Okay," Hannah said cautiously, and I couldn't tell if she was buying it or not, but I'd toed the line well and also told the truth. There had to have been footprints on the creek or path to match. That was what I'd thought when the technician went into the mudroom.

"You said they were digging for other evidence," I said. "What were they looking for?"

"I don't know, but they said they found her necklace with her key ring between the yards."

"The white lanyard?" I asked softly with dread.

"They said necklace."

I thought of the white braided cord, the key dangling, visible around the little girl's neck on Hillary's front door footage. Was that what had prompted the search of the house and then the yard? I felt sick to my stomach, like the bagel had ballooned inside of me.

"Mom?"

"Yes?"

"Did you see whether the police went to the wrapping closet?"

"The what?"

"You know, that big closet near the mudroom that Hillary uses for boxes and wrapping paper and stuff?"

"Well, I saw them in the mudroom, and they went upstairs and into the kitchen, but I didn't follow them. That wasn't allowed, you know."

"Okay."

"I'm pretty sure they went through the whole house."

"Okay."

Something about the way she chewed that bagel made me realize she knew something. That she was playing me a bit. I leaned in, lowered my voice.

"Honey, even if you don't talk to your sister, talk to me."

She took a deep breath. She held it a long time before she let it go, but it was a signal. A signal that she was coming around.

"Okay, well, Liza's mother told me there were presents under her daughter's bed. It was her birthday a few days before, and no one came to her party."

"Oh, that's sad."

"But someone gave her presents, and they don't know who. All they know is she hid them."

I felt a terrible chill go down my spine. I'm not one for theatrics, and I consider myself a tough old bird. But I tend to listen to my body and the occasional signals the universe sends me, and that one felt loud and clear.

"Dear God," I said.

"Yeah," she sighed.

"So they're looking for fingerprints, I suppose, or DNA, not boots." She was silent.

"I saw one of those shows on TV where the fingerprint showed up on the Scotch tape, on the sticky side. Clear as a bell."

"Yes," she sighed. "That would be too easy, though. They're asking all the kids in the neighborhood if they recognize them."

"But would a child remember wrapping paper?"

"I think so. Isn't that how most kids figure out Santa Claus is a fake?"

"Fair point."

"Mom, didn't you help the kids wrap presents for us a few months ago? For Mother's Day? When I complimented Miles on his technique, he said you taught him."

"Dear God, do you think I'm a murderer now? Really, Hannah."

"No, I just—did you help Morgan or maybe Ben, too? At her house?"

"Ben? Teach Ben to wrap presents?" I screwed up my face.

"Mom, how well do we really know Ben? I mean, we love him because he's charming and he's good with kids and he puts up with Hillary's crazy type-A shit, but plenty of fucked-up men are charming, right? Plenty of rogues and cheats and—"

"Hannah, I don't see where you're heading with this. You don't actually think they are involved? Dear God, that's beyond the pale. That's, that's—" I struggled to find the words, but what I was thinking, with great shame, was that that was how Hillary would think.

"Mom," she said abruptly and pulled out her phone. She opened up a photo and slid it across the table. "These are the presents."

"What, she…shared this with you? Just like that?"

"She's desperate for information. And she…trusts me. I don't know why."

I surveyed my daughter's open face. I knew why. Because Hannah Sawyer *was* inherently trustworthy. Hadn't we always known that? Wasn't that the primary difference between her and her sister? She was solid and open, where Hillary could shift and parry and move stealthily. And the relief, the relief I felt that another woman was listening to that little voice inside her that told her whom to trust and whom not to? It gave me joy.

Temporary joy.

Because when I looked at the photo, I felt sick to my stomach.

The ribbon. The ribbon.

I'd seen it before.

I met my daughter's eyes, and I didn't have to say it.

twenty-eight

HANNAH

On her way to the police station, Hannah tried not to think about the possibility of losing her gig at me3. She'd finished looking over the rough cuts of the high schoolers' interviews and sent them to Cat that morning. Cat would have to pay her for at least that half of the work if not the rest. She'd delivered, no one could argue that. But she knew that her family being caught up in a crime did not look good for a nonprofit devoted to nonviolence. It just didn't. And how long would it take Cat to connect the dots? Hannah figured she had a week before some kind of shit hit some kind of fan and there'd be more news trucks on her street than cars.

Inside, the station was both cleaner and emptier than she'd imagined it to be. A few people sat in a waiting room, drinking coffee, looking at their phones. They didn't appear to be particularly nervous or concerned or remotely guilty. They could have been anywhere, Hannah thought—a hospital, a car dealership, waiting for a friend who was getting a haircut, not charged with a crime.

She asked to speak to Detective Thompson, hoping he was around and not Carelli. She didn't like either of them, but Carelli set her teeth on edge.

After a few minutes, he came out, clearly surprised to see her, and invited her back to a small conference room, asked if she wanted a beverage. All the niceties but none of the charm. He was wary of her, she could tell.

"So you were in the neighborhood? Just decided to drop by?"

"No, I wanted to talk."

"Ready to cut a deal for your son?"

"If you think you're being funny, you're not."

"I am deadly serious, Ms. Sawyer. I can't think of a single other reason you would come here and feel so nervous you'd be twisting the hem of your jacket under the table."

Her hands went still beneath the green formica top, her fingers loosened against the wool. Damn it, you couldn't keep anything from these two. She supposed if she blew her nose, he'd assume she had a cocaine problem.

"Well, I have some information. And I feel a little uncomfortable telling you. Because I'm not sure. But you always say anything, even small."

"Okay, I'm all ears."

"I think my brother-in-law is hiding something."

"Well, obviously, we do, too, since we searched his house."

"Did you find the ribbon?"

He leaned forward, looking at her intently. "What ribbon?"

"The ribbon from the presents," she said. "Because I think it's there. My mother saw it. It might be in the recycling area and not the wrapping closet."

"If you think that coming here for a fishing expedition, to guess what we're looking for, is going to help you keep your son out of this, you are wrong."

"I'm not fishing. Kendra told me about the presents, and I showed my mother the picture, and—"

He got up and paced around his office. "I'm sorry, but this is police work, not neighborhood gossip, Hannah."

"Why, when women exchange information, do men call it gossip? I'm telling you something, Detective. That ribbon is in their house. My mother saw it."

"Okay, well, that's hearsay until your mother comes in. Now, is that all you have to tell me?"

"No. I also saw Ben behave inappropriately with a high school student. And I—just, well, I thought it might mean something."

She described the cozy behavior in the hotel room corridor, how wrong it looked. The lack of shoes. His hand on her back.

He asked a few more questions. How did Hannah know the girl was in high school? Was she fifteen, sixteen, eighteen? He sat back in his chair, sighed, rubbed his chin, considered her.

"This has to be anonymous," she said.

"Anonymous is for calls from pay phones, not people who stop by in person."

"I mean Hillary can't know. You have to find some other way to verify, or, or—"

"Oh, we will verify. We need more than suspicions and glances, Hannah."

She breathed deeply. When had she stopped being Ms. Sawyer and become Hannah?

"I thought you loved your brother-in-law," he said as he escorted her to the door.

"I do," she replied.

Those words were still in her throat when she walked out to her car and vomited in the parking lot before heading home.

twenty-nine

HANNAH

T here were no sirens. Later, she'd realize that was one of the many details no one tells you about law enforcement. That they pick their moments. That they choose their tools. That they don't throw everything they have at every situation, despite what you've seen on television. That most of the time, there are no SWAT teams and no tactical vests and no lights and sounds at all. Just the click of handcuffs at the agreed-upon date and time. *Surrender.* The softest word in law enforcement.

Hannah would find all the details out later. That her sister knew, and her mother knew. She didn't let on that she knew, knew the minute she looked at her mother's face as she surveyed the photo of the presents. The presents wrapped clumsily like a child did it—a child…or a man. A man with big hands, all thumbs, no practice. Ben's hands?

Her mother had seen that ribbon and remembered it. Whatever else she did or didn't know didn't matter; someone else had added them together and tied them in a bow with that ribbon. And her mother didn't need to unburden herself with her half facts and small suspicions anymore.

Hannah watched the police not from her porch—because that would be tacky—but from her kitchen window, curtain lifted, lights still out. The sun just rising over Kendra's house across the street, the orange light creeping its way toward her sister's side of the property, taking its time, the air ten degrees colder than it had been the morning before.

That light just catching the lift of Hillary's hair in the wind as she walked Ben outside solemnly. Already dressed at six fifteen. No robe, no boiled wool slippers. Both of them ready. They knew. For how long, Hannah wondered? Had Hillary known all along and just couldn't bear to tell her? To ruin the neighborhood, the dream, so soon? No.

Ben in his Lululemon pants and half-zip, sneakers on his feet, cap on his head. His rubber soles sluiced across the dewy grass. Jailhouse casual for his surrender. He stood beside his wife but didn't speak. Pale-gray puffs of breath were visible in the air, like empty thought bubbles. He got in the car and Hillary stood alone for just a second, then turned away. Hannah lowered the edge of the curtain. There was no way even her sister could keep this big of a secret for long. She must have a good reason for trying. But what reason, exactly, was that? If her husband was innocent, what was the reason for not talking?

A minute later, she heard Hillary's car going down the driveway, too. Following? Going to the lawyer, the arraignment, the bail bonds person, the media conference, what? There were no news trucks outside filming her. This wasn't for show; it was for real. Just a few weeks ago, Hannah would have known every item in her sister's calendar and agenda if she wanted to. Now she had no idea. She checked her phone to see if she'd missed a family text. To drive Morgan to school? To reassure her that all was fine, handled?

Nothing. Hannah felt sick to her stomach, knowing her sister was alone in this. That Morgan might know, might be in the car—or worse— might wake up to a note and have to catch the bus alone. No, she thought with a sigh, her sister had probably sent Morgan to a friend's overnight. Since she knew. Since it was arranged. Wasn't that why they did these kinds of things? Timed to happen at dawn. The wardrobe, the cast, all of it arranged. To protect the children from a scarring memory.

Hannah made a pot of coffee and struggled to make some headway of her notes from yesterday's interview. None of what she had written even made sense to her until she had half a cup of coffee. This particular morning, the world did not make any sense to her either; why should her work?

Two cups of coffee later, when her head started to clear, she looked up from her computer at the kitchen table as the alarm chimed in Miles's room and she heard his footsteps on the creaky floor. Every month, it seemed, his footsteps sounded heavier.

He came out to the kitchen, and she turned to face him. Before she could even say good morning, he spoke.

"Morgan's coming over for breakfast."

"What?"

"Do we have cinnamon?"

"Yes. Wait—how do you know this?"

"Mom, if I have to explain Morse code and flashlights to you, then our secret system will be revealed."

"Really?"

"No, she asked me yesterday, and I forgot to tell you."

Hannah pulled the butter out of the fridge, put four pieces of frozen bread in the toaster oven, and started to mix cinnamon with sugar. It was what Morgan always wanted when she visited, because her mother didn't let her have it, and Hannah had never felt any urge to reveal the secret.

"Do you know why?"

"Why what?"

"Why she wanted to come over?"

"Because she was hungry for cinnamon toast?"

He went back to get dressed and brush his teeth. Hannah didn't hear Morgan until the knock on the door, and she called out for her to come in, that it was open. And she did, stomping her little half boots and blowing on her hands and saying that it was colder out than she thought. She was wearing a down vest and scarf but no coat. Hannah offered her gloves, but she said no, she was sure it would warm up. She didn't seem troubled in the slightest as she called out to Miles before heading back to his room.

Hannah heard drawers shutting, laughter, and then a low murmur. Nothing unusual. Nothing out of the ordinary. When they came out and ate their toast and banana slices (her only nod to health, plus bananas were delicious with cinnamon), nothing seemed amiss. Hannah looked out the window as they waited for the bus together and talked companionably, Morgan using her hands to punctuate whatever she was saying and Miles keeping his in his pockets, as he usually did, unless he needed to adjust the flip of his hair.

She had to assume her sister hadn't told her daughter. It would be just like Hillary to believe she'd have it fixed and handled before there was any need to explain. No sirens, no lights, no publicity until they made bond. By then, she'd have her story straight and could explain. Was that possible? To keep it quiet, to have it handled? She supposed if she was Hillary that it might be. But what a risk, she thought. One wrong move, and the secret would be revealed at school, where kids had smartphones and could be merciless.

Her stomach knotted up at the knowledge her sister had taken that risk alone. That Hillary hadn't asked her for help. Morgan could have spent the night here, with them. Safe. Quiet. With family if anything had gone wrong.

She watched as the bus picked them up, looking out the front door in case Miles waved goodbye. But he didn't. She knew he wouldn't, but she still watched, still hoped. She just no longer allowed herself to be disappointed by this, this lack of looking back toward the house, this tendency to only go forward.

Maybe Hillary would come back. Maybe she'd want to talk. Maybe the guilt Hannah felt in the pit of her stomach, that she'd set all this in motion, given them the last piece of the puzzle, would recede. Or maybe it wouldn't.

Usually by now, the sun had warmed the kitchen, but she was still a bit chilly, so she walked to the back of the house to grab a sweater. She glanced in Miles's room perfunctorily to make sure he'd made his bed, and he hadn't. This was unlike him, but Morgan's arrival had probably thrown him off. She stepped inside and pulled up the sheet and both blankets, the thin cotton one, the heavier duvet, smoothed them. They were still warm, which astonished her. How the front of the house could be so cold and the back so warm, just because he'd been in it.

What made her go deeper, straighten his closet? She would wonder, always. Mother's intuition? She couldn't say that had been the case, not at all. She hadn't felt any thrum of electricity along her spine, arms, hairline. It had not been like that. But the closet also hadn't been that messy. It was no different from a hundred other days, but that day, she stepped in and started straightening, doing his chores for him, which she never did. Lifting the clothes piled on the floor, hanging the jackets, putting the rest of them aside to go in the hamper just to be safe. She wasn't snooping, she wasn't tingling, she wasn't anything. But as she lifted the T-shirts and jeans to go in the hamper, something in it caught her eye in the low light.

She put the clothes down.

She leaned in to look closer to be sure before she picked it up. Before she picked up the curled plaid ribbon and put it in her pocket, got in her car, and drove to a gas station, where she put it in the trash with a can of Diet Coke like it was nothing.

It had to be nothing, because it was her son.

It was only later that night that she realized the other possibility. Morgan.

thirty

EVA

S he called me and asked me to make supper for Morgan while she
tried to arrange bail. Didn't call Hannah, called me. *See?* I wanted
to say. If only I'd been the one in the carriage house, how easy this would
be. But no, you didn't want me that close. I tried not to be hurt by that,
that you'd choose your sister over me, because that would hurt Hannah.
Ay, what a pickle we were all in.

I made mac and cheese because I knew Morgan loved it. She came
home from school and did her homework while the casserole bubbled in
the oven. I knew Hannah was home, had seen her car at the curb, heard
Miles say goodbye to Morgan after walking her to her door. I knew they
were there but didn't invite them over. I thought Hillary and Ben would
have their hands full.

When the door chimed open and I heard the alarm code click off, I
expected to see two of them, but only Hillary was there.

"Don't ask," she said with a sigh.

"Dinner's almost ready," I said quietly, biding my time. I wouldn't ask,
but I certainly expected her to tell.

She poured a glass of red wine and drank an inch of it.

"They set bail too high. It's going to take a day or two to get the
money together."

I nodded. I didn't ask how high. I was sure I could read it in the papers
the next day.

"Have there been reporters? News vans? Any calls?"

"No," I said.

The doorbell rang as if on cue.

"Want me to get rid of them?" I asked, secretly delighted by the task of yelling at someone, at pulling the crazy old broad card.

"No," she sighed. "I'll face the music."

I walked out to the edge of the kitchen, just to listen. Just in case. I needn't have. The screech that arose from Hillary would have sent me out there anyway.

Outside in the circle, Hillary lunged at Hannah, almost knocking her down, screaming at her.

"What do you want? You're the reason we're in this mess, you and your so—"

"No, Hillary, I want to help. Can I take Morgan for the night, or tell me what I can do—"

Hillary clawed at Hannah's fleece jacket and flannel shirt, tearing the front panel. I heard a button hit the stone beneath my feet.

"You!" Hillary said through gritted teeth. "You're wearing a wire right now, aren't you? Cozying up to the police, trying to get me to turn on my husband to get your kid off—"

"No! Hillary, you're crazy. You've lost your fucking mind. Stop!"

"Girls!" I just kept saying that over and over, stupidly. As if that could possibly help.

"You think I don't know you'd lie to get your way? You think I of all people don't know what you're capable of?" Hillary screamed.

I reached for Hillary's arms, pulled at them, and she shook me off each time with a force that might have knocked me down but didn't.

"You're probably wearing one, too! Aren't you, Mother? Both of you! Turned against me!"

I yelled, I clawed, I stuck out my foot to trip her, but she was too wily, too quick. I ran to the side of the house and yanked the hose off its copper tether, unfurling it with a tug that nearly threw my shoulder out. I pulled it to the center of the driveway and aimed the cold stream at them like dogs.

They yelped, shocked, but didn't stop. Not at first. I walked closer, and the spray gained force. The water in the air curled in frosty whorls, like it had turned to ice.

"Jesus, Mom, okay! If I was wearing a wire, I'd probably be fucking electrocuted!"

"You would not," I responded. "That's batteries, not electricity."

As if I knew. As if I was up on the technological advances of field surveillance.

I took a deep breath while they dripped, took stock, wiped their eyes. I hated being in the middle. I'd rather they were ganging up against me, knocking me over. It was one thing to have accidentally told Hannah something and quite another to get caught having done so. Part of me felt relief that I wouldn't have to offer anything I knew about Miles in a quid pro quo.

If they'd been arguing over a doll or a book, I would have known precisely what to say. Even in high school, when they argued over something stupid that happened at school or a party, I could offer up a bit of wisdom. But now? I was shocked into silence. I had nothing more to offer, no punishment to mete out. All I could hope for was stopping. That and the glorious fact that Hannah was, in fact, not wearing a wire. Dear God, imagine if she had been?

They seemed to have forgotten that I was even there. They stood back, breathing heavily, eyeing each other. Neither apologizing, neither moving.

The *Eyewitness News* van rolled slowly up the street.

"Don't you think this is exactly what they want? A catfight on the nightly news? A family turning on each other? How's that for a story," I said.

"Mother," Hillary said, "you don't know what you're talking about."

"Oh, I know more than you think I do," I said.

Hannah turned and went back to her house silently. Hillary and I watched her walk across the lawn, getting farther and farther away, her dark shirt blending in to the navy of the night. Morgan's voice came from over my shoulder, wondering if the mac and cheese was ready. Wondering when Daddy was going to be home.

I looked at Hillary. I had plenty of experience telling a child that Daddy wasn't hungover, he simply had the flu. And zero experience explaining he was in jail for murder.

"We'll be right in," Hillary said.

In a few hours, the stars would be out, and all of us, I suspected, would have trouble falling asleep.

"Mom," Hillary said, "what was the name of Hannah's old neighbor, the one across the street who stopped talking to her?"

"Marley Klein?"

"That's right. Marley. I was trying to think of her name yesterday. I remembered it was kind of a cool name."

"Why?"

"Oh, no reason," she said breezily, too breezily for a woman who had spent the day at the police station. Too breezily for Hillary.

I'll tell you how naïve I was—at first, I thought she must be thinking of cool girl names because she was pregnant.

thirty-one

HANNAH

When she got back to the house, Miles came out of his room, asked her why she was wet.

"I…um, washed something off Grandma's car for her," she said.

"So you didn't have a fight and, like, fall in the pool?"

She surveyed him carefully. Could he have heard the commotion and come outside? She doubted it. He wore headphones. He was a boy.

"Morgan emailed me," he said, motioning to the iPad. "Said her dad was helping the police. Does that mean he's undercover?"

Hannah told him to sit down and tried to explain. About people being arrested but being innocent until proven guilty. That the police were under pressure to solve the crime. That there was plenty of evidence that they didn't have yet. And that they all hoped Ben would be cleared.

"So…he's in jail?"

"Temporarily," she said.

"Oh my God," he said. "But jail is…dangerous. He could, like, get knifed or something."

"I think it's not that kind of jail. It's smaller."

"Are you sure?"

"Um, pretty sure."

He stood up and started to pace. "This is, like, crazy. I mean, poor Uncle Ben. And poor Morgan. She doesn't even get what's going on. She thinks he's, like, a special witness or something."

"Miles," she said softly, "it's not up to us to tell her. Hillary knows what she can handle."

"No, she doesn't," he said. "Aunt Hillary thinks she knows everything, but she doesn't. When will he be home?"

"I don't know," she said, "but we hope very soon."

That did not satisfy him. He went to bed, but she heard him pacing in his room, back and forth, throwing a tennis ball against the far wall, over and over, long after she'd closed her computer and tried to go to sleep.

thirty-two

EVA

Hannah called me in a panic at four o'clock. Told me she was all the way in West Chester, at an edit for her new client, and needed someone to get to the house immediately so Miles wouldn't be alone with the police.

"Good Lord, Miles must be terrified. The police showing up like that while he was doing homework, alone!"

"Actually, Mom…he called them."

"What?"

"He told them he wanted to make a statement. But they're not allowed to talk to him without me," she said breathlessly. "They know that. That's why they called me. But I'm at least half an hour away, and I don't trust—I don't—I just—"

I told her not to worry. I told her to breathe, to drive carefully, to not worry. That I would go straight there. As I parked on the street, I noticed Hillary's car in the circle and couldn't help thinking about this rift between them. Wasn't that part of why they had wanted to be next door? To provide refuge for their children from bad weather, prickly neighbors, and police interrogations?

Inside, Miles was pacing across the length of the living room, and he told me quietly, without making eye contact, to go away.

"I'm not going away, Miles."

"This is between me and the police," he said.

The boy looked pale, paler than usual, and his hands were shaking.

"Can I make you a snack?"

"No!"

"Water then," I said and poured him a glass.

He took it, swallowed half, handed it back to me.

I was just treading, stalling, trying to figure out what on earth was going on. Did Miles have something to tell? About Ben?

There were two gray canvas chairs and a rattan table in Hannah's living room, nothing more. The detectives slouched in them, arms draped, bodies sunk into the down cushions as if they hadn't a care in the world. They were used to making themselves at home everywhere and anywhere, resting when they could, seizing information when it was offered, coffee, food, whatever presented itself. I almost envied their nonchalance. Still, I couldn't believe they weren't concerned in the least that a twelve-year-old boy was pacing like a wild animal behind them, sweating with fear and nerves.

"You should wait outside," I said, but they didn't move.

"We were invited in," the shorter one replied.

"By a child," I replied. "Who doesn't know better."

"I'm not a child," Miles said.

Still, I supposed it was better to have them in here where I could keep an eye on them. Who knows what they would do or find outside, where I couldn't see them.

"Miles, do you know where your mother keeps her jackets? I'm chilly," I said. "Show me, please."

I followed him back to Hannah's bedroom and closed the door slowly as he approached the cedar chest, opened it.

"Miles, what is going on?" I whispered. "I thought we had a deal!"

"Grandma, I told you—"

"The police are not here to help you. They are not on your side, but I am. Do you hear me? Now why don't you tell me what you want to discuss with them, and we'll figure out a way—"

"It doesn't matter what you think. I have to do this for Ben."

"Do what, precisely?"

"I'm a juvenile," he whispered, "and Uncle Ben is an adult, so he could go to jail forever. His whole life! You know he didn't do it, Grandma. You know that."

"But, Miles, surely you…didn't do it either, did you?"

"No, but if I confess, it will be better for everyone. For me, too."

My spine stiffened. That language did not sound like Miles. How on earth could this be better for him, too?

"Miles, I don't know who put these ideas in your head, but they could backfire horribly. Juvenile detention is just as bad as prison! Now I know you love your uncle, we all do, but this is madness. Madness!"

The door swung open, and I turned, expecting Hannah. But it was Morgan, dear Morgan.

"Don't do it, Miles," she cried and ran to embrace him. "I won't let her tell. I won't, I won't!"

"Won't let who tell whom what?" I said icily.

They didn't need to answer me. When I searched my mind and heart, I had my answer already from the day before.

That odd question. The look in my daughter's eye. *Marley.* The woman who knew something about Miles that he didn't want anyone at his new school to know.

thirty-three

HANNAH

This time, no amount of water would keep her away. She banged on her sister's door, screaming. *Let the whole neighborhood hear*, she thought. *I don't give a fuck what people think of me.*

Her mother ran up behind her, telling her to calm down, to discuss this rationally.

"Rationally? You want *me* to be rational?" she said, pounding on the mahogany door so hard her hand hurt, screaming her sister's name so loud her throat did, too. "What about her? She's the goddamn lunatic!"

By the time Hannah had arrived home, her mother had sent the police away and made the kids a platter full of grilled cheese sandwiches and put on a movie on Netflix. As if that could solve all the problems of the world. Still, Miles hadn't slept and hadn't eaten the night before and the police were not in her house, so maybe her mother was right. Maybe grilled cheese could solve everything.

One problem was solved, but another loomed. Everything Eva had told her led her to the same conclusion: Hillary.

"I know you're home!" She punched in the key code, the one they all knew, and the lock didn't open. She tried it again, then a third time. Changed the code? It felt as sharp a betrayal as a knife.

"Hillary! Don't make me break a fucking window!"

A few seconds later, Hillary raised the sash from the guest room on her second floor.

"Have you come back for more?" Hillary called to them below. "All wired up this time? Just tell me, because I'm not sure you can spare me ripping up any more of your precious fall outfits."

"What did you tell my son? Why did he—"

"I don't know. Why don't you ask your fancy lawyer for advice? Not me."

"Did you tell him to save his uncle? Did you…coerce him? Did you—"

"You're crazy. Mom, go put her to bed."

"How else would he know? How else would he think that he should take the fall?"

"I don't know. Maybe he feels…hmm, what's the word…guilty? Because he's killing animals and then playing with them afterward?"

"Is that what he told you? Is that what Morgan told you? Because that's not—"

"Apparently, it was common knowledge in your old neighborhood. Apparently, I, your sister, who welcomes your son into my home on a daily basis, was the last to know about your son's fucking dead animal fetish."

"So you blackmailed him. You told him to lie."

"Oh, you mean like I lied to save you?" Hillary spat.

Hannah turned away, her hands shaking as she flexed them, trying to control them.

"I don't owe you anything," she whispered.

"Really?" Hillary said.

"And neither does my son."

Eva shivered and shook her head. "Whatever this is about, girls, you need to let it go and move on."

"You clearly threatened him," Hannah said. "I know you did. How would he know about getting charged as a juvenile? Only you would be that devious—"

"Please, Hannah. Yes, he knows I found out his weird little secret, but the rest of it, he probably googled. And he loves Ben. You know he loves Ben. Miles is just smarter than you think he is, that's all. You should be proud of him for thinking of it, not yelling at me."

She felt her mother's hand touch her back slowly. A signal of sorts that she was there, a reminder to breathe. A touch straight out of Hannah's childhood that made her feel her mother was on her side, even if she didn't say so.

Jesus, they all loved Ben. Ben, Ben, Ben, Ben, Ben. But did they all love Miles?

She felt her back muscles settle back into some semblance of normal. She started to feel a little guilty herself. After all, she'd turned on Ben. Ben who had been wonderful to her, to her son, always. But that wasn't the same thing. She hadn't coerced him or lied. She'd only relayed facts. Hadn't she? She hadn't even told the police the other things that weighed on her, like Ben seeming odd on the path that day, like Kendra seeing Ben looking at the site where the body'd been found. And Ben had been out all night at poker! So drunk he couldn't remember shit! Ben was an adult. Miles was a child!

"Girls," her mother said. "We are going to all take a step back, try to get some sleep, and figure this out tomorrow. As a team. Like you always have."

"Mom, it's not that simple," Hannah said.

"Maybe not," Eva said. "But I for one don't really think either of your boys did this. I mean, I had my suspicions, with the fawn and the missing boots—"

"What boots?" Hannah said.

"What *fawn*?" Hillary said.

"Does it really matter? Because I let my imagination get the better of me. There's a child dead, and someone else did it, and if anyone can help find out who did, it's you two, together."

Hannah didn't like to admit it as she walked back home, but her mother was probably right. Separately, the two of them were just screwing things up, reacting, overreacting, spinning their wheels. Separately, they'd managed to nearly lose both Ben and Miles. Separately, they were jumping to conclusions and doubting themselves.

Together couldn't hurt, could it?

thirty-four

HANNAH

Two car doors slammed outside in quick succession, like the pop of guns. That was what woke her up and sent her to the window at midnight.

Her sister and brother-in-law stood outside each car door like bookends in the moonlight, screaming at each other. Hillary banged her fist on the roof of her car twice. Ben came around and tried to touch her on her shoulder, and she shrieked as if he'd burned her.

Hannah grabbed her robe and ran outside, crossed the lawn.

"Guys, stop," she said. "Someone will call the police."

"Oh, wouldn't that be rich?" Hillary said. "He just makes bail, and back he fucking goes. Fine with me!"

Ben took a deep breath in. "Look, I know you're angry with me, but—"

"But what? I shouldn't express it? I shouldn't act mad when I am mad?"

Hannah took a step closer. "Hillary, your husband is home, and your daughter will be thrilled. At least be happy for her."

"Happy that her father is a fucking cheater? And a liar?"

"I'm going inside," Ben said.

"Good! You can sleep in the goddamn basement!"

Hannah stood there, waiting until Hillary's breath settled back down, not moving, not speaking. She knew her sister wouldn't stay quiet for long.

"So it turns out Ben was having an affair. Or, as he corrected me, a fling. As if that was somehow better."

"With—the girl?"

"Dear God, no! She's six! Was. Six."

Hannah felt bile rising in her throat, then settling. Finally, she took a deep breath. "Do you know with whom?"

"Yes, with that stupid client of yours, Cat."

"Cat? No," Hannah said. "No, no, no, no. Are you sure it was her? Did you—"

"I suspected," Hillary said and sniffed. "He always seemed so…I don't know, excited when she called. So I thought maybe having you around would—"

"Christ," Hannah said softly. "You wanted me to spy? Jesus, Hillary."

"Not really. I just thought…I don't know. I thought you, you know, you're so observant, that you—"

"Great. Glad to be of service. So he just, what, confessed?"

"Yeah, to the police."

"What?"

"She lives down in the next neighborhood. They would meet on the trail and go to somebody's open pool house and—"

Hillary was waving her hands around and making faces I didn't recognize. She couldn't finish the sentence. Couldn't say it out loud. As if she couldn't quite believe it herself. That this most clichéd, ridiculous thing was happening to her. Finally, her face cracked, and tears rolled out.

I pulled her into a hug. She hardly ever cried, and when she did, it was even more heartbreaking for the rarity.

"Anyway," she said, wiping her face with her hands, "it turns out he was bribing little Liza to keep her mouth shut about it, that's all! She saw them together kissing, and he didn't want the word getting out. So he gave her money and candy. And she just…kept coming back. Kind of a weird little kid. Lonely, awkward. Maybe missed her dad, her parents are divorced, who knows. You know how great Ben is with kids. You know how he loves kids."

"So Ben did give her those…presents?"

"Wait, what? You know about the presents? Did Mom tell you?"

"No, Kendra told me. Liza's mother."

"Oh," Hillary said as if stung. That she didn't know Kendra. That her sister had made friends in the neighborhood without her, and useful friends at that.

"Well, he says he had nothing to do with the presents. No idea what that's about. And that wrapping paper and ribbon could be anyone's. They have it at CVS, for God's sake! Every house could have it!"

Hannah nodded. That much was true. Still, she couldn't help thinking about Ben at the hotel that night. Had she read the situation completely wrong? Or had Ben lied about Cat to cover up what was really happening?

"You don't have to stay out here with me," Hillary said.

"I'm not leaving until I know you're safe inside."

Hillary nodded. She walked to the front door and went inside. Hannah stood there on the circle and watched through the second-floor windows until she saw the progression of lights following her sister's path, illuminating stairs, hallway, master bedroom entrance. Only when the last light, on the bedside table that held Hillary's stack of books, flicked on did she turn and go home.

thirty-five

EVA

Yes, Ben had finally made bail and come home, but he was exiled to the basement. At least that was what Morgan told me when I picked her and Miles up from school and told them that homework could wait, we were going to get pizza and have a big party, all of us, together.

"Even Daddy?"

"Yes, of course. Your father loves pizza."

"But Mom said he's going to be on retreat for a while."

"Retreat?"

"Yeah, in the basement."

"Ah."

Interesting word, *retreat*. From one jail to another? Was that any way to welcome home an innocent husband?

We picked up three pizzas, one plain, one pepperoni, and one with veggies, to satisfy everyone, and headed back to Hillary's house. I parked the car and told Morgan to take the pizzas inside, then told Miles to go tell his mother that Hillary had invited everyone up to her house for a pizza party.

"Okay," he said warily, as if he knew I was lying.

Then I went inside and told one daughter that the other one was on her way and to open a bottle of red wine and get me a glass, that we were going to hash out a plan over pizza.

"Mom," Hillary sighed as she poured, "this is not how crimes are solved."

"Well, maybe if more police officers ate Italian food, they'd be better at cracking cases," I said, then sipped my wine. "This is delicious, by the way."

"It is, isn't it?" She took a long sip herself. "Well, maybe if Hannah drank once in a while, she'd be calmer."

"You drink, and you're not calm."

"I'm energized."

"Okay, honey."

There she went, trying to force me to take sides. I refused, of course. And I confess, I was not inclined to take her side anyway.

Hannah arrived, Miles went upstairs with Morgan, and three of us were alone in the kitchen. Hannah took her wine glass and poured some tap water into it, added ice from the freezer. At first, the silence was so deafening, you could hear the ice crackling in her glass. Was that the sound of détente? Or the sound that comes before everything goes to hell again?

"Hillary, you did find another good lawyer, right?" Hannah said finally.

"Yes. But the fact that he couldn't get Ben bailed out quickly makes me doubt I have the right one."

"There must be a reason."

"Yeah, there's a reason. They think he killed a kid. We know he didn't, but…"

"Do we? Know that?" Hannah said it as gently as she could.

"Of course we do! Jesus, Hannah, once again I ask, whose side are you on?"

"Yours. Which is…not the same as Ben's."

"It's all circumstantial. Bribing a kid to keep her mouth shut is not a crime. We bribed two of them tonight with pizza."

Hannah glanced at me. Bribery was bribery. It was not a great leap to think a man who gave a child money and candy might also give her presents for her birthday. I almost couldn't blame the police for adding it up either.

"But…what about DNA?" I asked.

"Oh, DNA takes forever. It's not like dry cleaning. So I don't think they have a damn thing besides her coming to the door to get more candy. Which proves nothing! And some stupid necklace they found. Which is why he should have made bail immediately! It's all circumstantial."

"They were probably just making him sweat a little."

"Well, maybe if he had the right lawyer. Maybe if someone hadn't swooped in and—"

"Stop," I said. "Don't you start this again. Hannah has as much right to protect her boy as you do your husband."

"Well, as long as we're sharing evidence, should I hazard a guess as to why there was a backhoe at your house?"

"I don't know. Are you going to use it so Miles can be blamed instead of Ben?"

Hillary shrugged defiantly. "All I know is, Ben is innocent."

"Well, Miles is innocent!"

"Is he, Han? Are you totally sure?"

"Of course he is, and he's not going to lie to help your…your cheating husband!" Hannah spat out finally.

They were facing each other now on one side of the island, another warrior moment. I took a step toward the enormous copper sink, the water spray with its self-retracting hose nestled into the marble. I had to prepare to arm myself again, just in case.

"Girls, just because you're mad at the world or your husbands doesn't mean you should be mad at each other."

"Mom, stay out of this," Hillary said.

"Listen to me. No one is going to take the fall and lie for anybody. If the two of you work together, you can accomplish any damned thing you want, and you both know it. Now the police have Ben, they'll be lazy. They'll stop. And whoever is out there will get comfortable, too, let their guard down. And you have an advantage over the police."

"What? We're smaller? We can fit through drainage pipes?" Hannah asked.

"No, silly. You live here. You know the whole neighborhood. And you're smarter than the police."

"Well, that's true," Hillary sighed.

"Now let's make a list of everyone who was at poker night and start there," I said, opening a drawer and taking out pen and paper.

"Also Kendra's ex-husbands," Hillary said. "And their closest neighbors. And older boys, teenagers who might party in the woods."

Hannah took a deep breath.

"What?" Hillary said. "You look like you were about to say something."

"If we do this, the kids can't know," she said. "We can't scare them about all their neighbors."

"Get Ben up here," I said. "We need his help with the poker list."

When Hillary came back with Ben, I walked over and gave him a hug, patting him on the back for a long time, for support. But Hannah kept her eyes focused on her feet.

He gave us the first names of everyone in the group, although he didn't know some last names and wasn't precisely sure where everyone lived. He also couldn't say for certain how many guys were there at the last game, since they had all been so drunk. He remembered talking to seven other men, and that was it. He didn't have their street addresses, but he had their email addresses and some of their phone numbers. Even as he spoke and we talked about each man, Hannah said nothing. Even when he spoke to her directly and asked her if she knew either of the people who lived behind her, she just shook her head and didn't meet his gaze. One thing was certain. If there was anyone who was guilty in that room that day, it was her.

thirty-six

HANNAH

Poker, poker, poker. Eva was convinced that finding out more about poker night was the only way in. And Ben had said some of the guys from their group went to the casino every Tuesday and played at the high stakes table. Hillary had downloaded some of their photos from Facebook, and they had decided to find them at the casino and see if they'd say anything useful.

Hillary had even discussed trying to attend one of the poker nights—to offer to substitute for Ben and hope they'd let her in, figuring they could win a ton of money off a woman. But that seemed like a crazy, risky strategy to Hannah. She knew her sister could flirt and charm her way into any situation, but a bunch of drunk men, one of whom could be a killer? That seemed a little crazy.

Hannah had ordered criminal checks for every man in the neighborhood, six streets' worth, and paid with Hillary's credit card. They were still waiting on those, but the chance that someone in the poker club knew or had seen something seemed pretty high. The only other lead—if you could call it that—Hillary was fixated on was Cat Saunders. Hillary kept saying she had as much at stake as Ben had and that the police had been sexist in focusing on him. Wasn't Cat perhaps part of the bribery of the girl? Where were Cat's handcuffs? Where was Cat's jail cell?

Hillary brought up Cat's name every evening they got together and kept asking if there wasn't some way Hannah could confront her at work.

But Hannah had very little face time with her. She was mostly interviewing girls out in the field, at various high schools, and was almost at the end of her list. The project would be over in weeks, and frankly, Hannah was lucky she still had it.

Cat hadn't said anything to her about Ben, and she didn't expect her to. Cat probably had a lawyer and had likely been told to keep her mouth shut. Still, Hannah decided to swing by Cat's office casually, with a concocted question about the videos she was doing, just to speak to her. To see what came up.

When she got there, she was astonished to see the young blond girl from the hotel in with her. She'd thought her face, which suddenly felt red and sweaty, might give her away. But Cat stood up, smiling, and calmly introduced her to her daughter.

"Your daughter? But your last name—"

"I use my maiden name," Cat said.

Afterward, Hannah felt like an idiot. She'd clearly misread Ben's solicitous behavior toward the girl. He'd been fatherly, she could see now; that was all. And Cat had taken her by the arm and apologized for the awkwardness with her brother-in-law, for the scandal. For any problems she'd caused her family. Her last words had been "It's hard to be married, isn't it?"

Well, how could she disagree with that? And God knows, it was hard to be married to Hillary, perfect Hillary. And, she had to admit, hard to be angry with Cat. Charming, warm Cat.

Still, Hillary insisted on a background check on Cat, too, maybe so she could use something against her personally at a later time, and Hannah reluctantly agreed. Maybe she was as sexist as the cops, but she didn't think any woman she'd ever met was capable of killing a little girl. Even her sister. Even her stone-cold sister.

The casino wasn't far away—half an hour, tops—but the still-rush-hour traffic crawled and sputtered in fits and starts, and Hannah wondered aloud why she was even going.

"I mean, Hillary's going to play, and you're going to take notes, and what am I going to do?"

"Help us carry home our winnings," Eva said.

Hannah was nervous, leaving Miles home alone. He had plenty of homework, the doors were locked, and his cousin and uncle were next door. Hillary had convinced her he was old enough to be alone. She'd said most boys stayed home alone at ten, not almost thirteen. But most kids didn't live in a neighborhood where another kid had been killed. Most kids also—she had to be honest with herself—weren't like Miles. But he'd seemed better. His therapist had said so, too. Appointments every week. Sleeping better, food habits back on track. Having Ben home, a father figure next door, was probably helpful, too.

She wrung her hands and sighed. The back seat of Hillary's car was warm and comfortable, because it had its own heating vents. And the leather seats of the Lexus seemed almost twice as big as her Honda's cloth ones. The traffic was clearing out a bit, and she tried to empty her mind, to not think about Miles. She should take advantage of someone else driving and someone else making this high car payment instead of her and just enjoy this spa of a car. She should relax and look at this more like a much-needed girls' night out. If Hillary could relax, with all that she had on her mind, so could Hannah.

But every time she closed her eyes, she saw the ribbon in her son's hamper. She pictured the girl's necklace lying between their houses. She saw Kendra standing on the path, innocently telling her about her daughter. She saw Ben confessing to the detective that he was an unfaithful asshole but not a cold-blooded killer. All of it added up to more unease. Just an overall thick cloud of nerves, jangling her in a way she hadn't felt since Miles was a baby. If both Ben and Miles were innocent, why did she feel so tense whenever she thought about her home?

"How long do you think we'll stay?" she asked.

"A couple hours maybe," Hillary said.

"I don't want to leave Miles for too long."

She was being ridiculous, she knew. But still, she'd called Mike and made sure he kept his phone on just in case. And she'd heard his annoyance in the tone of his voice, threaded with discontent. Mike saw things, heard things in her that he disliked. They were always there now, front and center. Still, at the end of the conversation, he'd asked if she wanted him to come over or take Miles for the night, which was nice of him. She'd said no. Not unless he calls you.

That was the last thing she needed, for Miles to think she'd sent his father over because she didn't trust him. She trusted him up to a point. But then she thought about a coyote howling from a corner of the Tamsen farm estate. Or the hoot owl she'd seen down in the gully below the path, calling out. Squirrels rustling in the bushes, leaping in the almost-bare trees. Would he go outside even though she'd warned him not to? Would he be able to control himself? Had the police told the neighbors to look out for any suspicious behavior with animals? Dear God, maybe they had.

Hillary pulled up to the circular entrance of the casino and was about to valet park when she spotted an empty space in the darkest corner of the front row of cars. She pulled in, and her mother jumped out eagerly.

"Maybe I shouldn't have come," Hannah said, wringing her hands.

"Calm down, Han," Hillary said, reaching for her handbag underneath her seat. "We just got here. It's practically still light out. He'll be fine. You can always call him. Or send Morgan over to check on him."

They got out of the car and walked up the long pathway to the arched entrance. It was garishly lit with gold and white lights that made Hannah squint.

"I don't want Morgan outside in the dark either."

"When did you get so fucking neurotic?"

Hannah almost asked her when she got so robotically calm, but that was a ridiculous question. Hillary had always been that type of calm. But Hannah had not always been neurotic. Her sister knew that, so did her mother, and so did Mike. She was a level-headed girl, almost to a fault. It was as if Miles's problems had rewired his mother's brain, not his. Miles was fine with himself precisely as he was. She was the one who had been altered.

A doorman wearing gold spats opened the door for Hillary, and she made a face of horror as soon as he wasn't looking. A face that said *Spats? Gold spats?* They stopped a moment to take it all in. Tables. Noise. Cheap gold chandeliers. And too many people, people who looked like they couldn't afford to lose any of the chips they clutched in their hands. It was as if someone had peeled open a flea market, poured the customers into this space, and sprayed it with glitter. It was down the road from one of the most upscale malls in the world, but there was nothing remotely glamorous about it. People weren't dressed up—it could have been Black Friday at Best Buy. It could have been—if you looked too closely and noticed some people's pants were dirty and they weren't wearing socks—the Salvation Army.

Hannah still didn't fully understand how watching their neighbors play poker would help them. Did they really expect the men to get drunk and spill their secrets to her sister? Hillary said yes, it was about gaining trust, about eavesdropping, but also about what they would say to her about Ben. How guilty they might feel. As if she could tell from the looks on their faces who might know more. Who might be glad Ben was being accused. Still, she was right about one thing—they couldn't just knock on doors and pepper their neighbors with questions.

They headed for the poker tables, mingling, watching. Most of the people playing were older men, a few older women. No one they recognized from their list.

A waitress stopped by, and Eva ordered two glasses of champagne, then asked Hannah what she wanted.

"I'm fine with water."

"Come on, Hannah. Live a little."

"I don't drink, Mom. You know that."

"Well, you might be calmer if you had a glass of wine now and then."

"Yeah, that worked really well for Dad, didn't it?"

"Oh, Hannah," Eva said with a sigh. "You have nothing in common with that man. When will you accept that?"

"It's a shame you never learned poker, Mom," Hannah said. "Looks like a good way to meet older guys."

"Oh, I know the bare basics. I'm just not good at it. I'm a terrible liar, as you may have noticed."

"Mike told me once that lying was the only reason women *were* good at poker."

"That sounds like something he should have discussed in therapy."

She'd never told her mother all the things they had, in fact, discussed in therapy. The way Hannah was raised, or non-raised as Mike sometimes called it. The way she and Hillary had tried so hard to be little grown-ups and help after their father's death was something the therapist kept focusing on, over and over. But she didn't know the half of it. All the stupid tests her sister had put her through to prove her strength. The ice-cold bathtub, with a timer. Eating tablespoons of Worcestershire sauce or soy sauce or the worst one, cocoa. Dry cocoa. She still gagged at the thought. Mike had always asked where her mother had been, and Hannah didn't know. She was there and not there. She told Mike he didn't understand because he didn't have a brother. Two of the same sex is like a cartel, she'd said, and the therapist had made a note, which irritated her.

Mike had a sister who had her own room with a miniature vanity and dressing room in her closet. She got a new dress for every prom, had her nails and hair done. Spoiled, in Hannah's view. Normal, in Mike's view. She'd had a childhood. She'd been a girl. A princess, Hannah thought. Loved, Mike said. As if all the fault for their marriage's divide lay with her childhood and not all the stupid things he did.

They strolled by the craps tables, wandered over to the roulette wheel, where they watched a group of women wearing tiaras shrieking and moaning over close calls and might-have-beens. The ladies were all dressed in black except for one girl wearing gold, and Hannah's mother leaned over and asked if they were all pageant queens.

"It's a bachelorette party," the woman giggled and showed her the straw in her drink, shaped like a phallus.

"Wow. Are there male strippers here, too?"

"If you see any," she replied, "let us know immediately!"

Hillary stayed at the poker table, dealing herself in, while Hannah and her mother circled and searched for nearly an hour. Every so often, they swung back to the table, and Hillary shook her head. No sign of any of them.

As they walked, Eva explained the various games in light detail to Hannah, as if sensing her daughter had exactly zero interest. Hillary was the competitive one, not Hannah. Hannah held tight to her phone in her pocket, afraid she'd miss the vibration, and every so often, she slipped it out and checked it just in case.

They were about to enter the ladies' room when Hillary came running up, out of breath.

"We have to go," she said.

"What? Why?" Eva replied.

"Ben just called. Morgan isn't in the house."

Hannah didn't ask if the cousins were together. If Ben had checked next door, looked in on Miles. She knew better than to make this about her kid. She also had a terrible, sinking belief as she gripped her phone that it *was* about her kid.

That those two were together.

Somewhere.

thirty-seven

EVA

I know it was an emergency, but really, Hillary drove much too fast on the way home. I kept gripping the leather strap near the window, trying to stay upright on the curves, praying the police didn't pull us over. The police, after all, were much too familiar with our family these days.

In the back seat, I heard Hannah's fingers tap-tap-tapping on her phone. She was emailing Miles to make sure he was home, I was certain. She didn't dare call him; she knew better than to insert her faux emergency into Hillary's real one. She didn't want to be on the receiving end of any more Hillary vitriol, and I couldn't blame her. I didn't want it either.

Stress does terrible things to people, but it does different things. When the girls' father died, I retreated. Hillary sought distractions—busied herself night and day so she wouldn't have to be alone or home to see me or my grief. Or her sister's.

And Hannah? Hannah took long walks and long baths and went out with her friends for solace. She was the only one, I realized later, who responded normally. Healthily. Going to parties, going out into nature. Soothing herself. The bonfires with other kids, the hayrides. Distractions. She was steady then, and she was steady as an adult. Until recently anyway, when she'd started obsessing over her son. Rightfully so, I might add, but still. It was so, so very unlike her that I can't imagine she was comfortable with it. It was as if the divorce had forced her to do the worrying for two people, not one. Still, I heard her tapping. We were two streets away when she finally spoke.

"I wanted Miles to go out and look for her, but he's not answering."

"Maybe they're together," I said.

"Great," Hillary replied. "We'll just call the police and tell them the entire fucking neighborhood of children is missing."

She pulled onto her street, zoomed up her driveway.

"Well, at least they can't accuse Ben of this one. He's the wounded party this time."

I thought about this for a few seconds before we opened the car doors and raced inside. How a smart person, a brilliant person in fact—for Ben and Hillary were both brilliant—could orchestrate something exactly like this just for that reason. I felt sick inside even having that thought. What was wrong with me now, looking at the world this way? Wasn't I the one who had said I thought he was innocent?

Hannah ran down to her house while Hillary and I searched hers. We spread out, her taking the upper floor while I took the basement, Ben trailing behind saying he *already looked there. And there. And there.* I swept my hands around the curtains, the blinds, opened the washer, the dryer, all the while thinking, *He didn't look here, I bet.* The difference between a woman and a man. I heard the doors opening and closing all the way upstairs, heard the slide of the shower curtain, the roll of the trundle bed, the swish of hangers against rod, Hillary thinking of every hiding place.

I looked at windows, doors, looking for anything loose or open. I went upstairs just as they were heading down to the front door, Hillary at full run, Ben trying to keep up.

"Are you kidding me right now? You didn't even open the door and call her name?"

"Why would she go outside?" Ben said.

"This isn't about why! She's in middle school. Who knows why any of them do anything!"

She ran outside, and I followed her. She screamed, "Morgan! Morgan!" in all directions. No answer. No anything, not even a dog barking or branch swaying in the wind.

She punched in the garage code, and Ben said it was locked, she wasn't in there. Couldn't be.

"Did you look?"

He shook his head; she seethed. It had taken only a few minutes for her and Ben to devolve into an argument. That was what having an affair did for a marriage, I suppose. Working apart instead of working together. I'd always thought of them as more of a team than this, but then, I'd never seen them in a crisis.

"Ben, did you even call her friends? Did you check social media?"

I didn't want to stay for the cross-examination.

"I'll go check the creek," I said and reached in my purse for the flashlight I used at dark restaurants. I switched it on and headed down the driveway.

Suddenly, Hannah's front door banged open, and she stepped onto the porch. She paced underneath the light, talking into her phone.

"Hannah?" I called out.

"Miles isn't here either," she yelled back. "I'm calling his dad, a few other parents—"

"I'm going down to the path. Unless you can think of anywhere else they might go?"

It seemed dangerous suddenly to consider what those two might do if they knew all that we had done. Had they put every piece of it together now, confided in each other? That Morgan's loyalties lay with Miles over her own mother was quite telling to me. And Miles's love for Ben stronger than I'd guessed. What would they do now? Were they trying to do exactly what we were, to help Ben?

I shuddered at the thought of them sneaking around houses, peering into windows, trying to collect evidence. I could just imagine Morgan imploring Miles to help her daddy, please. And of course Miles would be powerless in the face of his cousin's need. *No, please, dear God*, I thought. Let them be holed up somewhere with a Ouija board and a sleeping bag. Let them be playing cards, just as we had been.

"I'll come with you. Hang on."

She went inside and came out with two headlamps and two larger flashlights.

"I imagine we look ridiculous," I said as we walked across the street. As the beam bobbled and swayed with my gait, I was a bit nauseous until I got used to it.

"What is Hillary doing?"

"Yelling at her husband."

"That's helpful."

"Bet you don't miss that."

"No. No, I do not."

"I think they're going to get in the cars and fan out."

"That's a good idea."

The first part of the path was steep; I'd forgotten that. I held on to a tree with one hand while Hannah held my elbow. My right foot slid just a little, and I shrieked.

"Maybe you should wait here," she said. "I'll look."

"No, it's just this bit."

"It's steep toward the end, too."

"Well, I'll deal with that when we get there."

We called their names at first, then stopped. Hannah thought they might be hiding or be driven farther away if they knew we were getting closer. But suddenly, we heard footsteps behind us, and another light clicked on. Then another.

"Hannah?" a voice said.

I startled a bit, but Hannah didn't. The light behind her illuminated another person, younger, male.

"Hi, Kendra,"

"This is my son, Cameron."

"Nice to meet you. This is my mother, Eva."

I waved hello. The young man behind her was dark haired, tall, nothing like her. You'd never think they were related, and I supposed that was a good thing. She was so slight. That would be tough for a boy growing up, being so small.

"We heard someone calling."

"Yes, my son and niece are—well, I hesitate to say the word 'missing,' but...well, we don't know where they are."

"Maybe they just went out walking?"

"That's what we're hoping."

"Do they have cell phones?"

"He doesn't. She's not answering hers."

"Still, they have one in an emergency."

"I bet they're either up at the Bordens' playhouse," Matt said, "or the rock."

Even I knew where the rock was. There was a large, flat rock near the top of the path—a perfect place for anyone to sit and rest. I'd rested there myself.

"Where is the Bordens' playhouse?"

"There are two playhouses not far from the path," Kendra said. "One is the one that burned down. The other is farther away from the Bordens' house, on the downhill side toward Tamsen. Not really used since their kids left for college. They used to have a zip line that went from a tree near their house, but they took the cable down. The insurance company told them it was a hazard," she said. "My husband is friendly with them," she added, in case we were suspicious of her trove of information or the motivations of the family for keeping it, but we weren't. I just assumed she knew everything now.

If I were in her place, I'd know every square inch of this neighborhood. The houses, the stands of trees, the rocks breaking through, the pine needles littering the path. Yes, I'd have memorized it, walking it by day, lying awake at night, going over everything I knew. How would your brain stop the wondering, the guessing, the cataloguing? Was it even possible, or did you just have to let it go?

"The police said sometimes kids use it. When they searched it, they found candles, beer bottles."

"Beer?"

Hannah was clearly panicked. Miles was too young for those kinds of shenanigans. I'd read that kids were experimenting earlier—but this early? It didn't ring true to me, not for those two. The headlamp illuminated my puffs of breath against the navy blue of the sky, reminding me that it was cold, and these were kids, but they weren't stupid. They were smart enough to get out of the cold.

"I bet that's exactly where they've gone," I said.

"Why? What do you know, Mom?"

"Me? I don't know anything. I just know human nature."

"The last time you watched them, at Hillary's, did you—"

"Did I what? Let them drink beer?"

"No. I was going to say, did they go for a walk?"

"I don't remember," I said as fiercely as I could muster. But of course I did. They'd both been outside. I did not know where. Just prior to the deer incident, they'd been inside the house, but before? They'd been out for a spell. Walking? Running? Sitting? I wasn't watching them from the window. They weren't toddlers. What happened to children going out until the streetlights came on? Wasn't that precisely how Hillary and Hannah had been raised?

And even now, even after what happened, I don't know that I would change a thing. Lightning doesn't strike twice. I would not assume an adolescent boy would be stolen from his own yard just because a young child was drowned or strangled or God knows what in a creek a mile from her house. I would not. Did that make me a monster? An irresponsible, let-me-tell-you-about-the-good-old-days clueless adult?

"Then why do you think they've headed there?"

"Common sense," I answered. "It's cold. Why wouldn't they want to go inside?"

Kendra and her son ended up leading the way. I don't know if this was because of neighborhood seniority, the speediness of youth, the fact that they knew exactly where the playhouse was and we didn't, or because they wanted to let us have our little argument, but no matter. I wasn't about to question the judgment of a mother who had just lost her daughter. We followed them, perhaps more slowly than they'd have liked, but I didn't want to fall. That was the last thing this night needed, another emergency.

When we got to the steep pitch leading down to the playhouse, I swept my headlamp across it, trying to see if there was a less perilous approach. The little house looked boarded up, the windows covered with plywood and tarps. Was it damaged? Dangerous?

Matt offered to help me down, but I shook my head. Prideful old thing. "I guess I could just slide down if need be."

"Mom, maybe you should stay on the path and wait for us."

"Okay. Maybe you're right."

I sat on a low rock and watched them pick their way down, their flashlights sweeping and bouncing. It didn't look particularly safe for them either, but it had to be done. Where else would kids congregate in the dark? A barn? An underpass? Those things were much, much farther away. I couldn't imagine they'd try to walk to them.

I heard the shouting a few seconds later. High voice and low. Angry, followed by beseeching. Hannah and Miles. Aha. They were there. I don't know what I expected they'd be carrying as they all climbed up toward me. Beer, I suppose, since the idea had already been placed in my head. Snacks. A cooler, a board game, something. Not what they brought to me, bundled in blankets, Miles holding it out to me as soon as he saw me as if only I would understand, as if only I could make it all better.

"Look, Grandma," he said.

"Miles?" a voice called from behind us.

"Dad," Miles said, "come look!"

Mike ran down the path to meet us, his dark sneakers sliding in places but legs confident, helping him remain upright, his scramble goatlike the way some men simply were. Not as fit and trim or personable as Ben but just as strong and capable. Hannah didn't acknowledge him; he went immediately to his son's side. I shuddered to think how fast Mike must have driven after Hannah called him. She'd always said he was too calm, too unflustered, didn't worry enough. But maybe now his arrival meant my daughter had been wrong about him, just a tiny bit wrong. Would she admit this?

We all huddled beneath a tiny sliver of a moon, the headlamps cutting wide yellow stripes in the navy sky. We watched as Miles struggled to hold three squirming kittens, rolling against each other, too trusting, no fear of hitting the ground. But only one of us put his hands beneath Miles's blanket as a safety net. Mike.

But all of us watched. All of us witnessed. Calico kittens, long haired, blue eyed and green and gray, a riot of color and fluff. The neighbor, her son, my daughter, my former son-in-law. A beautiful moment in this broken neighborhood.

The look on my grandson's face was something I've seldom seen. It's in the photos taken of new mothers, of scientists clinching a discovery, of spelling bee winners. Love and pride, in equal proportions, as if these mewling commas in his arms were his flesh and blood.

"We have to keep them," he said. "Can we?" He turned to me first. I acknowledge that now, with tremendous pride. A gift: his first glance was mine.

"Well..." I answered.

"Yes," Mike said.

"No," his mother said at exactly the same time.

It would be a bit longer before I fully understood why.

thirty-eight

HANNAH

The kittens lived in Hillary's basement, next to the Ping-Pong table, in a tall, elaborate, fuzzy structure that looked like a carpet salesman with a drug problem had built it, at least to Hannah's eye. Ben had taken the kittens to the vet for all their shots, then gone to PetSmart with Morgan and bought every cat gadget in sight. Ben seemed incapable of saying no to anything Hillary or Morgan requested, as if he was on a quest to bolster his image as a nice guy, a soft guy, in case his daughter or wife started to believe he was a murderer. He'd stopped avoiding people, started going out in public freely again, walking, running, as if to say he had nothing to be ashamed of. Still, his poker friends told him they thought he should sit out for a while until "things calmed down." And Hillary told Hannah the book club had said basically the same thing to her, then removed her from their neighborhood Facebook group, which made her furious, since she'd done nothing wrong no matter what they thought her husband had done. Still, Hannah was grateful the neighborhood gossip had shifted away from her son and her property. The last thing Miles needed was those whispers spilling onto the schoolyard.

Ben had been forced to take a leave of absence from work—the hedge fund was a little less comfortable throwing their support behind him than his family—but with full pay, Hillary had emphasized to Hannah, and he was still working on selected projects from home, but nothing with Cat. Hillary made sure of that. He may as well have been wearing an ankle monitor, but as long as she knew where he was going, she was happy to let him do all the errands and pet and child care.

Miles was closely monitored, too. Hannah had to figure out new ways to get his mind off animals and onto other things. He was allowed to visit and play with the kittens three times a week after he finished his homework, and he begged to be allowed to go every day. Even though, as Hannah had pointed out, his cousin wasn't home every day, and there were other things to do after school, like sports or video games, this was still his top priority. She couldn't believe she was encouraging him to play video games. What was next, trying to get him to go to parties? Was she an inch away from buying her son beer or taking him to a strip club? But she was desperate for him to fall in love with something else besides animals, animals, and more animals.

She wanted him to have balance in his life, even if it meant bringing in a little darkness. Wasn't that what the therapist had said was the antidote to obsession? Balance?

She'd asked him if he wanted a trampoline in their backyard, and he'd looked at her like she had two heads. There wasn't room for anything larger, and she thought a hot tub was something she'd regret when he was older. That was just what she needed, being the house with the hot tub.

She'd brought home brochures from a rock-climbing place, go-karts, archery, art classes, photography. She'd left them on the kitchen table but never saw him pick one up. In desperation and against her better judgment, she'd even asked if he was sure he didn't want to go to the shooting range with his father.

"Mom, no," he said with a visible shudder. "God, you're as bad as he is, mentioning hunting or shooting every five seconds." He saw his father every other Saturday and Sunday, which cut into Mike's hunting schedule, but she supposed he was just looking for conversation ground with his son. This happened every fall, she supposed. And would continue each year, as if Mike waited long enough, Miles would change into an entirely new person. That or until Miles had the balls to say to his father that he considered him a murderer, he was turning vegetarian, and he never wanted to see him again. Isn't that where the love of animals usually led? To action, activism? Every time he came home from visiting the kittens at Hillary's, she expected him to refuse to eat chicken or to tell her milk and eggs were stolen property. It would happen someday. He'd pick up a drumstick, and suddenly it would all come crashing in.

She'd gotten her hands on four Eagles tickets (courtesy of her lawyer) and told Miles she would take him and Morgan, and did he want to bring a friend? From school?

"Can't Uncle Ben come?" Miles had said.

It had been the first positive thing he'd responded to, so she swallowed her discomfort and asked Ben. She was certain she'd never heard Miles happier about anything.

He bought the kids cheese fries and sweatshirts and persuaded Miles to cheer loudly and complain about bad calls. He taught him the Eagles theme song. He spoke of strategy, history, stats, and Miles was rapt. Morgan loved one of the players, a backup quarterback, and enthusiastically explained things about the team and the opponents to her cousin. Miles seemed totally engaged for a while, until he asked if Morgan remembered the Puppy Bowl last year, during the Super Bowl where the dogs played? Remember that? *Animals*, Hannah had thought with a sigh. *All animals all the time.* Where did this come from? What broken line of DNA made him prefer animals to people?

Still, they'd had a good night. And if it was uncomfortable between Hannah and Ben, especially when he had his second and then his third beer, it had been worth it. Miles had done something normal, with other people.

On the way home from the game, snarled in traffic, Hannah brought up the idea of fantasy football, hoping Miles might be interested in a more introverted way of following the sport. But he simply replied that yeah, he knew about that, knew some guys who did that. Hannah was relieved that at least he knew some other boys. That he had at least an anthropologist's perspective of what other boys did and liked. That he might have spoken to some other boys instead of spending all his time with his cousin's kittens. Oh well, she thought; now he could at least casually mention to those boys, whoever they were, whatever their names, that he'd been at the Eagles game the night before. She was giving him currency if not a hobby.

As they pulled onto Brindle Lane and said goodbye, the kids piled out of the car, and Ben stayed behind for a minute.

"Hannah, you have to believe me that I never meant for any of this to happen."

"Of course not," she said. "I know that."

"I'm going to be better. I am. I love my family," he said.

"I'm sure you do."

"All my family, Han. All of you," he said, starting to choke up.

She leaned in to hug him, instinctively, gratefully. For Ben had been more than an uncle to Miles, always. Ben was the reason they were living next door to Hillary as much as anything.

She said it was okay. He pulled away and wiped tears from his eyes. Said he was going to try to make up for it, all of it, somehow, and she nodded.

"Cat…is a very compelling person," she added.

"She's a force," he said.

"You like a force," Hannah said quietly.

"Yeah," he said, "I guess I do."

They both got out and went inside their respective houses.

Miles wasn't been punished for sneaking out the night of the kittens; he explained that Morgan was upset and needed a friend to talk to, and he'd suggested going for a walk. It was his fault, he emphasized. All his idea, he insisted. She should not be punished at all, he said. She deserved the opposite of punishment, he said, emphasizing this, because she'd been feeling sad. Punishing her might make her sadder, he said. They'd taken flashlights, he added, knowing that was the responsible thing to do. No, they hadn't told Ben or anyone what they were doing, but technically they were allowed to go outside. They hadn't broken any rules or laws really. That was really the extent of it. So the kids weren't punished, but they were admonished. They were not to go outside when it was dark without asking permission and waiting for it. Ever. Neither sister questioned Morgan's need to be soothed or Miles's desire to soothe her. They were happy the cousins were close. Wasn't that the whole point of living next door to each other?

After all, what child wouldn't be upset by what had happened to her neighbor—and her father? No, it all made sense. It all made sense at first.

Every night, Hannah had cried tears of gratitude for the innocence of the fire drill they'd just been through. That their children were safe. That they'd been found not with beer but with kittens. That her son and her niece were alive to go to the football game with her.

But that night, as she struggled to fall asleep after the game, the smell of popcorn and beer still on her clothes from the stadium, she couldn't shake the feeling that Kendra's daughter had also been on an innocent mission when she was killed. A creek. A bucket. Frogs. That a day could start out wholesome and end up deadly. You didn't want to say that to your kids, but adults said those things to themselves, daily, nightly.

thirty-nine

HANNAH

It had been almost a week, and there was no news. The police hadn't been around to harass Hannah or Miles. There was no new evidence that pointed to Ben, at least not that either of them was aware of. The background checks weren't back, and all Hannah had accomplished was compiling a broader list of all male neighbors in a two-mile radius, plus a map of registered sex offenders in their zip code (none of which overlapped). That the nearest sex offender was two and a half miles away, in Garrett Hill, should have made Hannah feel better, but all she could think of was the sweet little playground in Garrett Hill. How close it was. How small the neighborhood was. How awful it would be to live there, knowing the proximity, watching, worrying. But at least that was contained. How large, how impossibly enormous the world seemed, when you had no suspects. The man who killed Liza could be anywhere, not just in the neighborhood, as her mother continually pointed out. And there was no evidence the girl had been sexually assaulted, none that they knew of or had seen in the papers, so the sex registry might be of zero use anyway. Hannah was simply going off the numbers, the possibilities. But sometimes she felt like she'd have better luck at the casino roulette wheel.

Now it was poker night, and the sisters had concocted a loose plan to get inside and talk to the men. Ben wasn't welcome; they'd made that clear. But would they turn away a woman who wanted to play in his place? Someone who looked like an easy mark, someone they could take some money off?

They had no suspects, didn't even know some of the men's last names. They just had their suspicions that someone might have seen something. Just a nagging feeling that a drunk person had forgotten something important that happened on the way home and might remember now. And an overarching belief that it was absolutely no coincidence that poker night, the night all the guys walked home, always, was the night everything had happened. The police had to see that, too. And who knew? Maybe it was poker night that had led them to Ben. Maybe they'd find out something about Ben, too, Hannah thought. All Ben had been able to tell them was that some guys walked home on the road, like him, and some took the path. He couldn't even remember for certain everyone who had been there, just that two tables were set up. He'd had too much to drink and a wicked hangover the next day, as Hannah assumed most of them had. Was it even worth Hillary and Hannah showing up and preying on their sympathies, asking to play, if they didn't know what to ask or who to focus on? Should they just wait till the following month, when they had the background information? She didn't know. She was beginning to think her lawyer's idea to hire a private investigator and just hand it all to him was smarter.

Hillary had a box of cheesesteak sliders from a local restaurant and a bottle of whiskey for bribery. She put them in a tote bag, and they walked up the street to the Barkers' house. It was getting colder every night, Hannah thought as they approached the door and knocked. Just waiting the thirty seconds for the answer made her shiver.

Robert Barker was older—fifty-five, Ben had guessed—and the rest of the players were closer to Ben in age. When they'd started out, they'd rotated hosting duties, but over time, they'd settled in at Robert's. He liked to cook and he had no kids at home, so there were no distractions. Now they just shared costs and let Robert figure it all out. There were twelve regulars, but not everyone showed up every time. Occasionally, somebody brought their brother or a friend who was staying at their house, but Ben said he was pretty sure that had not been the case last time. Pretty sure but not totally sure. They were totally sure of exactly nothing, Hannah thought with a sigh as she stood on the porch.

"Smile," her sister said. "Stop sighing."

"I'm breathing."

"Well, then, stop breathing. Your hair smells like buttered popcorn."

"Now you know my moisturizing secrets."

The door opened, and Hillary's tone shifted.

"Hi there!" Hillary said. "These are from Ben. An apology for taking your money last time."

Robert laughed. "Ah, well, apology accepted. And if I might say so, we're all sorry for the predicament he's in. And we all believe in him of course."

"Thank you," Hillary said. "That means a lot to both of us."

She introduced Hannah, and they shook hands.

"So I don't know if you know this, but my sister and I are planning to do a ladies' poker night." She said *ladies* in a weird, lascivious voice that Hannah had never heard her use.

"Really? Great fun! Good for you."

"So I was wondering if maybe I could sit in for a couple of hands? Just to see how the boys do it?"

He hesitated, precisely as they'd imagined he would. And Hillary responded exactly the way they'd planned.

"Ben said he was sure it would be okay with everyone. Especially if I came early before things got crazy. Ha-ha. I'll sneak out and let you boys to it, okay?"

He smiled broadly. "Of course. Why not, right?"

Hillary flashed an equally wide grin as they swept inside. For a moment, Hannah looked at her in confusion and, frankly, admiration. What an actress she was. What a conniving liar she could be when she wanted to be.

The house was a sprawling split-level, redwood and glass, very unusual for this traditional neighborhood. From the outside, it looked right at home among the trees and winding paths, so it was easy to see why it had been chosen for the site. But inside, there were no curtains and blinds, and as they walked toward the lower level, Hannah wondered how a woman could feel comfortable living like this. Exposed. Vulnerable. Did his wife change clothes in her closet every night? Did she just turn out the lights and hope for the best?

They walked down cantilevered stairs to a room that overlooked a large stand of trees and a drop-off to the creek. There were a few subtle white lights nestled in the landscaping, illuminating aspens and lindens and maples, highlighting white bark and brown. It looked almost like an Ansel Adams photo. The pitch of the backyard was steep; the path was below them somewhere, but Hannah couldn't see it. She thought of what Kendra had told her, about the lanterns that used to be hung there, and thought what a shame it was they were gone. How pretty it would look from this vantage point, in addition to being useful. How welcoming, like a camp.

Two circular tables stood near the windows. They looked like real poker tables, not toppers; the felt was thicker and the bases sturdier. Hannah wondered if the room's sole use was for poker. Where could you store those tables when you wanted to have another, different kind of party? The men were congregated around the bar. A variety of beer bottles stood in ice in a copper tub. There were several bottles of whiskey, a lot of matching gold-rimmed glasses. And there was a lot of noise as they spoke and laughed and clinked ice, competing with the music in the wide-open floor plan. Nothing to absorb it.

So noisy it took them a few seconds to register that they had guests.

"Hey, guys," Robert called out. "You know Ben's wife and her sister?"

Everyone stopped talking at once. The Andy Grammer song in the background suddenly seemed too loud, too cheerful, childish. Like Robert's granddaughter had chosen his playlist.

"Hi!" Hillary said brightly. Every molecule in her body seemed to scream, *Don't judge me by my husband. I am my own wonderful person!* She'd taken care with her outfit, dressed casually in jeans and boots but with a cute, clingy green silk top underneath her suede jacket, and her hair in casual waves, the way Ben liked it, Hannah knew. He always touched her hair when it was like that, as if mesmerized. Hannah had witnessed that several times over the years, been jealous of it. Mike had never touched her as if she was a miracle.

Hannah stood by mutely, waving as Hillary explained her sister had just moved into the neighborhood and was next door, and wasn't that cool?

Hannah unwrapped her plaid scarf from her throat, sensing the room would soon be too warm for her embarrassment and nerves. Already feeling like the plainer, tomboy sister with straighter hair and a boring beige cable-knit sweater. She'd pulled it out of the dry cleaning bag and wondered if it was hers or Miles's. That was how not sexy it was.

She already knew there were only a couple of single men who came to poker night, a fact Hillary thought it was important to know, but she couldn't tell which ones they were, since most of them weren't wearing wedding rings. In Narberth, men wore their wedding rings.

Now she and Hillary stood before them, a group of men trying hard to look them in the eye and nowhere else. How long had it been since Hannah had been in a roomful of men? Years. Years and years. College probably.

"The girls are planning their own poker night. A little competition! So they're going to play a few hands so we can show them how it's done, whaddya say?"

Well, what could they say? Nothing, but their faces said it all. Their smiles fell, and the good cheer faded almost imperceptibly. They thought no one would notice, that they would get away with it, but of course the girls noticed. Of course. They'd also expected this reaction—*No fun for a little while. Watch yourself. Be careful. They probably know your wives.*

"Well," one of them said, "let's get started then."

The sooner we do it, the sooner it's over, his voice seemed to say.

Hillary pulled up to the table, selected her chips, and looked right at home. Someone brought her a beer. Hannah smiled and said she'd have a Coke. She sat in the back, said she was going to take notes.

"You're not going to cheat, are you?" Robert laughed loudly, almost a guffaw. "Whenever someone has a Coke, they're usually a cheater!"

Hillary laughed, too, brighter, more forceful, in a way Hannah hadn't heard her laugh in years. It was a bar laugh, overly large, meant to carry. She was flirting, Hannah saw. She'd almost forgotten what that was, flirting. She was single now; she'd have to relearn. It hadn't occurred to her that she'd learn from a married woman.

"Watch out. She's actually not my sister. She's from *60 Minutes*, doing an investigative piece on suburban gambling," Hillary said.

"I'm Lara Logan," Robert said in falsetto, and the two of them laughed. The other men, younger, didn't seem to get the joke at all.

"Clearly, she is your sister," one of them said. Barrett? He was taller than the others, maybe six foot five or six. Handsome in that unapproachable way that you notice a statue, looming above you, was handsome. Barrett. Hannah thought that was his name. "There's a huge resemblance."

Hannah smiled and considered thanking him, then stopped herself. Would Hillary do the same? No, she would not.

Hannah sat in the corner, taking notes in a small notebook in shorthand, just in case. She was behind Barrett's right shoulder, and she could tell he was uncomfortable with her being there. He kept stretching his neck, glancing slightly to the right, as if he didn't trust that she wouldn't look at his cards. She had the feeling he didn't trust women. Or maybe just didn't trust her. And who could blame him? They were on a very untrustworthy mission.

Hannah listed the names of everyone she'd met and their approximate ages and descriptions. Besides Barrett and Robert, there was Brian, who was married to Tara from book club. Sam, who was married to Susan from book club. Jason. Two Matts, one thin, one stocky. Will. And James, the only black man in the room. All of them well dressed with neatly trimmed hair, clean nails, and good manners. No floppy hair. No beards. Their hair colors ranging from dark blond to auburn to black streaked with gray. All of them on their best behavior, she supposed. But all of them drinking. She noticed that much. How many had they had before she arrived? One? Two? Impossible to tell, especially with whiskey. Some men savored it, and some were incapable of drinking slowly, of nursing anything. Those men should stick to beer.

The bar was stocked with two ice buckets, she noted. She also thought that was strange. Two ice buckets? Like they couldn't be interrupted to refill? Nine players plus Hillary, but only eight spaces at the tables. James and Robert stood toward the back, watching intently, as if they might learn something. And who knows, they might. Hannah knew there was an enormous industry built around people watching other people play games of all kinds, even though she didn't understand it.

Will, who had dark-brown hair and navy-blue eyes, was the first to get up and get a second drink. Hannah watched from the corner of her eye how he retrieved fresh ice for his glass. That struck her as odd, but she couldn't say why. He also didn't ask if anyone else wanted something while he was up. Was that just a girl thing? No, she'd seen both Ben and Mike do this. Common courtesy. Will refilled his own drink, grabbed a handful of peanuts from a bowl on the bar, returned to his seat.

The men were quiet. She'd imagined a raucous group, groaning at their mistakes, teasing each other, and she realized she was picturing, in her head, a group of adolescent boys playing video games. Not this measured, grown-up version where everyone was focused on the game. Was this how they normally behaved? Or were they just being good for her sake?

She watched their frown lines of concentration, their small, precise movements of cards to hand and table. Crisp, practiced. Her sister smiled and laughed, commented on her bad luck or another's good move, but they were much quieter, more serious. Hillary was trying to lighten things up, but they didn't rise to meet her.

Hannah realized suddenly what was actually going on. It was like watching people take the SAT. This was important. It was critically important to each man at the table that they beat her sister. That they not be bested by a woman! They were focused on her *losing*, not her learning.

Hannah spoke to the first player who folded: thin Matt. Dark-blond hair and brown eyes. Brown eyes with extremely long lashes, she noted, standing nearby.

"So the low chip is what, a dollar?"

"Five. White is five, and the highest is green, forty. Robert handles the bank," he added, as if that was her next question. "You should do that, too, put one person in charge of handling that."

"Okay," she said.

"Not everyone's good with money, so you need the right person."

"Right."

"I personally have trouble calculating a tip," he said and smiled. A nice smile.

"I'm guessing you're not an engineer?"

"No, I teach math."

His laugh was a welcome change in the atmosphere.

"Damn that long division," she said. "You never recover, right?"

"Right."

"So what do you really do?"

"I run a video and social media company. Which makes the no-cell-phone rule kinda hard for me."

"Ah, no cell phones allowed?"

"Right," he said. "And no sunglasses. No hiding your eyes."

"The phones have to be kept in your pockets?"

"What? No, hell, no—they're not even on this floor," he laughed. "Otherwise, we'd all be totally distracted. Plus at some places, people cheat. Especially women who don't know the game, they might be tempted to cheat."

"Ah," she said. "Those damned scheming women. We shall keep that in mind."

But what she was thinking was eight men, all drunk, all unreachable by their wives. Fascinating, she thought.

"So how is the evening structured? Do you play for an hour then go upstairs and eat, or…?"

"Yeah, I guess it's about an hour. Then Inge brings the food down."

The other Matt sitting next to him shot him a quick glance.

"Inge?"

"Personal chef," Other Matt declared.

Ben had overlooked this salient detail, that a woman might be present. She was about to say "I thought Robert loved to cook" but didn't want to sound combative.

"Oh, that's nice," she said.

"So we can all concentrate on the game," Other Matt added.

Clearly, this was regular procedure. They'd agreed? They'd voted? They'd chipped in?

"Yes, that makes total sense," she said. *Let them think I'm a logical thinker*, she thought. Let them not see how appalling this news was, that men gathered to gamble and hired a woman to wait on them, every other week, for months, and none of their wives were aware. Did Susan and Tara know but not Hillary? Was Ben so worried about his own affair that he hadn't dared to let on about this? Oh, well, she was probably an old maid in an apron, someone's childhood nanny who was an awesome cook, and Hannah was overreacting.

Hillary's brow was furrowed in concentration in a way that made Hannah believe she had a shitty hand. She didn't know much about the game, but she'd seen that look on her sister's face before, and it looked like she was trying to wrestle her way out of a corner. Finally, she folded, and the two of them were both free to observe the men. The men seemed to visibly relax after Hillary pushed away from the table, and the energy in the room lightened. At least they weren't losing to a woman!

When they took a break to eat, Hannah thought, she'd find out what everyone did for a living and where they lived in the neighborhood and how often they attended and if they had been to the last poker night. Those were her goals. Last names, location, job, attendance. Basic things the police might already know or not know. Hannah had read enough true crime and watched enough television to know that the basics were important, that solutions were often close by, right under your nose. Robert struck her as friendly and a little too trusting; he would probably answer anything she asked if she asked it innocently enough.

Ben had been zero help with most of this stuff—didn't even know most of their last names. She couldn't even imagine this, being in a small club and not knowing anything about the members. She'd thought it surprising, but even more surprising was that her sister didn't know. Hillary knew the book club husbands, of course, but she usually knew everything about where Ben went and what Ben did and who Ben associated with. Hannah had overheard some of those miniature inter-rogations. Hillary had known enough to sic Hannah on Cat after all.

She sat and made notes about the house and music out of boredom. She amused herself by trying to guess the names of songs that came on. The actual poker game, when everyone had a poker face on, was not exciting to watch at all. How did people find watching this interesting? She yawned and made a mental note to turn on poker tournaments the next time she had insomnia.

James won the hand, and almost instantly, there were footsteps on the stairs. Two sets, not one. In front, a woman around Hannah's age but with a much better figure carried a tray of food.

And behind her, an even younger, prettier woman followed with a tray of cell phones.

Inge and her sister, Anya.

forty

EVA

I wasn't as shocked as they thought I'd be. Or as they wanted me to be. They held on to their tidbit with the eagerness of the young girls they used to be, bursting to tell me, asking me if I was ready for it, like they were Margot, ugh. And could I believe it?

Well, yes, I could. Indeed I could. I'd met Robert Barker once at Hillary's house, at a holiday party, and his ironed blue jeans and hair-sprayed salt-and-pepper lion's mane and fingernails that looked as if they'd been buffed and oiled stood out to me as a man who loved beautiful details. If they'd told me the poker night was at his house—a detail they'd somehow overlooked the first time—I would have told them the evening was going to be curated and as close to house-magazine ideal as he could make it. That his idea of perfection was beautiful servers, well, no, that didn't really surprise me at all. After all, didn't married men go to football games to ogle half-naked cheerleaders? Didn't married men go to strip clubs with their clients? Wasn't their universal excuse that they all worked hard and deserved a little fun?

We drank coffee in Hillary's kitchen. The dew on her plants outside sparkled in the light, and I wondered, not for the first time, if Hillary appreciated all the beauty around her or if she just powered through her days producing it and arranging it and taking it for granted. Was Ben part of that? A handsome man, a kind man—or so we'd always thought—but did she look at him regularly and think that? Or was he just part of the landscape? Had she ignored him, walked by him so many times that he felt like a piece of furniture or a row of ordinary perennials?

We sipped and nibbled almond cookies and talked about men having sex with their nannies, men being in love with their personal trainers, and widowed men marrying the nurses who cared for their wives. You put women in a house, and anything can happen. Or, obviously, a neighborhood. Or a workplace. It's all about proximity. Hillary discussed these things with a coldheartedness that bordered on psychopathy, considering what she'd been through personally. As if the world was simply built this way and no one had any personal responsibility.

I agreed with them on one point, however—that it was astonishing Ben didn't think anything of it and hadn't mentioned it to his wife. That he thought it was ordinary to have a hot chef on call for the boys' night. That it was like getting a haircut from a female hairdresser or a workout from a female trainer. Not worth noting. All in the course of a normal day. Such a non-event that he hadn't even given her a heads-up.

Of course, in the scheme of things, Hillary being annoyed about this seemed petty. It would be as if Hannah was upset with Miles for carrying a living kitten instead of a dead one. Pick your battles, ladies!

We were assembled to pool our knowledge and decide on a next step, so we only spent a few seconds shaking our heads over this. It probably didn't mean anything, I kept saying. Just a fascinating, annoying detail.

"Now if beautiful six-year-old girls had served the food, that would be important," I said.

"What about if Inge was friends with, say, Cat?" Hillary said. "Would that be important?"

"Is she?"

"I don't know. I'm just weaving shit together."

"Well, it still doesn't lead to a little girl. Just big girls. Don't most pedophiles want nothing to do with grown-ups? Isn't that the whole problem?"

"Well, Kendra is awfully pretty," Hillary said.

"So?" Hannah looked up sharply.

"Maybe someone was in love with her, and the girl got mixed up in that."

"No."

"No? You spend, like, five minutes with her and you suddenly know everything about her?"

Hannah's face reddened. "No."

"Well," I added, "she was a tad obsessed with her dog, remember? With the monograms and whatnot? That was a bit strange."

"Not really," Hannah said huffily. "Her daughter also loved animals. She was probably indulging her."

"Okay," I said, shrugging. "Possible."

"Look, anything is possible, okay?" Hillary said. "The kid took a lot of walks and saw a lot of things. She was nosy. Who knows what else she nosed into?"

"We know, Hillary," I said. "We have Kendra's ex on the background check list, remember?"

"And there's a second husband. Two exes."

"So what?" Hannah said. "I could have a second husband."

"Yes," I said. "Of course you could."

"Not if she goes to poker nights dressed like she's going skiing."

"Oh, come on! You want me to flirt with murderers now? Am I bait?"

"They're just dudes! You could have put in a little effort."

"I think your unbuttoned blouse did enough for both of us."

"Girls," I sighed.

"Some of them were handsome and single. That's all I'm saying," Hillary said. "Barrett, for example."

"Too tall," Hannah said.

"Too tall? In my day, there was no such thing as too tall," I said. "Unless he's an actual giant."

"He kind of is," Hannah replied.

"Look, I just want to remind some of us to have an open mind. Including this having nothing to do with poker night," Hillary said with a flourish. "We have to remember that."

Hannah and I exchanged glances. She knew that even though I was sure to include the women in our investigation, I believed poker night was too much of a coincidence to be a coincidence. So, too, did the police. It was poker night that had led them to Ben after all. Of course Hillary was right—anything was possible. But we all knew the odds were against it. Strangers from out of state don't stray from the highways and stop by wooded suburban neighborhoods where everyone knows everyone (unless you are Ben, who doesn't know last names) to hunt for victims. It simply does not happen. And I for one preferred believing that human men behaved worse when they were blind drunk. The idea that men could just be walking around thinking about murder when they were sober was more than I could bear. Didn't matter if it was true. We'd follow the police, we'd follow the trail of beer caps and poker chips.

Hannah showed me a list of the men. She'd identified five people who told her they'd been at the last poker night; there were stars by their names. The others she wasn't able to ask, so they were maybes. She'd tried to keep it all conversational. She hadn't gotten everyone's last name and profession; Ben could fill in the gaps, or they could look at the neighborhood association booklet. And Hillary knew everyone's wife, so they'd figure out more names like a small, satisfying puzzle.

Ben came down for coffee, rubbing his eyes like a little boy, still in pajama bottoms and slippers. People spent entire days dressed like that now, and I had trouble getting used to this. One day in Starbucks, I had been astonished to see the entire coffee line composed of yoga pants and pajama pants. No one, not a single person, was actually dressed in clothes.

Ben was very little help; even after a full cup of coffee, he couldn't remember precisely who'd been there at the last game, or how many. All he knew was that there'd been two tables, and there had been no new people there. So it must have been at least eight men, including Robert and Ben, all of whom were among the twelve regulars. But when he'd looked at the list at Hillary's insistence, in case it prodded anything, he came up with one new piece of information.

Barrett Smith*—tall, divorced, works from home, lives ?
Robert Barker*—host, retired, married
Brian Feester—married to Tara, rents above Susan's house
Sam Wainwright—married to Susan, works in IT, lives below
    Robert on Tamsen Creek Lane
Jason Kempner—single, lives on Partridge Lane
Matt*—thin, video company, rents carriage house from Jason
    on Partridge Lane
Matt Carruthers—stocky, works in sales, divorced, lives ?
Will Turner*—lives next door to Robert
James—black, married to Janine

"James," Ben said suddenly. James was not there that night because he was getting an award at his company. Insurance, he worked in insurance, Ben proclaimed. He was so proud of himself for remembering this.

The one thing that came out of his hangover blackout provided relief around the kitchen island. None of us wanted the only black man in the neighborhood to be a suspect. That was almost more than we could bear.

The two people who weren't in attendance, who were on the list of regulars, were Evan and Eli, twin brothers who didn't live in the neighborhood but used to, Ben thought. He didn't know their last names, but they drank IPA.

Again, Hannah and I exchanged an amused glance at this. Even Hillary had to admit this was funny. That her husband wasn't certain of anyone's last name or where they lived but he knew what they all drank!

It struck me as we struggled to assemble even basic information how much more we would have if poker night had been an all-female event. If the fictional reason for our subterfuge was actually true and the women were assembling, and a murder occurred the same night we were walking home drunk—well, every woman would know one another's names, addresses, professions. There would be a spreadsheet of addresses and phone numbers as well as the names of their spouses and children. It's simply the way it is. Women know these things. We know our neighbors and everything about them. Of course, if we weren't so paranoid and secretive, we could have merely asked Robert Barker for the list, as the police had. But no.

But half an hour later, comparing the neighborhood association list with the poker night list, we had all the last names and addresses. I was relieved we had more detail on the two men named Matt, since there were nine Matthews in the neighborhood association.

Hannah retyped the list into a spreadsheet in alphabetical order, filling in the addresses. Hillary downloaded a map and put graphic pins of their initials on the locations where the men lived and organized any photos we had along the side, keyed to their initials. I looked on in admiration.

"Huh," Hannah said.

"What's that?"

"Barrett Smith lives in the house behind me," she said.

"And you never met him or saw him?"

"No."

"Well, that's not unusual. Men are clueless."

"But he works from home," she said. "He's divorced. He's there all day."

"But he's busy."

"But he has a security camera facing my house."

"No."

"Yes, he gave police the footage. Then the other night, he shook my hand like he had no idea who I was."

"Well, he probably didn't, honey," I said. "He didn't necessarily see the tapes. He didn't know what they were looking for."

Hillary walked over to the French doors leading out onto her deck. She stared out them at the stand of trees, starting to shed their first leaves. Then, wordlessly, she went into the pantry and came out with the binoculars.

She put them up to her face, and we stood there watching her watch something. I saw her swallow, hard, before she turned.

"He has a camera pointing this way, too," she said.

"Well, you have them pointing in all directions," I said. "You either have a bunch of them, or you have none."

"Yes," she said. "True."

I turned around and looked at Hannah. Her lips were in a straight line, and one eye squinted the way it did when she was thinking about something.

"Hillary," she said quietly, "did the police mention having footage of your backyard?"

"No."

She walked over and took the binoculars from her sister.

"Right over the pool," she said.

208

forty-one

HANNAH

One of the things Hannah liked most about Ben—besides how sweet he'd always been with her son—was how nice he'd been to Mike. They were polar opposites in many ways, from the way they voted to the way they dressed, but Ben had always treated him as an equal, approached him on common ground. Hillary said Ben had cried when she told him about their divorce.

Hannah thought of the two brothers-in-law in the kitchen at Thanksgiving, taking turns carving the turkey, helping with the dishes, one washing, one drying. Like they'd known each other forever. A holiday would arrive, inevitably, the first one when Mike wouldn't be there. Hannah breathed deeply. Maybe she should invite him? Or he could come for dessert? She'd have to think about that. She didn't want to be a jerk, but she didn't want to send the wrong signal either.

Ben had an easy comfort with other men; she'd noticed that before, at parties. She supposed it came from being in a fraternity, then working in a male-dominated industry. She imagined it was the same way at poker night. He would be the one who would offer to get others a drink when he folded. Yet he didn't know everyone's last name. Hannah couldn't help smiling at this. The guy in sales? Matt? She bet he knew everyone's name and email address. Necessary for his job.

She imagined everyone who knew Ben having trouble believing he was guilty. She could picture a parade of character witnesses coming forward, and the first one would be her ex-husband, and the second one would be her son.

Over the past few weeks, Miles had asked her so many questions about his uncle's arrest she'd had trouble answering them simply, in a way he would understand but wouldn't worry. She was concerned this was his new obsession, all right, and it wasn't a sport or a video game. Over a month of school had gone by, and he hadn't brought home a single friend. That was all she needed this autumn, for Miles to start downloading true crime podcasts or listening to the police scanner.

She stood at her kitchen counter, looking over at her sister's house. On the porch, the oversize verdigris planters were autumnal now, mums and gourds and greens that looked appropriate without looking stagey or like anyone else's. Nothing that Hillary did was cliché or wrong or too much. And Hannah knew that while she had been busy working and trying to keep calm, Hillary had been doing projects like assembling those planters herself, on the potting table in her enormous mud room. Hillary simply had an eye for things. She had plenty of cameras, but she didn't really need them—she noticed everything. How had she not known her husband was having an affair? Or, as he had apparently corrected her, a fling. He'd downgraded it to nothing, to a word you'd use to throw a sock. The sisters had laughed about that, and it felt good to laugh about something.

How had Hillary, all eyes and ears and radar, missed this early on? Hillary, who'd seen her sister's separation and divorce looming almost a year before Hannah had admitted it to herself? Hillary, who'd asked Hannah if she was pregnant a week before Hannah had even bought the at-home test?

It seemed impossible, yet here they were. Here they were.

Hannah sipped her coffee, dreading the day of work ahead with the Philanthropist's manuscript. It was the most challenging project she'd ever taken on—and the most lucrative. Lesson learned. She closed her browsing windows and settled in, told herself she had to write a thousand words before she got up for more coffee or checked her email. At the two-hundred-word mark, she started to squirm. This "memoir" was going to be boring no matter what she did, and the sooner she accepted that, the better. She almost wished the detectives would step onto her porch, just to take her away from this tedium. She hadn't heard anything about the forensic testing of the fox or anything else the police had unearthed. But she imagined it wasn't a priority now. That it wouldn't even matter if, for instance, they found animals had been beaten or, who knows what—smothered? strangled? Could you strangle an animal? She shuddered. The idea of it, the picture in her head, was more than she could bear. She shook her head as if to erase it. No. She had to keep working. Some things she did not need to know.

She had made it to almost nine hundred words when she decided to check her email. *Just a small break*, she told herself. *Then I'll go back to it and type an extra hundred words.*

But there, in her email, finally, were the background checks of nearly eighty men who lived in the neighborhood. Hillary had paid for them; she'd want to be there to help look at them now, Hannah knew, but she had a doctor appointment in the city. Hannah looked at her watch— eleven forty-five. She couldn't help herself. Hillary wouldn't hesitate—if she were in Hannah's position, she'd open them all. She decided to open only the files from poker night and save the others for Hillary.

As she opened them one by one, she felt a strange sensation of guilt creeping up into her chest. As if she were reading someone's mail, going through their drawers. There were some secrets in here, and anyone with a credit card could find them out.

She already knew there were no registered sex offenders in the neighborhood, but she also knew the system worked slowly and was based on convictions. So someone arrested but not yet convicted was therefore not registered. That was the kind of nuance she was looking for. That and any violent crime against women. Domestic abuse, rape. That would be an obvious red flag. But she'd also wondered about some softer violations. Stalking. Voyeurism. Public urinating. Nudity. And yes, cruelty to animals. That kind of unusual arrest could mean something, too. At least it could to a woman, a mom, a person suspicious by nature.

She opened the files one by one. Three years ago, Robert Barker had pled guilty to a DUI. She wondered if that was why he hosted poker night, because he got so shit-faced he couldn't walk home? Clearly, she and her sister had left too soon, way too soon, to tell if what had happened the night of the disappearance happened every night: that the men drank so much they stumbled home. The men had been on their best behavior during their visit, but it had been early. Still, Robert Barker seemed harmless.

She kept opening files. Nothing, nothing, nothing. She should have felt a sense of relief, but the dread kept growing. She wanted to find something but didn't want to find something. Who wanted their neighbors to be criminals?

Matt Carruthers, the one in sales? He also had a DUI and an outstanding warrant for speeding tickets. Rushing to the liquor store? Forty miles over the limit? She made a mental note to find out what his car looked like so she could avoid him. She worked her way through alphabetically. Barker, Carruthers, Gilbert. Finally, she got to the *S*'s. Cat Saunders, nothing. Kendra Harris's ex-husband, Bill Sinclair, nothing.

Barrett Smith. Her neighbor behind the trees. Her tall, handsome neighbor she'd never seen. The one she certainly would have noticed. The man who worked from home just as she did. Someone she could have a coffee date with on any given day, compared productivity, commiserated. That was what two women working from home in the same neighborhood might do. But he kept to himself.

"That isn't a crime," she said out loud as she clicked on his file. Violation of restraining order. She blinked, took this in. Nearly a year ago. A different address, twenty or more miles west, judging from the zip code. Willistown Township. Released on probation. He was divorced, so she automatically assumed it was his wife filing the order. She knew the Main Line was a very small place; you could accidentally cross paths with someone you were supposed to avoid on any given Tuesday. Was that what had happened? An angry ex-wife, punishing him? Should she give him the benefit of the doubt? He'd seemed polite at poker night, but she hadn't spoken to him for very long.

She quickly opened the last two files—Will Turner. Sam Wainwright. Nothing and nothing.

So she was left with two car-related crimes—DUI and speeding. And one that may or may not be violence against someone who may or may not be a woman. Barrett Smith. Restraining order. Probation. And only a thin stand of trees between them.

She got off the computer and called her sister, who answered with cotton in her mouth, like those wisdom teeth videos Miles loved on YouTube.

"I've got the background checks," she said. "We need to talk."

"I'm on my way home," Hillary slurred.

"Great," Hannah said.

"And I have painkillers."

"Even better," she replied.

Hannah never drank and had exactly zero experience with drugs. Even in college, she'd turned away, knew they weren't right for her. The Sawyer girls had to be better than that to succeed. Maybe Hillary could have a glass of wine with her friends now and then and hang out and smoke pot at a book club, but not Hannah. No. But now? They both might need to be medicated just to find the nerve to continue.

Because Barrett Smith seemed polite and nice.

But he was also the size of a tree. And someone out there was afraid of him.

forty-two

EVA

Hillary's den became, for lack of a better term, our war room. That we would continue to assemble there was unsaid but understood. She had space. She had homemade food. She had money to buy whatever we needed. And we certainly couldn't do what we were doing in public.

She had corkboard tiles on one wall that used to be filled with Pinterest-worthy photos that "inspired" her. She'd taken all that down so we could pin some of the men's photos with their descriptions and put a map up with all their houses designated with color-coded pins. It quickly became clear that both my daughters could have had careers in law enforcement, such was their natural enthusiasm and ability toward this task.

"Wow," I said, surveying the wall with a maple scone in one hand. I took a bite of it, and it was so creamy it didn't even crumble. "This is impressive, girls. But do you think—should we add their wives, too? Along with Cat, Inge, and Anya?"

"Why?"

"Well, women can be part of a man's motive or alibi, don't you think?"

"Well, of course. But, Mom, what are you thinking, though? Precisely? Do you have a theory?"

"No. Nothing. Just making the observation that women are also awful."

Hannah shot me a very specific look. She was chewing on the tip of a pencil in a way she'd done since she was a little girl. I used to worry about her teeth, the way she chewed on pencils. I called her my little beaver until the girls found out the alternative meaning and insisted that I stop. A month or so ago, I picked up her reading glasses in error, and the ends of them were chewed to bits, too. Some things don't change.

"Mom, spill."

I walked to the door, closed it.

"Well," I said, "the men were drunk and don't remember going home. That sounds like a group excuse. Like they devised it and agreed to it."

"Mom," Hillary said, "are you saying Ben is lying?"

"Not exactly. Several of them could be telling the truth, and the rest of them could be lying. It's a convenient excuse, and it protects them all. Bandwagon excuse, that's what I'm saying."

"Okay, so?"

"So the men were drunk, but the women were at home, stone-cold sober. Some of them are probably protecting their men. Or they might have seen or heard something that's important, and they don't even know it."

Hannah reluctantly agreed this could be useful and started searching Facebook and Instagram, combing through friends lists, printing out the wives.

"But," Hillary said, "by the same token, anyone in the house could know something. Kids. Live-in nannies."

"Are there live-in nannies in the neighborhood?"

"Of course there are. So where does it end? Do we have to consider everyone in the poker dudes' houses?"

"Maybe," I said. "Start with the men, but don't discount the others."

Ben helped us pull in a long table from the basement, and we put it in front of the corkboard wall and spread out our laptops and papers.

We grilled him about Barrett Smith, but he wasn't much help.

"The guy never talks," he said.

"That's suspicious right there," Hillary said.

"A man not talking? I believe that's rather normal," I said.

"No, I mean, he doesn't even say hello. He waves or nods. Sometimes he opens his mouth as if he's saying the word 'hi,' but no sound comes out."

"He spoke to me though," Hannah said.

"A, you're a woman. B, you probably asked him a direct question."

"Yes."

"So answering a question isn't the same as talking."

Ben was a garrulous man, it was true, and so was Robert Barker. Based on Hannah's notes, thin Matt was also extremely friendly and talkative, and so was James, but he had not been at the poker night in question. He'd been out of town at a dinner, getting an award.

"Why don't you try to get the chatty ones to tell you more about the quiet ones?" I said suddenly. "They probably spent hours trying to draw them out, asking them questions. So they know some answers."

"Well, if that were true," Hillary said, "then Ben would know more."

"Well, are there any talkative ones who don't drink themselves into oblivion the day before their daughter comes home from camp?"

"Ouch," Ben said.

"You deserve it," Hillary said. "You're lucky any of us still speak to you."

The tension in the room with those two sometimes just shifted into ice. It was as if everything was fine until Hillary suddenly remembered what he'd done, and she lashed out.

He cleared his throat and said he had some yard work to do. Hillary agreed. There was plenty of yard work to do. *Go do it.* It was another awkward moment, and I couldn't help thinking we could have avoided it by collaborating at Hannah's. But then I took another bite of scone and changed my mind.

We all agreed to focus on Barrett and Matt Carruthers. We all felt a need to find out the circumstances of the restraining order and the DUI. First things first.

"Well, both of them are divorced and live alone, so my theory of including the women is not helpful," I sighed.

"Wrong," Hillary said. "The ex-wives could prove helpful for sure. Especially if there are no kids involved and they have nothing at stake for retribution."

She opened the window and called out to Ben, inquiring about children. He seemed both surprised and grateful to be summoned back. No kids, he said, shaking his head. Hillary asked if he was sure, and he said yes. It had been an issue in both marriages. Matt's wife was infertile, and Barrett's wanted kids but he didn't.

"I thought you said Barrett didn't talk."

"Well, he isn't completely mute."

"When we asked you in the beginning, you didn't know their last names, and now you're telling me he told you he didn't want kids? That seems pretty intimate."

"It came up somehow."

"How?"

"I don't know."

Hillary sighed, cranked the window shut, and sat back down without thanking him. I couldn't blame her, really, for being angry, but she had to soften. If she wanted to save her family, she'd have to do more than keep Ben out of prison. She couldn't save him from one cage only to put him in another. She would have to forgive him. Surely, she knew this. Surely, she planned to, just as soon as she was done punishing him?

We stared at the men's photos up on the corkboard as if they would suddenly come alive and reveal themselves. Their ages leapt out at me suddenly. Stocky Matt was only twenty-eight. Plenty of time for children. Maybe he wasn't ready. But Barrett Smith was thirty-seven years old. I felt a chill sweep across my arms suddenly.

"Hannah," I said, "when the police told you about the footage of your house, what did they say?"

"They said they'd asked for surveillance footage from all the houses."

"Is that true?"

"Well, they asked if I had any," Hannah said.

"But you clearly don't. Anyone can see that."

"But they asked Hillary, too."

"Yes, but did they, in fact, ask everyone?"

My daughters blinked, looked at each other.

"I mean, that's something we can ask the wives, right? That's something we can know by the end of the day."

"Mom, what is your point?"

"My point is, maybe Barrett Smith *offered* the footage."

"To protect himself?" Hannah said quietly. "Because he had a police record."

"No, just to be a good citizen," I smiled. "Just to have an excuse to go talk to the police because he likes to talk so very much."

forty-three

HANNAH

She woke just before dawn, as she often did. Still dark, but there it was again, the familiar streaks of pinky-orange just beginning to spread across the sky. She looked out the front window as if she could watch the color grow, see the light as it changed, like watching someone paint. Already she knew how the sky looked in the neighborhood depending on the time of day, the angles, the colors, what she could count on. But every week, it would shift now, depending on which trees had started releasing their leaves.

Liza Harris's house had been shrouded when she first moved in. And every day, it revealed a bit more of its stone contours as the bright maples shed their leaves and the oaks stood firm, toasty leaves wrinkled but clinging, refusing to drop. *Marcescence*, she thought suddenly. One of those words on her high school list of words that she wanted to use. *Well, there you have it*, she thought. *Cross one thing off.*

Now, if she wanted to, she could count the glossy gray shutters, the black framed windows, the lights that blinked on and off on timers. Now she could see the expanse of the heavy front door, twice as big as Hannah's, painted a color somewhere between black and brown, with copper planters flanking it. Black, brown, gray, rust. Colors that weren't colors at all. She found herself hoping Liza's room was brighter, neon pink, purple, something. As if it mattered anymore.

The spruces and firs that ringed the property stood green and firm as a fence. They looked wrong now without other leaves around to soften them, out of place, as if they were just waiting for their season, for snow.

Hannah was more attached to what was outside her new house than what was inside, she realized with a start. Would that change in time? Would she become more affectionate toward the creaky wide-plank floors of the kitchen and living room? The pale paint that changed depending on the light, the way her fiddle fern stood sentry against one window? Or would she always look around and see what she could or should do—change the backsplash to something brighter. Buy curtains instead of cheap blinds. She imagined her sister in her big house. Did she think of Hannah as just being on her property, convenient, in an outbuilding down the hill? She shivered, thinking of the term *servants' quarters*. Had she been put in her place? And she wondered, for all of Hillary's decorating prowess and money, if she was ever satisfied in her own home. If she spent mornings restless, unattached as well. Was this just how the Sawyers were, always searching for more, never quite settled?

She heard it before she saw it. A rustle, the sound of a flag or windsock. She stepped out onto the porch, thinking it was a flyer or paper lifting in the wind.

On one of the Adirondack chairs, tethered with a bungee cord, was a plastic suit bag. Inside, two different Halloween costumes. Mike must have dropped them off—Miles had probably told her, but she'd forgotten. The costume on top was a pilgrim, which made her smile. Wholesome. Sweet. When your son is named Miles, why not be a pilgrim every year?

But underneath, another brown felt get-up, more elaborate. Fur cuffs. Fur hood. An animal. A fox?

Jesus fucking Christ, Mike, she wanted to scream. Hadn't it been costumes almost exactly like this on those boys last Halloween that had sent Miles into despair? Had Mike forgotten that awful week, his refusal to go to school, the search for the therapist, the phone calls to the other parents seeking apologies for something they couldn't even articulate or name? *They ganged up against him. They all dressed as animals to taunt him. They called him Fur Baby.*

But then she stopped. Maybe the costumes weren't Mike's idea. Maybe they were Miles's? She took them out of the bag and looked more closely. The fox costume was half the size of the other one.

Of course, she thought. *It must be for Morgan. Miles must have asked him for both of them.*

Still, she thought as her heart settled and she went inside, made the coffee. Whose idea had that been? She said a small prayer that it had been Morgan's, trying to connect with her cousin, and not the other way around.

forty-four

EVA

I didn't set out to interfere. I really didn't. I was simply minding my own business, picking up groceries, when the *Action News* van passed me, heading in the direction of Tamsen Creek.

So I threw the grocery bag in my car and followed them. Why wouldn't I? I was hopeful of adventure involving someone who wasn't in my family. I wanted to revel in someone else's drama. And if that something happened to break the case open, that this Barrett person was barricaded in his house, a police standoff, something, some action to live up to their name, well, so much the better. I could tell the whole story to my daughters and the kids, and they'd hang on every word.

When the van turned on Brindle Lane, I had a brief surge of joy. Until I saw two other vans, all camped outside Hillary's house. *Eyewitness News* was there. *News Night* was there. I felt deflated as I parked in front of the line of vans. Had something happened with my girls or the kids and they hadn't told me yet?

No, it was actually worse. That woman Susan, who was in the girls' book club, was giving an interview. She had on a blazer and a scarf with her black jeans, and her hair fell in waves to her shoulders in a way I knew took hours to prepare, because I'd seen Morgan try to replicate the same style. Holding on to the microphone with her manicured nails, she claimed to be a "close friend" of Hillary's. Emphasizing how she and her husband had been so shocked about Ben's arrest, and it had reverberated through the neighborhood.

"Unfortunately, they're no longer welcome at our book club or our poker night," she said. "We have to put the safety of our children first."

I waited patiently until this idiot was done and thought perhaps someone should step up and take her down a notch. I went up to the reporter, a young woman wearing so much makeup it looked like it hurt to smile, and asked her if she wanted an exclusive. A scoop.

"A scoop?" she said, as if she didn't know the term.

"New information no one else has?"

"Are you a neighbor?"

"No, I'm their mother."

"Wait, what? You're Mrs. Sawyer?" She looked at her notes. "Eva Sawyer?"

"Indeed I am."

"Are you willing to go on the record?"

"Of course," I said, straightening my own handknit scarf and smoothing my cotton tunic dress. This woman was dressed up in that silly way news people are, stretchy dresses and high heels that look fine on camera but ridiculous on the street, where they just had to run after people who didn't want to talk. Oh, I'm being too cynical now. They were occasionally doing important work, not just waiting to prey on people like they were now. I could see the inside of their van was littered with coffee cups and bakery wrappers and socks. As if they were living in it, and I suppose, for part of their day, they were. Nothing glamorous about this work except for the false eyelashes and lipstick.

The girl who pointed a microphone in my face was exactly that, a girl. I could see now, in the daylight, that it was only the clothes and makeup spackled on, a spit coat, making her look older. She was so slender and small and smooth skinned she could have been in high school.

"I'm Becca Campion, and *Eyewitness News* is in Radnor Township, covering the Liza Harris murder investigation. With us is Eva Sawyer, mother-in-law to Ben Mattock, who is out on bail for the crime."

I confess, I was surprised by the rapidity and force of her sentences. I hadn't expected her to be good at her job.

She turned the microphone over to me.

"Mrs. Sawyer, do you have new information to share about the case?"

"Yes," I said. "Some initial investigations have turned up some interesting things about the neighborhood."

"Can you elaborate?"

"The police seem to have overlooked the neighborhood poker night where drunk, married men are serviced by younger women unbeknownst to their wives and girlfriends."

"Are you suggesting—"

"Oh, I'm not suggesting. I'm flat out telling you. Susan's husband is one of the poker night regulars. He could maybe tell us all about Inge. She's supposedly a personal trainer. Such an interesting label, that. But I think you'd have a more interesting story talking to her. Because if the Tamsen Creek poker night boys are hiding Inge, who knows what else they are hiding."

I tried to stifle a smile as I walked back to my car and they called behind me with follow-up questions and requests for my phone number. As I pulled away, they followed after me, microphone pointed toward my windows, Becca in her high heels, followed by her cameraman. Chasing me as if to justify they did their job. They didn't follow me, though. They didn't do anything but pretend to. But they don't show that on TV.

Still, it's always good to leave people wanting more, I thought. *And maybe spur them to do a little digging for us instead of against us.*

And if the phrase *Tamsen Creek poker night boys* became a GIF or a meme or whatever the heck those things are, well, wouldn't that make Miles proud of his grandma? I smiled, thinking of my own graphic design, what I would do if I knew how. Animated wolves sitting around a poker table, being served by Little Red Riding Hood.

That was a far more interesting story, surely, than my two girls trying to do the most natural thing in the world: save their own.

forty-five

HANNAH

Hannah needed a break. She stood up from her computer, stretched her arms overhead, walked circles around her living room. Another person would set up a yoga mat and do some exercises, then finish her work and start on her investigative tasks. That was probably what Hillary would do. But for the last few days, she'd felt trapped in her house, like it was too weather tight. Like she wasn't getting enough air. Her own house, the house she'd longed for and chosen, was strangling her now.

She'd promised Hillary she'd make half the neighborhood phone calls, as soon as she finished her pages for the Philanthropist, but she couldn't concentrate.

It was the fall festival that night, and she'd already let down the whole neighborhood apparently by telling Susan that she had not procured the ingredients for a "signature fall cocktail" but had bought tequila and lime juice. The disappointment in Susan's voice came through even over text. Oh, but we always do something original! Otherwise everyone will be stuck with the IPA the guys brewed in their garage! Oh well, you're probably not attending, right? Because of Ben being arrested and all, but we were still counting on you two to be creative. We still need your contribution!

Oh, could this woman be any more annoying? Why didn't she just say *We don't want you, just your fancy expensive cocktails?* Like they didn't all have more important things to do, like saving the neighborhood from a murderer, when there were cocktails to be designed.

But people love tequila, she'd texted back.

It's fine as a base, Susan texted. But you need a twist!

Okay, I'll think of something, Hannah sent, then added Hillary has glow-in-the-dark napkins. Susan squealed with delight over this, with a string of shocked-face emojis.

Hannah would have to get Hillary to think of the twist. She didn't know anything about cocktails. She probably needed an herb or strawberries frozen in ice cubes, something. Maybe there was a poisonous herb to slip into Susan's.

The last thing Hannah wanted to do was worry over this stupid, inane task.

Ever since she'd learned where Barrett Smith lived, she'd had trouble sleeping. She imagined him seeing right through the walls of their houses, knowing what they were doing, breaking into their war room and killing them all. Quietly. Without a word. She now understood why people didn't take justice into their own hands; there weren't enough security systems and guns in the world to make the average citizen feel safer than a police force. Ben had run out to the hardware store and installed a simple alarm system for her, and she and Hillary had emailed all the women in the neighborhood to gauge their interest about a female poker night, keeping up the subterfuge so no one suspected them, but still. Still.

They were going to be asking questions. After Eva's absurd performance on *Eyewitness News*, the vans trolled by several times a day, as if hoping to catch one of them outside. Robert Barker had called Hillary and moped about this betrayal, stating that Inge and Anya were completely innocent and were friendly with his wife, for God's sake. Hillary had played dumb and blamed her mother for being unhinged, for having old-fashioned views. She'd even gone so far as to use the word *senile*, she'd told Hannah. They did what they had to do, because they still needed people's help. And as soon as you rippled out to others, you were in danger of getting caught. Hannah had even thought about sending Miles to Mike's house for a week or so but then told herself she was being silly on every level. First of all, he was so excited about the fall festival. And when she was thinking clearly, she knew that if Barrett Smith was involved, wouldn't he be crazy to hurt either of the two main suspects? No, she was being illogical.

Still, when she texted Kendra to see if she was open to taking a walk somewhere else, anywhere else, she was surprised when Kendra told her she was in California and would be staying there, probably until Thanksgiving. She said she couldn't handle the fall festival this year. Hannah was about to wish her an early happy holiday when she stopped, her thumbs hovering about the screen, then adding:

> Can I ask you something?
> **Of course.**
> Did the police ask you for surveillance footage?
> **Yes.**
> Do you know if they asked your neighbors?
> **No.**
> No, you don't know?
> **No, they didn't.**
> Are you sure?
> **Yes. Why?**
> It might be nothing.
> **But it might be something?**
> Yes.
> **You'll let me know?**
> Yes.
> **Text me anytime, Hannah.**
> I will. And, Kendra, please don't tell anyone I mentioned this until I know more?
> **I promise.**

Well, she thought, if you can't believe the word of a grieving mother, who can you believe? She locked the doors, set the alarm, then drove herself to the path at Haverford College. She walked a mile and a half loop in the cold damp air, missing the trees of her neighborhood but enjoying the anonymity. The college students laughing and looking at their phones while they walked. The retired people swinging their arms, wearing their Fitbits and Apple watches. *Everyone walks now*, she thought to herself. It used to be a way to get away from the world, but now the world was walking.

After she finished, she went to her car, wiped her face with a napkin, and grabbed her laptop from the trunk. She walked down the street to a coffee shop and plopped down among the students and freelance workers. All people from another neighborhood at least. Thank God. She had the same sensation she sometimes felt at out-of-town shopping malls—the comfort of all these people, none of whom knew her or recognized her.

The buzz of the restaurant provided just the right amount of white noise, and she hunkered down and finished her chapters, then went back to her car. She was running behind; the walk had taken up too much time. Miles would be home soon, and she couldn't make those calls around him. She'd have to go to Hillary's and shut herself away. Then she'd have to explain why she was running late. Hillary would have all her work done, she was sure. Then she'd have more ideas, and Hannah would get pulled into doing more, and she was tired. This was important, but she was tired.

She pulled out the list in her messenger bag and decided to just make two calls quickly from her cell phone before she went home. That way, she could report some progress to her sister.

That morning, she'd found a phone number listed for Barrett Smith in Willistown Township. She assumed it was where his ex-wife lived and that if she hadn't disconnected her landline, maybe she could still reach her. Otherwise, with a last name like Smith and no first name, they might have a hell of a time finding this woman they hoped would rat out her ex. Unless they had a marriage license in the county, or if they could find someone at Barrett's office who knew. It struck Hannah as an awful lot of work for what could be a useless dead end. She was much more interested in her mother's theory about the surveillance footage.

Still, she made the call. As it rang, she practiced her spiel in her head.

When the woman picked up, Hannah almost couldn't contain her surprise.

"Mrs. Smith?"

"Yes?"

"This is Karen from the county commissioner's office. We're just following up on the order of protection filed last year?"

"What?"

"The order of protection? Just a follow-up call to make sure there have been no issues after the first violation?"

She'd practiced the script, but still, even she was surprised with the ease of the words as they came. How simple it was to lie when you set your mind to it.

"I have no idea. You'd have to talk to—I'm not married to him anymore. We're divorced."

"I realize that, but—"

"So I have no idea if he's in compliance with that or not."

It hit her not like a ton of bricks but like one actual brick. *The restraining order was not taken out by his wife.*

"So I should follow up with…I'm sorry, the paperwork is…uh… smudged…"

"Alathia's mother. I can't remember her first name. But I'm sure the school would call you if there was another issue."

"The school," Hannah repeated. She swallowed carefully, trying to frame another question. Did she dare?

"Wait," the woman said. "Who did you say you were again?"

"Thank you for your help, Mrs. Smith," she said breathlessly, then hung up. Part of her was elated, and part of her couldn't breathe. Alathia. A school. A child. And part of her was furious. She had no last name. And no school name. Just Alathia. Fuck!

Hannah called her sister from the car. *All hands on deck. New information.* They would gather at Hillary's while Miles and Morgan did their homework upstairs. They'd been promised if they did their homework and behaved, they could go to the festival later and stay up late.

Hannah had gotten skittish ever since they'd started talking about

Barrett Smith, and now, she was terrified. Hillary, as usual, was the calm one. Was Hillary afraid of anything? her sister wondered.

As they started to assemble their plan, Hannah said that this was how people who lived near registered offenders felt every day. Always on the lookout. Never a chance to rest. Hillary googled the unusual name of Alathia plus Willistown Township while trying to remember if they knew anyone who knew someone there who might have a school directory. It shouldn't be too hard to find a girl named Alathia, she said.

"Wait a minute," Hillary said. "What difference does it make?"

"What difference does it make?"

"Yes. We already know it happened. We already know there's an incident involving a child. The police could find out who she is in a heartbeat. If they wanted to know. If they cared. My point is, we already know this is a red flag. We don't need more information to make it more of one. So focus elsewhere."

"Like where?"

"Like what Mom said. If our neighbors were asked for their footage or not. If he offered his footage *and* he has a secret, then you should go to the police. That's all you need. As nerve-racking and as exciting as this is, you don't need to know the name of the girl Barrett was bothering."

Hannah's face froze, her eyes focused on something over her sister's shoulder.

"What?" Hillary said.

She turned. The door had swung open a foot or so, and Miles, skinny, narrow Miles, stood in the wedge of light. He swallowed and hung his mouth open a second before he spoke.

"Can...um...can we have more cookies, Aunt Hillary?" he said.

forty-six

EVA

Margot's calls were always a bit thrilling to me. She knew this; I knew this. She never called to check in, to wish me a happy whatever, no small talk, no nothing. Unless she had something useful to say, I never heard from her.

So when she rang me before I went to Hillary's and said, "Are you ready?" that silly, classic opening line that preceded something she knew I would love to hear, I simply sighed and said yes, as I always did.

"Are you sure?"

"Yes, Margot," I laughed. I was always ready. I was always sure. Why did she persist with this odd tag of hers? Maybe this little peculiarity was why she wasn't married.

"So the property behind Hannah's? Two years ago, the owner considered subdividing a half acre. Talked to a contractor about putting up a cottage."

"Really?"

"Yes, ma'am. Sounds like he didn't want to take on the investment of building at the time, but…"

"Maybe he'd sell the half acre," I said.

"That's what I'm thinking."

"Let me ponder this," I said.

But what I thought was, let me go over and eyeball that property. And while I was at it? Maybe I could snoop around and make myself useful for a change instead of just baking cookies and riding shotgun.

Terrible phrase, isn't that?

forty-seven

EVA

I'm not going to say that I knew my grandson well enough to know something was wrong. I certainly didn't understand all his peccadilloes and quirks. But I know a fair amount about people and children in general, and when I got to Hillary's after swinging by Barrett Smith's property, I believe I saw something in Miles's face when he answered the door. Something that haunted him.

Hannah and Hillary had made a yeoman's effort to keep the door closed when we were in our war room and locked when we were not. They did not want their children dragged into the drama around their uncle and father, and they certainly didn't want to scare them about bad men in their neighborhood.

I hadn't seen anything out of place when I'd peeked into Barrett Smith's front and side windows. No weapons, no pornography, and no innocent things that could be deadly, like shovels, duct tape, rope. I knew there were cameras in the back, but I saw none in the front, so I was emboldened to look in anywhere my little eyes could reach. His house was orderly and neat and clean, too, with vacuumed rows in his area rugs, and he didn't appear to be home. I tried the door, just in case he was foolish enough to leave it open, but it was locked. Still, I took some pictures of his land from the street. I had my eye on the parcel to the northeast of his house, tucked into a corner of the woods, catty-corner to Hannah's. On the opposite side of his garage and pool. Perfect, I thought. Far from him, but with just enough shade, just enough sun. I'd have to report back to Margot in the morning.

By the time I arrived at Hillary's, I figured Miles was probably on his umpteenth cookie. He'd opened the door with one hanging out of his mouth like a dog, probably throwing crumbs everywhere.

The girls came out of the war room, and we sat around the kitchen island talking about who would make what for Thanksgiving, like it was just another day. Just an ordinary family planning the holidays. But Miles seemed quieter than usual. He only ate one additional cookie. When I asked him if he knew yet what he was going to be for Halloween, he shrugged as he picked up cookie crumbs with his thumb. He wanted another one but didn't ask. The last time I'd been with him, he had eaten six cookies. And yes, I'd let him. Sue me. He weighed ninety pounds soaking wet.

The girls had decided to use the fall festival to their advantage. Nearly everyone would be outside, walking along the torches set up along the street. They could try to sidle up to their neighbors over cocktails and pretend they cared about the pumpkin carving contest or the bluesy duo playing guitar to an audience sitting on hay bales at the top of the street. I was of course persona non grata among many of them after my stunt telling on their hubbies and their poker night. Some of the bitchiest women from book club were certainly gossiping and speculating about Hillary and Ben now, but maybe, just maybe, they would be fine talking to Hannah. Now that Miles seemed innocent and Ben seemed guilty. They could try at least. They could ask the women, grown chatty after their signature cocktails, about surveillance footage, maybe allude to new information and a new suspect to get their imaginations going. And they could leave Ben at home with the kids until they were done eating, till their homework was done, and they were ready to come out and walk around for dessert. The girls could finish their interviews, meet the kids, bring them out for caramel apples or whatever.

And in that moment, when they were getting dressed and heading out, which should have been my cue to go home and leave them to it, something in me said I should stay, too. That something was in my grandson's eyes, not my granddaughter's. Morgan, it seemed, was far more inscrutable, like her mother.

"I'll make dinner for everyone," I said valiantly. "So you won't have to rely on whatever junk they have at the festival. How about chili?"

Hillary shrugged and Hannah smiled and Ben said it sounded good, and that was that. Chili. Easy. Hillary had everything in her fridge and pantry. I could do it in my sleep. The girls went out on their mission. I bided my time. I browned everything, even the spices. I roasted the peppers over the indoor gas grill. I waited.

Ben was upstairs, the kids downstairs. And then finally, Miles was in the kitchen.

"Grandma," he said.

"Yes? Did you come for a taste?"

"Not really."

"Try it anyway."

I held out a spoon. He nodded.

"More salt?"

"Maybe."

"A maybe is a yes," I said. "When it comes to salt anyway. So, another cookie? Is that what you came for?"

"No."

He rubbed one hand over his upper lip as if hunting for the mustache he'd have someday.

"Grandma," he said, lowering his voice, "is it okay to tell someone's secret sometimes?"

Another woman's heart might have stopped right then, but I'd already raised two children. And I was there, standing in front of a stove so complex I barely understood how to turn it on, precisely because I expected him to say something remarkably like this. I knew something was wrong!

"Yes," I said calmly. "If there's a good reason."

"Like if it hurts more people to keep it quiet than it does to tell it? Even if the person whose secret it is doesn't know it?"

This was quite a sentence to unpack, as the kids say, but I got the gist.

"Yes. That's what's known as mitigating circumstances. That's a great vocabulary word, by the way, mitigating."

"Well, I might be wrong, but…um…I heard you talking before. In the den? And Barrett is a pretty unusual name, don't you think?"

I put down my wooden spoon and reached for the red chiles. I wanted, more than anything, to look at him, but I had the strong sense that he would tell me more if I just kept doing what I was doing. I sliced the chiles in tiny, slim little circles, just as Hillary did.

"In my experience, yes, yes it is."

"Well, so, there's a guy named Barrett who is kinda friends with Morgan."

"Is there? Well, I know you want to be helpful, but the person we were talking about, sweetheart, is a man though. Not a boy."

"I know."

At that point, I couldn't help myself. I turned from the stove.

"Miles, are you saying—"

"Yes," he said, lowering his voice even further. "Her friend is a man, too."

All this education. All these talks from concerned mother to responsible child. Where had it gone? When had they forgotten that adults aren't friends with children? That the world, when it's properly fastened, doesn't work that way?

Before I could respond, he started to tell me that night when he and Morgan had gone out to the path? And found the kittens? She'd been upset about him. He'd been mean to her. He'd threatened her.

I held up my hand. "Miles, has this man…hurt her? Has he—"

"No, he's just…well, he used to be nice, and now he's mean, and she was upset."

"Nice…how?" My heart was indeed perilously near my throat at that point. You don't fully understand that expression until something terrible is on the line.

"He gave her presents," he said.

I took a deep breath. Oh, he had no idea. He had no idea, and neither did Morgan of course, how these things could connect. I felt terrible for both of them then, but especially for Morgan. That it had never occurred to her to connect the dots. That one thing could mean another. I thought of the ribbon, that wide plaid ribbon, too nice to throw out, recycled in Hillary's gift closet down the hall from where we were standing. Good, responsible Morgan, who knew she should always save the prettiest ribbon and gift bags, to not put them in the landfill. Sweet, adorable Morgan, who perhaps wanted it to put in her hair during spirit days.

Oh, Morgan, I thought. *The therapy you are going to need!*

I told Miles to stir the chili. Then I went outside to the patio. Above me, the band's voices from the fall festival were harmonizing but each distinct. Two beautiful voices, one male, one female, singing about weather, singing about sky, singing about coming home. Laughter and conversations from up and down the street broke over an occasional soaring word, and I wanted to scream at these people to listen, to be quiet. *For once, everyone just hear what is in the air.*

I took a deep breath and made the phone call.

Not to his mother. To the police.

forty-eight

HANNAH

For just a moment, Hannah walked slowly behind her sister, taking in the beauty of Brindle Lane, lit by lanterns in the trees, luminaria on the ground, and pumpkins grinning on tables, fenceposts, and the wide arms of Adirondack chairs lining the path. At intervals along the way, there were pale yellow banners that said FALL FESTIVAL in small orange block letters bridging the trees. Their neighbors had planned every bit of it, pitched in, carried, lifted, assembled. For years, she'd idealized this neighborhood, fetishized it, and nights like this one could almost convince her she'd been right. Hillary stopped and turned back, motioned for Hannah to hurry up, and she was brought back into reality. Not a glowing star of a neighborhood at all but a dark one now, dented, stained. And they had to dig into the tender parts to figure it all out.

The music floated down from the small gazebo at the top of the street, lit by a hazy harvest moon peeking out from the fog and trees. Two singers, both playing guitars. They couldn't have picked a better evening, Hannah thought. Under other circumstances, Hannah would have loved to sit and listen and just relax. But no one was sitting on the hay bales set up around the singers; everyone was mingling and talking, and they had to get to work.

Logic told Hannah to concentrate on speaking to the women who lived on the west side of the street. After all, it would make sense that the cops would ask anyone on the creek side for footage; the girl had been walking there and found there, on the east side, not the west. However, if no other homes on their side of Brindle Lane had been targeted, that would mean something. That would bolster their case about how the police had obtained Barrett Smith's footage. Barrett Smith's house address wasn't even on their street; his front door faced the opposite way, onto Brigham's Ford Road.

But the festival wasn't organized by address. People didn't congregate near their houses, and they weren't wearing name tags. It would take a fair amount of mingling and neighborliness to accomplish anything in this environment without her sister's guidance.

There were a series of tables (or stations, as Hillary kept referring to them) up and down the street, and they'd have to move through them one by one, identifying the right people at each.

There were cocktails, of course. Hillary had immediately added cranberry juice and a cinnamon rim to Hannah's tequila, which had delighted Susan, who had hugged them and pretended everything was perfectly fine with them and that she hadn't kicked them both out of book club. There was home-brewed beer, hors d'oeuvres, pumpkin carving, a make-your-own-scarecrow game similar to pin the tail on the donkey, a used Halloween costume swap table, and a mini pumpkin pie station with four flavors of whipped cream.

Most people stood near the cocktails, ignoring everything else. If it hadn't been for Hillary identifying the women and pointing out who to speak to, trying to do this the night of the fall festival would have been madness. So much easier to just ring doorbells, Hannah thought. But Hillary had said this would feel more natural, more low-key. It would feel more like making conversation and less like interrogating their neighbors.

As it grew dark and they wove up and down the street, Hannah thought of Liza wandering between neighbors' houses. The map of her world, one where she thought she knew the borders and the terrain. The things she saw when no one knew she was there, hiding in the slipstream. The stories she carried in her little head. She was lonely, Hannah knew. Searching for frogs and worms. No children at her party, no father at her house. This neighborhood that seemed so friendly and inclusive with its poker nights and book clubs and fall festivals didn't include everyone and couldn't include everyone. Someone was always in the margins.

Hillary wandered around the stations, sampling foods, remarking over the pumpkins, making the smallest of awkward small talk with whoever was nearby, while Hannah asked the real questions. They'd agreed it would look better that way, less self-serving. No one wanted to shun Hillary outright—they were all raised better than that—but on the other hand, no one felt comfortable talking about the case with the prime suspect's wife. They weren't quite that two-faced.

Hannah had her spiel down pat, saying *It was such a nice neighborhood, and she was so happy to be there, but it was a shame about all the police in their quiet little hamlet, all the visits, and the requests for footage! Did that happen to them, too? Or just the ones close to the Harrises?*

The first four neighbors she spoke to told her they had front-door cameras pointing straight down to the gully, just as Hillary did. And no detective had asked to look at their footage.

"You're certain of this?" she said to all of them, and one by one, they said yes. One even said it was a good thing they hadn't, because she couldn't remember the password to her security system anyway.

Hannah walked back and reported this all with a shake of her head to Hillary. And all the while, trying to keep her eyes open, searching always not just for the women but for where the men were. She had glimpsed almost all the guys from poker night except the two Matts and Barrett Smith, who wasn't at the beer station, who wasn't at the pumpkins, who wasn't anywhere. He was tall enough that she knew she could spot him anywhere. Barrett Smith who had maybe, just maybe, tried to frame an innocent boy.

They walked all the way to the top of the street, where the musicians were playing. Looking back down the street, from this vantage point, it looked like the world's smallest but best-lit street fair. The warm orange glow of torches, pumpkins, candles. The distinct smell of singed pumpkin and melted beeswax you only get once a year. The people holding children with one hand and Solo cups in the other, the frosty breath of their laughter rising up, gray mist in the dark sky. The hay bales set out for the music audience were empty except for one couple, who listened and held hands. Hannah was pretty sure these were the newlyweds on their list, the millennial couple who'd just bought the house five houses up from Hillary, but as she was about to approach them, a siren started up in the distance. As it grew louder and syncopated, two sirens, three, it came closer, and the rumble made Hannah's bones vibrate up from the blacktop. *The earth is moving*, she thought. *The earth is moving beneath my feet.* She glanced down at her sister, lingering near the farthest bale.

"It's just a coincidence," Hillary said. She sounded precisely like their mother in that moment, and Hannah wondered how she'd never noticed this. Their shared tendency to say everything was okay when it was clearly, definitely not.

When an ambulance turned onto their street, though, they were in sync again. Their heads both swiveled, and they broke into a run at the same time, although, Hannah was certain, it was for different reasons.

That neither of them was right would not prove to be much consolation.

forty-nine

EVA

They remembered me, I'll give them that much. I wasn't invisible. I had a name and a role and a place in their memory after all. And they listened. And they agreed. Both of them on speaker phone, talking to me. I could picture them nodding their heads, exchanging glances with each other as I told them.

Yes, it was significant information. Yes, my grandchildren had to be interviewed. Yes, they would take steps with Barrett Smith. But the sticking point was when I insisted on subterfuge. That the reason for it had to come from them. Not Miles. Not me. Anything less and they'd tear our little family apart further. This has to be in confidence, I said. Pretend I'm an anonymous tipster, I said. What do you expect us to do, they asked.

I stood in the night air, shifting from foot to foot, trying to stay warm in my clogs and down vest. I was tempted to brainstorm, but wasn't that their job?

Finally, I simply said, "You'll have to cook something up. Say you found something."

"Despite what you may think, ma'am, the police are not in the business of lying."

I chuckled then. "Oh, I think you can do it. I have confidence. And children are pretty gullible, in case you haven't noticed."

They said they'd be right over, and I believed them. I had no reason not to. I didn't know that they'd do anything else first. Make a pit stop.

Make a phone call. Look at the sports scores. No, those things didn't occur to me. I took them at their word. I went inside and took the spoon back from Miles, told him to finish his homework. Told him not to worry, that all was taken care of. And the relief in his narrow shoulders! The way they lowered with his breath, like wings folding in! I knew I'd done the right thing by him. Now the police just had to do theirs.

Had I said Barrett Smith's name out loud, in the dark, on the patio? Yes, of course I had. I must have; how else would I have told the story to the police? Was it possible Mr. Smith had cameras trained on the front of his house that I hadn't seen? That kind in the doorbell, something? I suppose it was. I can't picture the front of his house now, only the corner of land that I wanted. I remember parts of the conversation, about lying and subterfuge, but not all. Some things are missing. Bits of it I must surmise, piece together now. I don't remember anything special that happened as I spoke, not additional sounds or lights, spotlights through trees, streetlights, moonlight, flashlight. I wasn't focused on where I was and what was around me but rather on what I had to say. I acted viscerally, and it needed to be said hastily. I wasn't thinking everything through. I wasn't paying close enough attention, before, during, or after.

For instance, I left the French door unlocked. How long was I there, tending the chili, with that door unlocked? Not long. The chili was almost done. But it was bubbling, steaming my face, so I didn't feel the rush of cold air. And I had the exhaust fan on, sweeping away the scent of garlic and chiles.

Which is why I didn't hear that beautiful mahogany door with its gleaming brass hardware creak back open, letting in the soaring sounds of the nearby singers, along with everything else.

fifty

HANNAH

She called the same movers, requested the same team of guys. Everyone was happy to see one another. It was like a little reunion. The only bright spot in a terrible autumn. Miles got to use the hydraulic lift again. Hannah reused most of the same boxes, which were still like new. And the apartment they moved into, in Wayne, walking distance to school, was brighter than her old street, facing south, not east, and overlooking trees that didn't seem to be hiding anything or anyone. Friendly trees, she thought, and then the phrase *mature trees* came to mind and grew in meaning. Yes. Mature trees.

The apartment wasn't large, but square footage wise, it wasn't much smaller than her house. It really wasn't. The only thing missing was the porch, and she figured the town would be her porch. Miles would like that better, all that freedom. He could run errands, go to the movies, go out for pizza with his friends. Hannah had seen the clusters of kids walking everywhere in town. Like a college town, but with middle schoolers and high schoolers everywhere. All that freedom but more people than animals. That would be better.

When she'd called Kendra to tell her she was leaving the neighborhood, Kendra had mentioned she loved the village of Wayne. That she'd often thought of moving there, too, for Liza. And, she'd added, it's close by. With plenty of places to walk. She'd promised that after the holidays and traveling to see her brother and parents, she'd call Hannah to schedule some walks.

Ben and Hillary put their house up for sale almost immediately, too. They went beyond cleaning the kitchen and patio—they gutted the floors, redid them with wood in a herringbone pattern. As if the zigzags could distract from what had happened there, the spilled red sauce and chili, and yes, her mother's blood. All of it mixed together, indistinguishable. As if her mother had been injured by the pot of food.

She supposed it would be years, a dozen or more, before she or Hillary or Miles could ever think of eating chili again. It would become a kind of joke in their family, if Eva had anything to say about it.

So far, her sister hadn't gotten any offers on their house. Their move would take longer, be more considered, and require more equipment, but Hannah still passed on the names of the moving company to her sister. She wanted them to have someone kind to help them go through their transitions, too. Morgan was having nightmares. She dreamed that Barrett had broken out of jail. She dreamed that Kendra tried to kidnap her. Hillary and Hannah had even called Kendra, to FaceTime with her, at Morgan's insistence. She wanted to apologize. And Kendra, of course, said there was no reason to. She told Morgan nothing was her fault. She held her hands together like a benediction and there were tears in everyone's eyes. This made everyone feel a little better.

But Morgan still felt terribly guilty, Hillary had said. But how could she have known? How could she have understood that she was being groomed the same way Kendra's daughter had been? That a man had been watching her jump into the pool while thinking of another little girl? Another girl who didn't want to talk to him anymore, who didn't want his presents, who yanked herself away and died because of it?

Hannah couldn't bear to think of Barrett Smith, so tall and broad and silent, watching the neighborhood from his perch. And Ben? Ben was angry with himself. How could he not have known? How could he have had beers with that guy for years and not seen any sign? But Hannah knew it was possible. How little you can know someone you see every day.

You can do all the wrong things and feel terrible forever. But you can also do all the right things and still find something more you could have done. Even a small knuckle of guilt can weigh on you. Hannah should have said something about the ribbon a long time ago. She was so focused on protecting her son, it had closed her mind. She was as bad as the detectives, locked into a theory.

And Eva? Well, she was a tough old bird, but even she agreed that she needed to live in a smaller place with more people around. No more stairs. No more raking leaves, shoveling snow. No more driving, perhaps. A skull fracture will do that to you. After she finished rehab, Hannah and Hillary would move their mother somewhere close. An apartment. Assisted living. But close to which one of them, neither could say.

Hillary was talking about moving to another state, starting fresh. And Hannah couldn't blame her. But she also thought she was bluffing, doing it for show, parroting what her husband wanted to do. Hannah knew her sister would end up back near her someday. She just didn't know when or how close.

She told the whole story, all of it, to Jay DeSanto over a drink at a little bistro in Wayne. She surprised herself, discussing it in public. But it was early, not quite five o'clock on a Saturday. There were curtains on the windows. Jay had known the bartender, greeted him by name. He seemed older, discreet, like bartenders used to be, barely glancing at them as Jay kept asking Hannah questions, delighting in the details, shaking his head. Even a lawyer who had heard it all enjoyed a good crime story with a happy ending. Well, happy enough.

She'd been surprised when his number came up on her phone. He'd called to ask her how she was, said he'd been thinking of her. In his penthouse office, in his suit. She pictured him there, looking out the window. She said she was fine, but it had been quite a month. Complicated. Crazy. And then he had said, well then, we need to discuss it over cocktails.

When she walked into the restaurant, she almost didn't recognize Jay in ordinary clothes. A sweater with a leather pull, dark jeans, loafers. He could be a dad from school, a man at poker night. His suit and tie had sharpened him, and now he looked softer, more approachable. Younger. Kind of handsome, now that she saw him out of context. She and Hillary used to discuss the differences in men's looks by assigning them labels from TV shows and movies. Rhett and Ashley from *Gone with the Wind*.

Charlie and Bailey from *Party of Five*. As if all the love triangles they'd seen had taught them there were only two poles, two types. Their father, the drunk. Their husbands, the nondrunks.

Seeing Jay now, she saw clearly the in-between. Not big and muscled, like Mike had been, not classically handsome like Ben, but a softer kind of manly and confident. Something in-between. Someone who could nurse one whiskey and didn't think anything of you ordering sparkling water. Didn't even ask you why.

When she got to the part about Barrett Smith and his restraining order to keep him away from another child in his old neighborhood, a child he'd also given gifts to, just like Morgan and Liza, Jay leaned in, and his face creased with concern. As if it were his own child, his own daughter, grown and in college. And when she said he lived behind her, with cameras facing her house and Hillary's, he covered his face with his hand. Then he took a long sip of his whiskey.

"Hannah, who did you buy your house from?"

She blinked. "A couple who was retiring, moving to Florida."

"So if they had kids, they were much older. That's somewhat of a relief, isn't it?"

Hannah sucked in their breath. "Wait. They…had a granddaughter," she said. "Seven years old. She was staying with them when I first looked at the house."

He reached out and took her hand, told her to breathe. Told her it was probably all fine but that she should probably make a phone call. Just in case. A heads-up.

"I don't know—I don't know why I didn't think of that," she said. "It was selfish. I should have—why didn't that occur to me?"

"No, stop. You had your hands full, Hannah. You're just a person, not a cop, and you were under tremendous stress. You should have hired a PI, you do know that, right? I mean, what you and your sister did was ridiculously dangerous."

"Of course I should have. But then…then I wouldn't have had a story to tell you," she said, smiling finally, shyly. "I wouldn't have had anything to say to you over dinner."

"Sure you would have."

"No. I'd just have a street full of suspects, a kid even his own family doesn't understand, and an empty bank account."

"I have a feeling, Hannah," he said, "that you are full of stories. More than you know."

She thought of that sentence as she said good night to him after coffee, after he kissed her on the cheek and asked if he could see her again. After she said yes.

She went home and folded laundry and did the dishes and told her son to put away the iPad in the charging station and go to sleep. As she closed her own computer and walked away from all the storytelling work she did for others, not herself. As she looked out her window, facing the trees that hid nothing, and the first flakes of snow started to swirl and got caught in the streetlights, shining. The ordinary days and nights when nothing happened but everything did. The unglamorous life she lived and mostly loved.

She didn't tell anyone the story of why she didn't drink. Didn't tell them about the night in high school she'd passed out at a party, and when she'd woken up with vomit in her hair, and seen, down the hall, two boys taking off the clothes of another unconscious girl. A girl in her Spanish class, a year younger, the younger sister of Marisa Gothie. Her pale bare legs, her slim toes, her feet dead weight as they moved her. Hannah's head was spinning, and she could barely move. But when they dragged and pulled at the other girl, she felt it on her own skin. She'd sneaked into the back of the kitchen, found a phone, and called Hillary, her older sister, her beacon, and told her about the girl, had asked her what to do. And Hillary had told her to leave, immediately. To walk to the corner and find a cab and come home.

Hannah hadn't questioned her sister's directive that night, not once. And she didn't question her own actions for a long time. They both knew her mother's heart would break if there was another alcoholic in the house. And if Hannah had opted to stay and call the police and make a statement about those boys and that girl, shit-faced, tongue so thick in her mouth the words came out swollen, it might not have even mattered. No one listened to drunk girls anyway. And the other girl? Marisa Gothie's sister? She'd survive. Or had she? Who knew where she was. She had disappeared midsemester, gone to another high school, and Hannah's secret had slowly faded into the background of her life. It had only resurfaced when Hillary threw the fact of it in her face: that Hannah would do almost anything to save herself and her family. That Hannah would do what her sister told her to do, even if she knew it was wrong. Those things were true. That was part of her story, but that wasn't all of it. Hadn't she stopped drinking that very night, forever, to try to prove that? Didn't that count for something?

Maybe, she thought, she needed to add to her own story now. Not her sister's. Not her mother's. Not her son's. She didn't share a property line with anyone. She didn't share her bed or her room any longer. No.

She'd done some smart things and some idiotic things and, yes, some criminal things in her life, but now she saw it clearly as she wiped down the counters and refilled the soap dispenser. All these things, all these moments, they all belonged to her. No one's sister, no one's daughter, no one's wife. Just someone's mother, trying to help her boy. And now, finding the strength to finally help herself. *Rock, paper, scissors, Sawyer.*

fifty-one

EVA

He was a boy who did all the right things the wrong way. That's a fair statement, looking back, isn't it? In their own peculiar way, his mother and aunt had loyalty mostly to each other. Over me. Over their husbands. But Miles, well, Miles seemed to have empathy and loyalty for all creatures in the universe.

Still, it was no wonder it was hard to know him. Hard to get too close. He wasn't cuddly. As a baby, he didn't arch his back, squirm away, but neither did he nudge up next to you. No. He simply wasn't the kind to lay his head on your shoulder or hug you back. There was an awkwardness to how he moved, how he thought. Watching him sometimes, when I'd pick him up from school or take him out for ice cream—these things we might never do again, at least not in my own car if my daughters have their way—I often thought of giraffes. Of sloths. Long-necked things. Ungainly things. Not without affection, mind you; not with complete judgment. More with detachment mixed with wonder. What was it like to raise a boy? What had I missed out on and never learned? The Mars of males, so alien to me. So much I could see that I didn't know. So much.

Would there always be awkwardness in Miles? Possibly. Hard to say. Girls certainly grow out of that stage. But there was more to it with him. It was as if he wasn't part of our human world. He was indeed more of an animal perhaps. Closer to the other species than ours. That's one way to look at it. That what I saw, he felt. He knew, in his bones.

My daughters, though, were as faultily human as humans could be. Making terrible mistakes. Miscalculating. Trying to create their own rules. I swear, if I didn't possess a piece of paper that said my husband had died of heart failure, I might have been tempted to find a private investigator and track down those two's whereabouts the night he died. What those girls were capable of used to exhilarate me, but sometimes now, it also frightens me. The clarity of old age isn't always so rosy.

When you're near death, everyone says that two things happen: either a light appears, beckoning, or the events of your life appear in quick cuts, a slideshow of gratitude. Neither of these happened to me. I suppose that's how I knew for certain I would live.

But Miles didn't know this. Miles didn't know what was inside my head any more than I knew what was inside his.

After the French doors opened and Barrett Smith stepped up behind me and raised his hand to strike with the hammer, I saw his shadow. In the gleaming brass of the stove hood, kept so shiny by my daughter, with the gleam of the Murano pendant lights washing across it just so. It was almost beautiful, this last thing I saw for a week. As if Hillary knew the perfect lighting would come in handy someday. And in that moment, so too did I see my mistake. The camera out back. Facing. What he could have seen or heard or known.

But in that split second, when I saw what I saw, I did one final intelligent thing at least. I didn't turn around, didn't offer my face, my forehead, my throat. I parried a bit left, knocking the chili pot, and he missed his mark, caught the side of my head. That was what saved me, the surgeon said.

I was knocked out cold, saw stars circling before it faded to black. But then no light, no slideshow of life. Blanker than night. Footsteps running, maybe a scream? I don't really know. The sound was muted, turned low. Blood in my ears, I suppose.

And then, just those thin, awkward arms picking me up, rocking me, holding me like he had that broken fawn. I couldn't see him, but I imagine he had the same look on his face, that eternal calm like his mother. Making sure I wasn't alone. That in the journey between life and death, another warm body would be near me. His mother and aunt had found him there, sitting in my blood, tears in his eyes. I thought I heard their voices, murmuring as they ran in. I felt a tear slip from his cheek and land on mine. There is no other feeling like it, a warm tear landing.

I understood him then, finally. All the boy knowledge I never had, the crash of ball against backboard, the bang-bang of pots and pans, the screeching wheels, the chiming trains, all the animal wonder of bears and wolves, the adventures my girls never carried in their heads, never shared in our heart-to-hearts, all that he possessed in his small body that I had never understood, it flooded me, filled me. How I wished I could spread it around, share it. How I could explain! How I now knew what his therapist and mother and father had all struggled to know. This oddity. This compulsion. This crazy hobby that belonged only to Miles, no one else. It all made sense.

It was simple, so simple. It was the opposite of wildness. A million miles from strange. To be with someone when they are hurting. When you are so very awkward, you don't ever know what to say or what to do, because you are too young and too unformed and too different from other people. When all you know is that you don't have the power to help it and you don't have the knowledge to change it or the courage to fix it. But you have to do something, because you are inherently good.

You don't give up. You don't walk away because you don't know what to do.

No. You just hold them. You give them nothing and everything you have. And you abide together.

You simply abide.

where
she
went

DON'T MISS ANOTHER
UNPUTDOWNABLE STORY
BY KELLY SIMMONS!

As the woman approached the glass door of Maggie O'Farrell's salon at quarter to six on a humid Saturday night in early November, all Maggie saw was hair. Not her dark clothes, not the rain gloom of her face. No, Maggie saw chestnut curls, so voluminous they appeared to grow sideways out of the woman's head, the kind of hair you needed to buy a separate seat for on the trolley. Hair like that traumatized women. They were celebrated as infants—"look at those curls!"—then mocked in middle school for not knowing how to straighten them, control them.

Sometimes Maggie believed she could understand all women's thoughts and experiences as she massaged shampoo into their scalps. They sat in her chair hour after hour confessing their wrongdoings, spilling their sad histories, but she was seldom surprised. The overarching story Maggie had almost always guessed.

But on that weekend, her bone-deep exhaustion got in the way. Instead of motive, secret, narrative rising from the stranger, there were coiled, springy strands that would take over an hour to smooth, precisely when she was ready to go home and put her feet up.

Why hadn't she turned off her neon *Bubbles & Blowouts* sign? Maggie had chosen this location on the edge of the Philadelphia suburbs because of its visibility—all glass, set on an extended curve so people could see it, pink and glowing, in every direction. She wanted women to come in off the street and feel welcome. But not ten minutes before closing at the end of the week.

Maggie's assistant, Chloe, was putting the last of the empty mini champagne bottles in the recycling. Her blunt bob had been blond last week but was currently strawberry red, and her large, blue eyes scanned the salon constantly, taking in every little thing that needed to be done. A few pink-striped paper straws were scattered on the whitewashed wood floor, bent at unfortunate angles. Chloe picked those up almost the second Maggie noticed them. They reminded Maggie of her daughter Emma's Barbie dolls, still stored in a box in her crawl space for when she graduated college and had a daughter of her own.

There was no more chilled champagne for this woman approaching the door. Maggie looked back down at the till, counting twenties, planning to announce this as soon as she stepped inside.

The door opened with its wind-chimey jingle, but then Maggie heard something equally familiar. A sound she'd heard late at night, ear tipped toward the door, for years. Holster slapping against hip. Nightstick swinging from a chain, squeaky rubber-soled shoes. Not the *tip tap* of high-heeled girls at all.

Maggie looked up. *Great,* she thought, surveying the dark shirt and shiny badge. Huge-haired cop? She'd probably expect a discount, too. Maggie knew the drill. Before her husband, Frank, was killed, he took every advantage being a lieutenant afforded him. They'd laughed about these things, the small flirtations and badge flashing that had resulted in saving the family money. Now? *Payback,* she thought. *Payback.*

"Mrs. O'Farrell?" the cop said.

Maggie froze. Every hair on her arms stood at attention at the sound of her name. The formality of the *Mrs.* The gentleness of the punctuation. What a question sounded like when you damn well knew the answer.

She closed the till slowly, as if she could make time stop. She knew how this would go. When a cop came to your door and said your name, there were only a few seconds before everything changed. And here it was again—the last precious moment, the unknowing.

Maggie knew the next question was not going to be *How much for a blowout?* but *Are you the mother of Emma O'Farrell?*

She met the woman's eyes, which were large and long-lashed and might be expressive under other circumstances. Circumstances that didn't require you to keep your cool.

"Ma'am?"

"Yes."

"Detective Carla Frazier. Is your daughter's name Emma?"

Behind her, the soft swishing of Chloe's broom stopped. The clock ticked louder. The last shampoo bubbles popped in the sinks. And Maggie's heart beat against the cage of her chest like a small, desperate bird.

"Yes," she choked out. "Yes."

"We were contacted by an officer in the second district, following up on a wellness check?"

Maggie knew from all the years married to Frank that the second district was the farthest reaches of North Philadelphia. Where Semper University was. Where Emma was, on what the city called a blue scholarship, for the children of officers killed or gravely injured in the line of duty. Not a full ride, because so many officers were killed or hurt nowadays, Maggie supposed they couldn't afford it, but full tuition and half room and board, and that had been enough to make her grateful. Emma had always planned to go there—a state school was all they could even think about, and Maggie couldn't bear her being far away in Pittsburgh—but she was facing work-study and loans or possibly a gap year to work and bank some money. And then, suddenly, it all melted away. Semper meant *always* in Latin. And Emma had pointed out that meant their school slogan—"Once a Semper, always a Semper"—made no sense. Her smart girl. Her witty girl. A child who was wholly deserving of a scholarship.

The day the mayor announced Emma's scholarship, on a podium in front of half the police force of Philadelphia, Maggie sat in the front row and wondered if the reporters there would ever print the real story, the reason for this generosity. That Frank had been gunned down in front of his mistress, who was also his newly assigned police partner. So two of Maggie's deepest fears had come true at once.

She had found out about his affair not by going through his pockets or finding texts on his phone but by being ambushed in an interrogation room. Could Maggie tell Captain Moriarty about her own whereabouts that day? Had she known where her husband was and what he was doing with a female detective in that car parked in an alley? Had that bullet missed its intended target, the woman next to him?

She'd had to admit, with tears streaming down her cheeks, that she hadn't known Frank was having an affair. That she'd had no idea. She had to confess not to being a murderer but to being a goddamned fool. And then the look on Moriarty's face. That he'd spilled a secret about another cop. That he'd broken the goddamned code. Did he think she wouldn't notice his guilt?

That woman, her husband's partner, would never be called by her actual name in their house. Maggie referred to her as Salt. As in salt in wound.

"Is she dead?"

The officer looked around the salon.

"Is there somewhere we can sit?"

"*Is she dead?*"

"No, but—"

"Is this your first time?"

"My first time?"

"Delivering bad news?"

"I never said it was bad news."

"You asked me to sit down."

The woman took a pen and notebook out of her pocket, scribbled something. Maggie wanted to hit her over the head. Taking notes, like that was important right now. How would she feel if Maggie started *sweeping*?

"Look, my husband was on the force, so just spit it out. Now."

"Your daughter's friend Sarah—you know her?"

"Yes, Sarah Franco."

Sarah was the only person from Lower Merion High School who also went to Semper University. The girls were good friends but thought it might be a bad idea to room together—after all, college was about meeting other people, expanding your horizons. But that decision had cost them—their dorms were far apart, anchoring the ends of the sprawling campus. Sarah in Graystone, Emma in Hoden House. How they'd groaned when they had gotten their housing assignments. A big campus was always so exciting until you were hungry, late for class, or in need of a friend. But the girls had vowed to meet midquad in their pajamas if they had to, to keep in touch. Emma's dorm was near Bairstow Stadium, and given the school's fanaticism over the football team, the Semper Sabres, Sarah said she'd be over there all the time anyway. Maggie had been happy, thinking of the two girls dancing with the sabre-toothed tiger mascot, faces painted yellow. In Maggie's mind, they looked like something lifted from the college brochure. Still, Maggie was a pragmatist, and yes, a worrier; the sheer number of students, the ring of frat houses, the jogging paths obscured by trees—were there enough blue emergency lights in the world to make up for all that? She had loaded Sarah's number into her phone, just in case. If she couldn't reach her daughter; if she didn't respond to repeated texts or calls, she could call Sarah, and she could run and check on her. Wouldn't Sarah's mother want the same safety net? She still remembered the set of Emma's lips when she'd asked Sarah for her contact info. She was embarrassing her daughter. She was being ridiculous.

But now this.

READING GROUP GUIDE

(Note: The author wants all of you to know that she did not base "the world's bitchiest book club" in her new novel on ANY of the hundreds of reading groups she has visited!)

1. Have any of you ever dreamed of a "family compound," with relatives nearby, like Hannah and Hillary? Did your dreams change over time, and why?

2. While both Hillary and Hannah love their mother, Eva is sometimes kept removed because of the sisters' closeness. Have you observed this pattern in other families? And at what cost to the others?

3. The novel contains a number of observations about parenting boys versus parenting girls. For parents—did you notice any differences in the way you or your friends approached this? Do you think Hannah's attitudes toward Miles's proclivities and her ex-husband's interests were justified or are a product of her own prejudices?

4. Miles's relationship with his cousin, Morgan, is one of the reasons the sisters wanted to live near each other. As readers, did you worry about the closeness between them and what might happen as a result? Did you agree with Hannah's decision to downplay Miles's issues in order to keep that friendship intact?

5. If Miles were your son or grandson, what disciplinary choices or parenting decisions would you have made differently? Should he and Hannah have stayed in their former school district and toughed it out? Should Hannah have disciplined her son more harshly? Or protected him more fiercely?

6. What were your feelings about Eva's real estate quest? Do you think it was wrong not to confront Hillary—and inform Hannah—about the illegal financial transaction? Should Eva have threatened her?

7. Even in the midst of an unsolved crime, the neighbors don't consider cancelling the fall festival. How did you feel about this decision?

8. The relationship between Ben and Hannah is one of the most fraught in the book. Do you think Hannah did the right thing by going to the police with her concerns? And do you think, after the final chapter, that she and Ben will be able to be close friends again?

A CONVERSATION WITH THE AUTHOR

Many of your novels are set in the Main Line area of Philadelphia, which you have said you find endlessly fascinating. Do you think *Not My Boy* could have been set in another place?

The desire of close-knit sisters to raise their children together is pretty universal, so I think there are many towns in America where this could work. But the other elements—one sister's house much bigger than her sister's next door, neighbors who seem friendly but aren't, the history of the estate, the hilly topography with a creek running through it—all made it seem right to be set in Pennsylvania. I guess I could have found a neighborhood in Pittsburgh, but I was too lazy, haha! (Although I love Pittsburgh and lived there for a few years.) There were lots of neighborhoods nearby that I used as a roadmap.

You have three daughters. Was it a challenge to base a novel around a young boy?

Yes, in a way, because there was not as much personal history to draw from. But Hannah was a woman with no brothers, raised by a single mother. Her experience was a girl-centric household, and she was not innately in tune with the world of boys. So I related to that aspect of her and channeled it in writing.

Not My Boy is your sixth novel. In what ways do you think your work is different from when you started out?

Stylistically, sentence for sentence, I think all my work is pretty much of a piece. But I think I've grown better at crafting well-rounded male characters, better at tempering anger, better at offering hope within the darkness. I'm all about the hope.

You've written novels in first person, in third person, and with multiple points of view. Do you prefer one over the other?

I feel most comfortable writing in first person. I just love the intimacy and creating a singular voice. But it's so limiting, especially when writing about crimes and secrets (which I always do!). So I've grown to enjoy and embrace all the flexibility of third person, too.

What's up next for you?

I'm plotting out a book about three sisters who commit a crime in high school and hide it from their mother, who stumbles onto clues ten years later. My daughters are not particularly happy about this!

ACKNOWLEDGMENTS

I owe a debt of gratitude to the family and friends and exercise buddies who endured my whiny complaints and disappearances for months at a time, as this novel swallowed me whole. And also to the writing communities, like the Tall Poppy Writers, the Liars Club Writers Coffeehouse, and the Binders, who gave me ideas, resources, and support. And then there are the book bloggers and Bookstagrammers who rally around my new releases (one of whom is a character in the book because she won it in a charity auction!). And, of course, readers, who invite me to book clubs (many of whom have read all of my books!) and write to me with their questions and pleas to write another book, quick. I'm going as fast as I can, people—I promise!

I also have to acknowledge the beautiful neighborhoods around Philadelphia. It was so fun exploring, using aspects of them to create the world of Tamsen Creek. I apologize for anyone frightened by my slow driving with the windows down, taking photos. If you think that's creepy, you should see my search history...

ABOUT THE AUTHOR

Kelly Simmons's novels have sold in twelve countries. She teaches in the Drexel University MFA program and is a member of the Tall Poppy Writers, Women's Fiction Writers of America, and the Liars Club, where she co-hosts a weekly podcast for writers and readers. Follow her on Instagram @kellyasimmons or Twitter @kellysimmons. Sign up for her newsletter with book recommendations at kellysimmonsbooks.com.

PHOTO © BILL ECKLUND